THE ART OF INSANITY

For everyone taking on the challenges
presented by mental illness. You rock.
Keep rocking.

Published by Peachtree Teen
an imprint of Peachtree Publishing Company Inc.
1700 Chattahoochee Avenue
Atlanta, Georgia 30318-2112
PeachtreeBooks.com

Cover design by Maggie Edkins Willis
Composition by Lily Steele
Edited by Jonah Heller

Content Advisory: This narrative contains mentions of a suicide
attempt, mental illness, hospitalization, surgery, prescribed medication,
therapy, emotional trauma, bullying, personal and familial shame,
delusions, hallucinations, anxiety, and panic attacks.

Printed and bound in August 2022 at Lake Book Manufacturing,
Melrose Park, IL, USA.
10 9 8 7 6 5 4 3 2 1
First Edition
ISBN: 978-1-68263-457-8

Cataloging-in-Publication Data is available from the Library of Congress.

Dear Reader,

It is my sincere hope that I've crafted a story you enjoy. There is a lot of fun in it—the ridiculous pug is a personal favorite of mine. There's friendship and romance and characters taking on complex challenges.

There are also some sad bits to the story. This is a story that deals with themes of suicide and mental illness. I have made my best effort to present the illnesses and disorders in this book with nuance and in a way that respects and honors the characters dealing with them, just as the people who deal with these things in real life deserve honor and respect.

For the character of Natalie, I have drawn on my own experience of having bipolar disorder as well as some of the experiences of friends from the mental health community. While Natalie's experiences are reflective of some of mine, by no means can any individual speak for all who have ever wrestled with this disorder. If you or someone you love is affected by bipolar disorder, their experience could be very different from Natalie's. No one story could ever present a complete picture of what it is like to have a mental illness. This is only one story of many.

— C. W.

THE ART OF INSANITY

CHRISTINE WEBB

PEACHTREE
Teen

Chapter 1

The car accident this summer wasn't an accident.

Secrets have weight, and this one's heavy. Most of my secrets are light. For example, I dropped a bottle of nail polish behind the couch last year. Now my mom will find a small puddle of Lime-So-Sublime on the floor if she ever decides to remodel. I plan to blame it on the cat.

Which reminds me: I need to get a cat.

Let's see . . . other secrets . . . I pretend high heels are comfortable even though I get blisters whenever I wear them. My recovering ankle has given me an excuse to wear tennis shoes to school for the foreseeable future, so turns out the accident had some perks after all.

One more example: My brother's beta fish is not the same one he asked me to feed when he left for spring break.

The pet store had a near-perfect match, and Brent isn't very observant. Rest in peace, original Finny.

See? Pretty tame secrets. Until now.

"Natalie," my mom says. "Remember what we discussed—not telling people about . . . you know."

She's sitting with my brother and me as we eat our traditional, first-day-of-school omelets. Brent still got up to make them even though he graduated in the spring and his classes at the community college don't start till the afternoon. What's odd is that my big secret—the car accident—isn't the one Mom's warning me to keep this morning. According to her, I have a bigger one.

"I'm not going to tell, Mom." My face is hot. "Pass the orange juice?" I pour myself a large glass in an attempt to drown this conversation.

"I want what's best for you." She picks a microscopic piece of lint from her secondhand Chanel cardigan. "To avoid questions, be careful about where you take your med—"

"Mom, seriously, I got it." I can't keep my voice from rising.

Brent focuses on cutting his omelet. I pull out my phone and jab at the screen, fully aware of Mom's disapproving scowl.

"Natalie, it's not appropriate to text at the table."

"I'm not texting, see?" I flash the screen toward them. "I made a note for myself: Don't tell people I'm a nutter."

Her carefully composed expression doesn't change, but her face pales. I want to confront her right then about what I heard the night before my accident, but Brent grabs the

2

carton and says, "Who wants more orange juice? Nat? Have more juice." He flashes me a stony glare while he pours into my almost-full glass. The moment passes, and I know I won't say anything.

"Mom? Juice?"

"Thank you, Brent. That would be lovely. Vitamin C is so important." The tension leaves the table, and Brent exchanges a glance with Mom. I know what they're thinking: Crisis averted. We're just a happy family having breakfast.

It's one of the biggest things I've learned from my mom: appearances are everything. It's like our family is a designer knock-off: it looks fine on the outside, but something about it isn't authentic. My phone note reminds me that I haven't taken my pills today, but taking them at the table would bring the whole thing up again. I eat my omelet quickly so I can go take them in the car.

Once safely alone in my "new" fifteen-year-old Camry, I take out my orange pill bottle. I put it on the dashboard, and it's as ugly as the peeling gray vinyl around it. The white lid, the white label, and the harsh black letters are familiar in the same way that an obnoxious uncle is familiar: you don't want to see him, but he keeps showing up.

The pill bottle and I have a stare-down, which happens most times I take my pills.

Pill bottles always win staring contests.

One day I will stop taking them, because either a doctor lets me or I decide I'm simply not doing it anymore. Apparently, stopping treatment is a terrible idea, because without these drugs my brain does weird things, like make me want to drive full speed down a road and then crash into a tree.

I blink out the memories and quickly take my pills before the flashbacks can overrun my mind. I reach for my old gearshift and realize it's not there. Oops. The new one is by the steering wheel. I hit the gas a little too hard when I speed out of my driveway, but no matter. I'll get away from my house that much faster. Home is a weird place to be lately, so hopefully school will feel normal.

Students buzz around the one-story brick school like bees near a hive, and it looks the same way it always has. Most of the windows are open in a desperate attempt to catch a breeze. The gazebo to the right of the glass-walled entryway still has peeling white paint on the sides. Students mill about in their first-day-of-school outfits, looking like the best versions of themselves.

But are they talking about me? Are they talking about what happened? It was two months ago, so they've probably forgotten.

"Oh my gosh, Natalieeeeeee!"

Before I get to the front door, Alyssa Jackson envelops me in a hug. I had physics with her last year (I think). She knocks me off balance so that my full weight is on my bad leg, and I wince.

"I'm so glad you're okay," Alyssa says. "I was worried sick! I checked Twitter, like, once every five minutes looking for updates about you. For *weeks*."

Whoops. Never underestimate the power of a gossip chain in a school with only a few hundred students. What were people putting on Twitter? Note to self: Get a cat, and also get on Twitter.

Alyssa pulls out of the hug and gives me a once-over. "They said you almost *died*." She seems disappointed that I'm not in a body cast. She can't see the scar on my chest where a plastic tube fixed my collapsed lung, or the scar from the surgery to clamp the internal bleeding. She can't see the hours of physical therapy I've done to fix my whiplashed neck and strengthen my broken ankle. I only got the boot off a few weeks ago. My crutches are in my car, so she doesn't see those, either. My mom made me take them to school, but she can't make me use them. School's mostly sitting anyway. Alyssa also doesn't see the hours of talking I've done with a psychiatrist and a therapist, trying to be mentally ready to come back to school again.

"I'm fine." I smile, trying to look convincing. "Really. I'm great. Thanks."

As Alyssa gave me her once-over, more people started coming up to welcome me back/gawk at me. My friends and I usually have quite a few people hanging around us before school, but this feels awkward. It's different when I'm more of a spectacle than a friend. I start to walk inside.

"You're limping!" says Alyssa. "That's awful. Here, I'll carry your backpack."

I try to protest, but she already has the bag over her shoulder. "Move aside, people! She's in pain!"

My face flames. Dozens of eyes turn my way, and I want to sink through the floor.

"Wait up! I'm fine, seriously." I try to rush after her, but my ankle slows me down. My salvation comes in the form of Cecily, one of my two best friends.

"I can take the backpack. I've got first hour with Natalie." Cecily's blonde hair is in a curled ponytail, her smile is wide and white, but her eyes are demanding. She stands straight up, a full head taller than Alyssa, and puts out her hand to take the backpack.

Still, Alyssa persists. "Are you sure? It's really no trouble. . . ." She turns to me, looking for a verdict.

"Cecily can take it. It makes more sense. Thanks, though. I'll catch up with you later, okay?" Not sure when I'll catch up with her. If we're not friends, what is there to catch up on?

Alyssa reluctantly hands the backpack to Cecily.

Cecily waits until she's around the corner and then throws the backpack to me. "Carry your own backpack, weirdo." She smiles.

I roll my eyes. "Thanks for that." It's more than gratefulness for the backpack bailout—finally someone is acting like things are the way they were before the accident. It's like a small breath of untainted air.

"I've got your back." She readjusts her ponytail.

Once I'm inside the school building, everyone has something to say.

"I heard you flew fifteen feet into the air!"

"Were you really in the hospital for two weeks?"

"What caused the accident? Be honest: Were you drunk?"

"When we thought you were going to die, I put flowers by the tree you hit. Just so you know."

"Thank goodness your face didn't get smashed in. You still have a shot at homecoming queen."

That might have been encouraging at some point in my life, but right now the priorities of my peer group disgust me. Have they always been this shallow? Have I?

By the time I get to my locker, I'm ready to turn around and drive back home.

"Brynn, I'm going to kill you," I mutter as I open my locker door. She's already there, waiting for me and Cecily. Brynn is our other best friend. She's a shoo-in for "Biggest Gossip" in senior specials. I assume everyone knows the details of my accident because of her.

"Not my fault." Brynn holds up her hands in defense, as if she bears no responsibility but also as if she's not sorry it happened. "This is the twenty-first century. It was on the news and a thousand different internet platforms. I didn't have to spread a single thing."

I was the juiciest gossip of the summer. As one of my best friends, Brynn played both the part of the insider and the part of the grieving friend. She didn't mind the attention from either.

"That's not to say you didn't spread anything," Cecily teases.

"I absolutely did not spread things." Brynn seems indignant. Then she looks up as if she's trying to remember. "Not much, anyway."

I raise my eyebrows, and she shrugs.

"Come on, Nat. You're headline news. Big drama. Like, celebrity-breakup big. It's not like I could say *nothing*. People care, so I had to keep them informed for you."

I couldn't logically expect Brynn to keep any sort of gossip to herself. She doesn't have it in her. All people have Achilles heels, and part of being a friend is loving them anyway.

Cecily gets out her phone. "We need to do our annual first-day-of-school selfie." Her smile turns a bit sad. "Aw, this will be our last one."

We've been doing first-day-of-school selfies ever since sixth grade, when Brynn was the first one of us to have a cell phone. That was also the year we stopped letting my mom take a first-day-of-school picture of us outside the school building (which she'd done since kindergarten). Junior high was too old for that.

"Say 'seniors'!" says Cecily. We all smile, and Cecily taps the phone a few times. She looks at the pictures. "My hair looks weird. We have to do it again."

Cecily's hair never looks weird, but I smile again and brace myself for the dozen or so takes that Cecily will need before she deems the selfie acceptable. It doesn't help that Brynn starts making goofy faces around the fifth take. Some people are whispering and pointing at me. My smile tightens.

8

We finally get a picture acceptable to Cecily.

"Nat, you're so lucky you're a natural blonde. I've spent zillions on highlights."

I assure Cecily her hair is gorgeous. I even try to act like it's the first time we've had this conversation.

"How did Brent do his hair today? Did he use mousse, or did he leave it natural?"

Cecily's had a crush on my brother for the past year, and it seems that his graduating did nothing to dampen her fervor. If anything, it made it worse.

"I have no idea," I say. "Do you really expect me to pay that much attention to my brother's hair?" I exchange a disbelieving look with Brynn. Crushes turn Cecily's brain into spaghetti. It's embarrassing for all involved.

Shelley from the track team walks up and welcomes me back. We were kind of friends before I dropped out of track last spring, and now, with my busted ankle, I probably won't be running this year either. Without running, Shelley and I don't really have much to talk about.

"Where were all these people when I was in the hospital?" I whisper to my friends. The only people who visited were Brynn, Cecily, and my art teacher. Not my school art teacher, but the one at the Vicksburg Institute of Arts, a haven in my Michigan hometown. I've had lessons with Soo Ahn once a week for the past three years. She was concerned about my overall health, but also I think she was concerned about my fine motor skills. I'm bad at a lot of things in life, but art isn't one of them. Luckily for Soo, the accident didn't change that.

A guy I don't know stops by my locker. "Hi, Natalie. Sorry about the accident." I smile and say thanks. As soon as he walks by, I turn back to Brynn and Cecily. "Who is that guy? This is getting creepy."

Brynn squints as she accesses her mental database. "Ben Jones. Sophomore. He's dating Andrea Sark. I *think* he's the one who got caught cheating on an algebra test last year, but that might have been his brother. Not sure."

I stare at Brynn, who widens her giant blue eyes. "You seriously need to get a life," I say.

The warning bell rings, and we have three minutes to get to class. With my bad ankle, I'm going to need all three. I shut my locker door. "See you at lunch?"

Brynn and Cecily agree before joining the hustle of students trying not to start the year off with a tardy. I check to make sure I have everything in my backpack, then start making my way to my first-period classroom. Things feel almost normal, but not quite. It's like someone took my friendship with Brynn and Cecily and put a photo filter on it. The colors have changed just a little bit. Is it because this is the first major secret I've kept from them? What would happen if I told them that the accident wasn't an accident? I wish I could sweep the filters right and left to see what the different results would be before I choose one.

"Hi, Natalie?"

Someone taps me on the shoulder. I don't have time for another round of assuring someone I'm fine, but I need to be polite.

I stop limping, turn around, and smile. "Hi. Ella, right?"

She's a sophomore. Her sister, Chloe, is in my class.

"Yeah, uh, sorry about your accident." She meets my eyes but then looks away.

I force yet another smile. "It's okay. I'm fine now." I turn forward and hope she'll let it go. I have got to get to class on the other side of the school, and running there is an impossibility.

"Uh, Natalie?"

I turn around again, my smile still plastered on. At first I thought she was nervous to be talking to a senior, but there's something more to it. "The thing is, I was walking home from my grandma's on July seventh . . ."

I get goose bumps even though there's no breeze inside. Where's she going with this?

"I take Martin Road," Ella continues. She nods the slightest bit, like I should put together what she's trying to tell me without her having to say it.

My stomach drops. My smile disappears.

She takes a deep breath. "I know what really happened."

Chapter 2

After school, I stand in the parking lot squinting into the harsh sun. I feel sick. Maybe I can skip this meetup. When Ella told me to meet her by the football field at 3:00, I barely had a chance to say "Okay" before she was off to her first-period class. Now my stomach's all twisty. And do I detect a faint headache? There! Yes! A faint headache! Who could expect me to show up when I have a twisty stomach and a faint headache? Plus, my ankle's practically a cantaloupe. It hasn't been this swollen in weeks. I should have used the stupid crutches. Tomorrow, I'll tell Ella I had to go straight home after school. She won't mind.

But what if she really knows?

The leaves on the trees are beginning to change colors, and there's a spark of joy in realizing the horrible summer is almost behind me. My only obstacle to going on like it never happened is sitting over there in the bleachers, waiting for me.

Ugh. I might as well get this over with. I look at my watch. Talking to Ella could make me late for art class with Soo, but the risk is worth it. The breeze whips my hair around my face, and I manage to tame it into a haphazard ponytail. I'm self-conscious about this until I get close enough to see Ella.

Her mess of frizzy hair is blowing up into an arc around her head, making her look like a brunette medusa. Two chunks of hair are firmly secured behind her ears, tucked into the sides of her glasses. She watches the football team and then furiously scribbles in a notebook. Her plaid skirt with neon tights and brown combat boots is an interesting fashion choice, and it doesn't even remotely match her burnt-orange T-shirt with the periodic table printed on it. Is she allowed to wear that shirt while taking chemistry tests? The fact that she owns it, though, means she probably doesn't need it.

"Hi." I hobble up the bleachers to where she's sitting.

"Hey." She's still writing in her notebook. I'm quiet, but my heart pounds. I can act nonchalant, right? I can do this. I channel my freshman year drama-class skills. Nonchalant, Natalie. *Non-cha-lant.* I peek over at her notebook. There are a bunch of arrows and Xs.

"What are you doing?"

"Keeping track of the football plays. I watch the team practice. When I know their plays, I use a combination of logic, probability, and psychology to predict which play they'll run at any point in a game. My sister always drags me to the games. My mom says I have to go in order to 'be social,' so this keeps it interesting."

"Oh." What else is there to say? For some reason, I thought she was like the other girls at school who like to watch hot guys run around.

"So, um. . . ." I'm not sure how to broach the topic. "You wanted to talk to me?"

"Oh yeah," she replies, as if she just remembered why I'm here. She closes her notebook. "I'm wondering why you lied, that's all."

That's all. As if it's no big deal. As if I have some easy explanation for my lie.

Okay, don't panic. I need to figure out what she saw.

"You were walking home on Martin Road?"

"I walk home that way every time I go to my grandma's. I saw your car and knew it was yours because it had that bumper sticker that says EARTH WITHOUT ART IS JUST EH. That's a cool sticker, by the way."

"Thanks." I miss that sticker.

Ella takes her glasses off and tucks more hair behind her ears before putting them back on. She stares straight ahead. "I know you didn't swerve to miss a deer. There was no deer."

Shoot. Even with just that, she knows enough to sink me. The lie has become my security blanket over the past two months. Even when Mom and Brent found out the truth, the lie kept it hidden from everyone else. I would feel naked without it.

Her statement hangs in the air. I consider denying it, but I don't see a point. She was there.

I'm quiet for a minute. "Did you tell anyone?"

It's like my entire life crashed with that car. But while the car is sitting broken, forever out of commission, I have to go around trying to run my life as if the crash didn't happen. It's difficult to run on broken parts.

"No, I didn't tell anyone." She shrugs. "I ran home to plug in my phone and call 911, but they already knew. I told my sister we should come visit you in the hospital, but she had camp. Plus, you and I aren't friends. It would have been weird."

It's a little jarring to hear her say we're not friends, but we're not, so I can't disagree. It's the opposite of Alyssa, who pretends like we're super close when we aren't. This is better, I decide. At least it's honest.

"Anyway, when the news report said that you hit that tree because you were avoiding a deer, I figured maybe you had a reason to say that. It's none of my business, really."

"Yet here we are talking about it."

"Well, yeah, but that's just because I wanted to ask you. Since I was there and all."

"You could have emailed me." It's disconcerting to have this conversation in person. I don't have adequate time to think up good responses.

"We're not friends. I don't know your email."

"Snapchat?"

"Are we friends on Snapchat?"

"I don't know. I'll check." I pull out my phone, glad for a diversion from the topic at hand. We are not friends on Snapchat. "I sent you a request just now." I put my phone back in my knockoff Kate Spade.

"Cool. I'll check it when I get home." Ella opens her notebook again. "Hold on. I think this is a new play. I need to write it down."

"No problem." This is one of the most bizarre conversations I've had in a while. Or ever. What's her angle? What is she trying to accomplish here? My heart pounds, but I pull my phone back out because that's what everyone with a phone does during an awkward silence. A text pops up from Brynn, and I text her back.

Where r u??

Thought you left. Sorry. Call you tonight.

I don't want Brynn to come out here and join this weird exchange. Ella is still watching the football players run around, and she's scratching down arrows and Xs.

"Couldn't you just ask the coach for his plays? Or one of the football players? They'd probably tell you all of them."

Ella rolls her eyes. "Are you the kind of person who looks in the back of the crossword puzzle book for the answers? I bet you are."

She shakes her head, finishes writing, and closes the notebook again.

"So." She looks at me. "Let's pretend I emailed you. Let's pretend it said, 'Dear Natalie, I know there was no deer involved in that car accident. Why did you run into that tree? From, Ella.' How would you have responded?"

I watch the football players, pretending to discern the play. What would I have said? Nothing, that's what. I wouldn't have responded to that email. And I would have done a better job of avoiding Ella for the rest of my life.

"I should probably add a 'P.S. I'm glad you're not dead' to that email, because I'm glad you're not dead and stuff."

"Thanks."

"It would have been really freaky if I'd watched someone die. Watching someone almost die is not nearly as traumatic." Her hair flies all over the place. We make an odd pair. I wonder what the football players would think if they looked up here.

Ella is quiet now, clearly waiting for me to answer. I look away.

The moment of the crash is fuzzy at best. A concussion ensured that I don't remember much of it. Leaving my house that day is clear, though. *This is it*, I remember thinking. My street looked normal, and it was sad to consider that was the last time I'd see it. Leaving a note seemed like a good idea, but I didn't want to give myself the chance to change my mind. Before I could overthink it, the keys were turned in the ignition. I wasn't scared or nervous. Just numb. For months, maybe even years, I had been suspecting that my life would end by suicide. Then, after hearing my mom tell my aunts her suspicions about me, there was no more reason to battle at all.

At least a car crash would look like an accident. People would be sad at first, sure, but they'd get over it. That's what I thought when I got in the car that day: They'll all get over it. My foot pushed all the feelings I had left into the accelerator: 60 . . . 70 . . . 80. . . . This will all be over soon. The fight is over. Maybe I lost, but at least it's over.

"I was texting." I tuck some flyaway hair behind my ear. "Texting and driving. Such a cliché, you know? My mom would never let me drive again if she found out."

Hopefully Ella will buy that. It's embarrassing, but it's better than the truth. Come on, Ella. Buy it. I try sending a brain signal through her halo of hair: Buy it.

Ella's eyes narrow. She tilts her head and appraises me.

I try to arrange my face into the most innocent, honest expression I can muster. I even fold my hands demurely.

Ella stares at me as if she can see into my brain. She purses her lips. Finally, she says, "You weren't texting."

Dang it.

"How do you know? You weren't in the car."

"First, you were lying when you said that. You got all jittery and wouldn't look at me. Also, you were going really fast when you crashed. No one texts while going that fast. You were the junior class president last year, right? I'm sorry, but you're just not that stupid."

"I absolutely could be that stupid." It feels ridiculous to defend my theoretical stupidity. "Lots of people text and drive!"

18

"Lots of people do, but you didn't. That's all I'm saying."

The declaration hangs between us, and I'm out of energy to defend my lies. I'm also not ready to tell the truth. "Please don't tell anyone about the deer thing, okay? Wait. Have you told anyone already? Your sister?"

"I already told you, I didn't tell anyone. I barely even talk to my sister." Ella is quiet. "So you're not going to tell me what really happened?"

"Nope." I overenunciate the *p*. She wants to be blunt? I can be blunt, too.

"All right."

I appreciate that she doesn't push me for more information. Brynn and Cecily would never have accepted that answer.

Ella stands and puts her things in her backpack like she's ready to leave, then stops. "Hey, can you do me a favor?"

"What is it?" What would Ella want? Maybe she wants me to set her up with a guy or give her a makeover. A hair straightener and some mascara could be transformational.

"Can you adopt my grandma's dog?"

"What?"

Is this a weird sophomore joke? I give a small laugh, like I understood the joke, but she doesn't laugh back. My quasi-laugh deflates to a sigh, and then I'm quiet, trying to figure this out.

It appears she's serious about the dog. She's getting more excited. She bounces on her toes while holding the straps of her backpack. "You're eighteen, right?"

"Yes . . ."

"Perfect!" She plops back down. "My grandma sent her dog to the pound yesterday. She says it's too 'high-maintenance.' My grandma is the one who's high-maintenance, if you ask me, but no one ever asks me anything. Anyway, I really like the dog. She was the only reason I liked visiting my grandma. I asked my mom if we could keep her—the dog, not my grandma—but my sister's 'allergic.' She *says* she's allergic, but I think she hates the dog. She sneezed once while at my grandma's house, and from then on she declared herself allergic. The shelter in town kills dogs if they're there too long, but apparently this bothers no one except me. You can adopt her though, right? Because the shelter will let you adopt since you're eighteen, and you can't play sports now that your ankle's all jacked up. You'll have time for a dog."

I blink a few times. This is the most Ella's said in our entire conversation. She looks so hopeful, and I want her to keep my secret. I've never wanted so badly to impress someone two years younger than me.

Because I don't answer right away, Ella fills the awkward silence. "Was it too much for me to talk about your leg being jacked up? Maybe I shouldn't have said that. My mom says I can be socially awkward. I say I tell it like it is, and the rest of the world is socially awkward. Still, that was probably harsh about your leg. Sorry."

"It's okay. You're right. I'm still supposed to be on crutches, so I'm not playing sports this fall." I pull up my jeans to show her my swollen ankle. I'm hoping for some sympathy, but she ignores it.

"Right. That's what I was saying. So you'll get the dog? Can I come visit her sometimes?"

"Um, sure," I say.

"Great! Thanks! Here's a picture." She pulls out her phone and starts to scroll.

I try to backpedal. "You know, it might not work out. My mom might not let me keep a dog."

"She'll let you because she feels bad about your accident." Ella's still scrolling. "Just play the sympathy card. You can't imagine the crap I got away with when I had pneumonia. Two more days in the hospital, and I could have asked for a 3D printer. Ah! Here it is." She holds out her phone and shows me the most ridiculous-looking dog I've ever seen.

"Is that even a dog?" I take the phone and put my hand over the top to shield it from the sun.

"Yes, it's a *dog*." Ella rolls her eyes. "She's a pug. Her name's Petunia."

"*Petunia?*"

"Yes, Petunia. Make sure to brush her snaggletooth at least once a week; don't squeeze her too hard, because her buggy eye almost popped out once; and clean in between her wrinkles so they don't get infected." She puts her hands on my shoulders and gives me a serious look. "Believe me. You do not want the wrinkles to get infected."

"Right. Um, I don't know if this is the best—"

"Great! Thanks a million. Whew, that's a load off my mind."

Before I can say anything, Ella grabs her phone from me, picks up her backpack, and tromps down the bleacher seats. "I'll come see her later this week," she calls over her shoulder. "I really appreciate it!"

She gets to the bottom of the bleachers, turns the corner, and disappears from view. I sit speechless. What just happened? Have I been blackmailed? I kinda feel blackmailed. I look around, as if something in this situation might look black-mail-y. It looks like a high school bleacher on a sunny day.

I only agreed in order to be nice, I say to myself as I stand up and stretch my sore ankle But if someone's being nice only because they want someone else to keep a secret, isn't that kind of blackmail? Sort of? I look at my phone and realize that I'm late for my after-school art class. I almost fall in my rush to get down the bleachers. Maybe by the time art class is over, I can think of a good excuse for why I can't adopt this dog.

Chapter 3

"Excuse me?" A guy in the art gallery is trying to get my attention.

I don't have time to talk. I'm already late. Can I get away with pretending I didn't hear him? Probably not, seeing as there's hardly anyone else in here.

When I turn, he's striding toward me. He's in a hurry, but his eyes are darting around the room like he's stuck in a maze—lost and a little scared. I haven't seen this guy before, because I'd definitely remember him. He's about my age, and his curly brown hair peeks out from beneath his Detroit Tigers baseball cap. His eyes are framed by long lashes that Cecily would kill for, but they don't look feminine. Perhaps it's because his strong eyebrows, currently knitted in concern, balance them out. His broad shoulders make the strap from his messenger bag seem small. He's wearing a forest-green jacket that fits him perfectly, and his jeans are frayed at the bottom where they hit the ground by his bare feet in Birkenstocks. I don't usually see Birkenstocks worn with baseball caps. I'm pretty sure artistic jocks are like unicorns: great in theory, but nonexistent in real life.

"Excuse me, where's Soo Ahn's studio?" he asks. "I'm supposed to be there right now, but this place is huge and I can't find it." He adjusts his canvas messenger bag and shoots a nervous glance at his watch.

"You're going to Soo's?" I'm surprised. There are only five people in my art class, and that includes me.

"Yeah. I'm the new studio tech. I hope she's not big on punctuality, because I'm already five minutes late." His mouth turns up in a dimpled grin, as if a smile will make up for his lack of promptness. If I were Soo, it would work, because I'm suddenly nervous about my hair.

I pretend to itch my ear so I can try to smooth out any flyaways. Did the humidity make my hair all frizzy? Shoot. Yes, it did.

"We're both late," I say. "The bad news is that Soo *is* big on punctuality. The good news is that I'm headed that way also, so hopefully we'll split her wrath in two."

"Crap." He adjusts his hat. A few curls get flattened onto his ears, and they look as discouraged as he does. "Is she really going to be mad?"

I walk toward the back of the gallery with the new guy trailing close behind. "Yeah, but she's pretty soft-spoken. Her 'wrath' is going to be a glare toward us, a stern look toward the clock, and then she'll say, 'Better late than never, but better to be never late.'"

"That's it?" His broad shoulders relax, and his smile returns.

"Most likely. She's a woman of few words."

We're at the back of the gallery now, and I push on the white door that looks flush with the wall. This leads us into a hallway that's off-limits to gallery visitors. The rooms are mostly office spaces, but there are a few studios for artists-in-residence.

"Hey, do you need a hand?" He nods to my noticeable limp and holds out his arm. I slide my fingers into the crook of his elbow, sad that the weather isn't warm enough for T-shirts today. I wonder if his skin is smooth under his jacket. His cologne smells fresh and woodsy, like the air outside a log cabin right after a summer storm. I try to take a deep breath to smell it more without seeming creepy.

"Thanks. I left my crutches in the car."

He suppresses a laugh. "You know, they don't do you a lot of good there."

"Yeah . . . it's a long story."

We make it to the end of the hallway as quickly as possible, which isn't very fast. He's surprisingly patient with me even though we're later by the second. Soo's studio is the last one on the left. All too soon, I drop my hand from his arm and put it on the handle. "Here we are. Ready?"

He shifts his canvas bag from one shoulder to the other. "I guess."

The studio feels like my second home. I've spent count-less hours in here, but the new guy whispers, "Wow." I remember my own reaction the first time I walked in, when it seemed like my dream of being an artist took its first real breath of life. It was like finally finding my way home.

The studio has sky-high ceilings and a bank of windows on one wall, giving the illusion of space. The sun streams in today, casting rays on the paint-spattered floor, which may have originally been gray. My classmates are already working at the three rectangular tables in the center. Sinks and cabinets line one side, and all available wall space is covered in student work—framed pieces, canvases, even murals.

"Pretty neat, huh?" I feel proud even though most of it isn't mine. I did paint the mural of a marine scene by the far window. His gaze lingers on it for an extra second, and I want to say, "I made that! Do you like it?"

In the interest of not sounding like a first-grader, I don't say that.

Soo is at her desk in the back corner, typing something into her computer. She stands and walks over, crossing her arms when she gets close.

She first addresses the new guy. "You must be Ty." Her stern glare is intimidating, which is impressive considering she's only four foot eleven. She's a tiny Korean woman with gray hair that's always striped with shades of paint. It's like she matches her floor.

"Yes. Sorry I'm late."

"Yes." Her eyes narrow. "The apology is appreciated." She looks at the clock as if to check exactly how late we are, but she already knows. She sighs and relents. "Well, as I always say, better late than never, but better to be never late."

"Right." Ty looks appropriately chastened. "I will keep that in mind."

"All right, then. Moving on. You can put your things over here." Soo walks toward her desk.

As soon as she turns around, I give Ty a small grin and an I-told-you-so nod. He grins in return and runs the back of his hand over his forehead. His smile is really something—his teeth like snow-white acrylic straight from the tube and framed by perfect lips.

My lips feel chapped. I should put on some lip balm. As soon as Ty puts his things down, I fish a tube out of my purse. It's shimmering tinted gloss, but that's basically the same thing. There. Now I can have the confidence of the women in lip gloss commercials. Or something.

I grab my easel and set it up in my usual spot next to Jill. She's painting a grasshopper, but she stops when I sit down.

"Who's that?" she whispers, tucking a piece of her dark bobbed hair behind her ear.

"Not sure." I shrug. "He says he's the new studio tech? Have we ever had one?"

Jill wrinkles her nose. "No. Why do we need a studio tech? There are only five of us."

"Beats me."

Jill stares at Ty, who's now talking with Soo in hushed tones. "If we have to have a studio tech, I'm glad Soo picked him. He can help me clean paintbrushes any day." She wiggles her eyebrows up and down.

I roll my eyes. "Jill, focus. Paint your grasshopper."

I think of the fact that Cecily would be on Team Jill for this one. She would probably have his number by now. Brynn would be unable to resist the lure of a new guy and would need to know his life story by the end of today's class. Sometimes I wish Cecily and Brynn were more into art, but today I'm grateful that they aren't here. I need to completely focus on painting my piece for our upcoming fall art show. It's my last chance to impress the Kendall College of Art and Design—my dream school.

Starr walks by to borrow one of Jill's green paint tubes. "Who's the hottie?" she whispers, twisting the bottom of her scarf around her finger, and nods toward Ty. Starr always wears scarves around her neck, and today's is light pink and flowy.

"A studio tech," Jill answers. "Because apparently we need one now?"

"What?" Starr picks up the paint tube. "We've never had a studio tech."

I jump in. "That's what I said!"

"Well," says Starr, "if we have him around here to help clean up messes, I might accidentally spill some of this green paint in my lap."

I wrinkle my nose. "Ew. That's disgusting."

Starr giggles. "Whatever. Just because you've basically sworn off men doesn't mean the rest of us have."

"I haven't sworn off men." I give her a mock glare. "I have a nasty habit of attracting losers, and I'm sick of it."

"Then he must be a loser," says Starr, "because he's looking over here."

"Shoot, really?" My stomach gives a little jump. "Should I look over? He'll know we're talking about him."

Soo calls to us. "Ladies? Is this art class or gossip hour?"

"I had to borrow paint." Starr holds it up as evidence. "And I'm asking Nat what to do about my fox's face."

Soo gives us an incredulous look, but she goes back to talking to Ty.

Starr turns to me. "Legit, actually. Can you come help me with my fox's face?"

I glance at Ty. He catches my gaze but then looks embarrassed and nods enthusiastically to whatever Soo is telling him. Why is my stomach so jumpy today? I grab my water bottle. Maybe I'm dehydrated.

Soon, I'm looking at a bulldozer that's about to flatten a den of baby foxes.

"Should I paint fear or serenity on the mother fox's face? Because fear is logical in this situation, but serenity could be symbolic of the fact that none of us know the havoc the new Industrial Age is about to wreak upon us."

"Uh, maybe go with surprise?"

"Ah." Starr nods enthusiastically. "Brilliant. Because she's caught off guard, and she hasn't had time to form a reaction.

Genius. It's a statement about how life will run over us before we even have a chance to properly respond." She throws the end of her breezy scarf over her shoulder to prepare for serious detail work.

"Um, right." I nod like that is exactly what I meant.

The other students ask me for help a lot, especially when Soo's busy with something else. I don't mean to say I'm the best in the class, but let's put it this way—everyone else thinks I'm the best in the class.

Karl calls me over and asks for help with a Robert Seldon Duncanson piece he's trying to replicate. Something looked wonky with a pear (it was the stem). Karl's work is almost always inspired by famous Black artists. He doesn't know how good he is, but I think other painters will be looking up to his work someday like he looks up to Black artists from history.

Tim paints candy. His parents own a candy store downtown, so he's around it a lot. They display his work in the store, which is pretty cool. He asks for my help with a Jolly Rancher because "something about it looks odd" (it was the left side of the wrapper), and I get a few M&M's for my trouble. Tim likes to eat candy while he paints candy, and he's always willing to share.

"Think the new guy would want an M&M?" Tim asks.

"Not sure," I say. "You could ask."

Tim's kind of shy. He doesn't ask.

I get my own canvas all set up and begin work on the winter scene I've been painting for a while. Almost all my projects are landscapes. Other people love them, but I don't.

I keep painting them because Soo says it's where my real talent is. I did abstract art a few times, which I love, but she always steers me back to landscapes. "There are no scholarships for abstract art," she says. "People like things they *know*. Scholarship boards don't have time to interpret." And then the conversation ends.

I wonder what the potential unicorn over there with Soo would think. She finishes talking to Ty and claps to get our attention. She even turns down the classical music that's always playing in the background, so this must be important.

"Class, this is Ty. He'll be our studio tech for the semester, and he's here because I'm going to be busy. I have some very exciting news."

She pauses with her hands clasped at her chest and a smile on her face so big that her mouth wrinkles meet the ones by her eyes. I didn't even know wrinkles could do that.

"Our usual fall art show is canceled."

How is this good news? This sounds like really bad news. I need this show. My heart stops.

"It's canceled because I have been chosen as a featured artist in this year's Art Connect showcase."

Whoa. That *is* huge.

The class claps and cheers—we make about as much noise as five people can make. Karl even throws in a "You go, girl!"

"Okay, okay, calm down." She motions for us to be quiet. She tries to regain her usual stoic composure but can't quite get there. "It's not that big of a deal."

31

Except it totally is that big of a deal.

"That's not all," she continues. "Because I'm a featured artist *and* an art educator, I will have the opportunity to showcase some of my students' work. Since you are my top young adult class, each of you will have the opportunity to display three pieces."

My eyes bug out. Starr literally gasps. Jill brings her hands to her mouth and knocks over her palette. Tim and Karl look like someone has frozen them in place, jaws dropped open.

I'm going to have work in Art Connect? Art Connect is an international art show held in Greater Falls, the large city about an hour from where we live. People come from all over to view the art, and thousands of people enter for a limited number of spots each year. For Soo to have been chosen as a featured artist is a huge honor. For us to have the chance to showcase as her students? Unheard of.

We stare at one another, stunned.

"Wait," Jill says. "Seriously? Are you serious? That would not be a funny joke."

"I never joke," says Soo, and I believe her.

Suddenly, we're all out of our chairs, screaming and hugging. I accidentally knock over my paper plate full of paint globs, but who cares? Tim and Karl do a manly handshake-to-bro-hug thing, but the three of us girls tackle them with real hugs. Easels get knocked over.

I'm jumping (on mostly one foot) and cheering. I look around for people I haven't hugged yet, and I see Ty standing by himself next to Soo. I'm tempted to hug him, but then I'd have to deal with the awkwardness after. He makes eye contact, and I pump my fist into the air.

Did I seriously do that? A fist pump?

He raises his eyebrows, then laughs and does a fist pump back.

I'm going to die of embarrassment. My face flames, and I hug Jill again so that I have a reason to get out of this ridiculous exchanging of fist pumps.

"Class!" Soo yells. "Class! Pull yourselves together!"

We stop long enough to look at her. She looks stern. Or, rather, she looks like she's trying really hard to look stern.

"Sit down. Now more than ever, you have work to do. There'll be plenty of college scouts at the pre-showcase event, and there could be scholarship money on the line if you do well. You need to let me know by October twenty-fourth which pieces you plan to enter, and they have to be in my hands by October thirty-first. They will go up for the pre-showcase on the evening of November first."

"Is Ty an artist?" asks Starr. "Will he be presenting, too? I'm Starr, by the way," she adds, beaming at him.

He nods and returns her smile.

"Ty isn't in high school," says Soo, "but I'm going to see if they'll let me include him anyway. He attends community college, but you never know what kind of four-year university might snatch him up."

"I'm not in college for art," says Ty, "so I doubt I could get a scholarship for it."

Soo sniffs. "You should be in college for art. I've seen your portfolio. Maybe some money for it would change the minds that need to be changed."

My mind spins. This is the biggest opportunity I've ever had. I've known since I was in elementary school that I couldn't afford to go to college unless I got scholarships. My mom, who manages an upscale consignment store, has always told me to study hard. "My job at Runway Flair puts food on the table, darling," she says, "but it won't pay your tuition." Surely someone at Art Connect will like my art, right? My family loves it. I won the school's art show. I've been on scholarship at the art institute for years now. I can't be awful.

Except, wait. My stomach sinks. No matter how talented I am, a show this big is a lot of pressure, and my brain doesn't handle pressure very well. It would be so typical of me to have beautiful pieces prepared and then somehow crack and ruin the whole opportunity. That's what happened before the ninth-grade art show.

My chest tightens. I try to take a deep breath, but it gets stuck somewhere. I shake one of my hands, like it's possible to physically shake off the memory, but it doesn't work.

I'd won in my seventh- and eighth-grade art shows, so my odds were good. My high school debut was so exciting that I decided to try a new medium. I made a clay pot— worked on it for weeks. Two nights before the show, I had a panic attack. I thought thousands of spiders were about to crawl up my wall, so I threw the pot at them in self-defense.

All my hours of work were smashed in a thousand pieces over nonexistent spiders. I told Mom I threw the pot because I was angry at Brent. To this day, they're both still confused about what made me so angry.

I haven't worked with clay since.

It's harder to ruin paintings in a panic, right? So I should be fine no matter what happens? Unfortunately, there's a lot more riding on this than there was on the ninth-grade art show. But I'm three years older and three years more mature. That has to be worth something, but is it worth enough?

I'll make it be enough. My brain has stolen a lot from my life, but I will not let it take this opportunity. Deep breath, Natalie.

Shoot. That one got stuck somewhere, too. Stupid lungs. I take another swig from my water bottle. The key to my success will be to stay cool and calm. Super chill. I'll keep everything else in my life as low-stress as possible, and maybe my brain will be able to handle the pressure of this competition.

Then I have to make sure Ella doesn't throw my secret around school like confetti. In order to do that, I have no choice but to adopt that ridiculous dog. I take out my phone and quickly look up the hours for the animal shelter—I might just make it after class. Plus, didn't I read somewhere that people who own dogs have a lower heart rate or lower cholesterol or something? This could be a two-for-one: keep Ella quiet and keep my anxiety down. My mom always taught me the value of a good deal.

Oh, shoot—how am I going to pitch this to my mom?

Soo's voice breaks my reverie. "The pre-showcase will begin at five o'clock sharp on November first. Whatever you do"—she looks pointedly at me and then at Ty—"do *not* be late."

Chapter 4

Mom's car isn't in the garage when I get home.
Petunia needs to be settled, calm, and maximally adorable
before I present the happy news that we are now dog owners.
Carrying the dog crate, the supplies, and Petunia all at once
proves impossible. Also, my ankle is killing me, and I don't
want to put any more weight on it than I have to. I settle on
carrying only the dog inside. There's nowhere logical to put
her, so she ends up in the middle of the carpet.

"Stay." I point at her authoritatively. Has Ella's grandma
taught her basic obedience commands? We're about to find
out. Petunia doesn't move, so this is promising.

I stare at her for a minute, and she's possibly staring back at
me. It's tough to tell since her buggy eyes are pointed in different
directions. They're set into a black face that matches the tips
of her ears, and the rest of her body is tan (or "fawn," as the

paperwork from the shelter says). There is a small yellow tooth sticking out from her lower jaw, and it seems that her mouth is too small to hold her tongue, because the tip of it sticks out by her tooth. She's cute in an alien-creature sort of way.

The stare-down is broken when Petunia barks.

Bark is a generous word for the sound that comes out of her. It's more of a *charp*. No one teaches kindergarteners that dogs say *charp*.

She does it again: *Charp!*

"Hi, girl." I kneel down and put my hand out so she can smell me. She ignores my hand, hops on my leg, and starts jumping up and down to lick my face. She keeps slipping off, falling to the floor, and then jumping with new resolve. Lick! Lick! CHARP, CHARP, CHARP! Lick, CHARP! I stand up, because how embarrassing would it be to let a dog break her leg within five minutes of bringing her home from the shelter?

When I move to get the rest of the supplies, she immediately follows me. "No!" I pick her up. Her body is awfully bulky for such a small dog. It doesn't help that she's wiggling like a short, fat caterpillar. Finally she's back in the middle of the room.

"Stay. Here. Stay right here."

She sits down and stares up at me.

"Good girl."

My hand is on the doorknob before I feel a hot snorty breathing on my ankles. Her curly tail is wagging, and she looks up as if to say, "Cool, where are we going?"

"Nooooo." Urg. We'll do more training on *stay* another time. For now, she can't be in the living room. But where to go? Kitchen? No, she'll eat stuff. Bathroom? No, she might lick the toilet—sick. Bedroom? Bedroom it is.

In my bedroom, she wiggles so much that I accidentally drop her in my pile of dirty clothes. She's completely unhurt, which says something about my laundry habits.

My bed looks like the comfiest place in the room, so that's where I put her. I've never had a pet. The only pet that's really been mine was the goldfish my dad won at my preschool's Roundup Carnival. At home, when I took the goldfish out of its bowl to snuggle it, it died. In my defense, I was three. I thought you could *pet* pets. My dad helped me dig a goldfish grave with a serving spoon and then put dandelions on the tiny mound of fresh dirt. It's a little sad to consider that one of my only vivid memories of my dad includes a dead goldfish. My dad died when I was four. I guess there are worse childhoods, but I feel like the ghosts of a million father/daughter memories got buried with him.

Petunia's fur is soft, and it's relaxing to pet her. She, unlike the goldfish, enjoys this attention. She is staring at my wall.

I nod to the flag hanging there. "That's the Union Jack. It's from England."

It appears that at least one of Petunia's eyes is looking at my "Yellow Submarine" poster.

"And that poster is for a song by the Beatles. They're also from England." My mom studied in England when she was in college, and she still loves all things British. She bought me the flag and the poster.

Petunia puts her head between her paws and licks my green comforter.

"That's not from England. It's from a Target Black Friday sale."

She seems calmer, so I try again.

"Stay, okay? Please?"

I inch toward the door, channeling my inner ninja. Silent, stealthy, only a few more steps. Crap, she saw me. I reach the door first and shut her in.

"I'll be right back!" I call. She immediately starts whining and scratching at the door. Her *charps* give me pangs of guilt as I limp down the stairs, but when I get to the car I can't hear them anymore. The supplies are heavy, but nothing I can't handle. My ankle is very unhappy with me, but with two arms and one good leg, I lug it all upstairs and stuff it behind my bedroom door.

As soon as I open the door, I see Petunia gnawing on a painting in the corner of the room. "Ack! Petunia, no!" I drop all of the supplies and rush over to her. She runs away with the canvas in her mouth, but it's a 24x36. She's more dragging than running.

I snag the back of the canvas and pull it out of her mouth. She smiles at me, panting happily, like she's excited to see what game we'll play next.

"You're a bad dog," I reprimand while examining the chewed-up corner. When I look back at Petunia, her tongue is almost entirely back inside her now-frowning mouth. She's sitting on a tucked tail, and her eyes are (if possible) bigger and buggier, like she can't understand what she possibly did to deserve such a harsh condemnation.

"No, it's fine. You're still a good dog," I amend, guilt outweighing my frustration. "Kind of," I mumble under my breath while I take a closer look at the bite marks.

They're mostly on the side of the canvas, and the parts that hit the paint can possibly be covered with some thick acrylic. Maybe Soo can replace a strip of canvas on the side. I set the painting up on the easel in the corner of my room, and I take my current work in progress, a smaller abstract piece, and put that on my dresser. Good thing the piranha dog is short.

Once the crate and food dish have been set up, Petunia ambles over for a snack. While she snorts and chews, I stand in front of my full-length oval mirror. My brightest, most optimistic face stares back at me as I say, "Guess what, Mom? We got a dog!" No, that will never work. Need a plan B. "Can we keep her? Please? She was homeless! There was nowhere else that I could take the poor thing. She would have died in the streets, covered in mud, starving to death!" Except, wait, Petunia's kind of fat. Ugh, that strategy won't work. Plus, my mom has no rescue complex. She's more of a suck-it-up-you're-fine kind of mom. Ella's suggestion of playing up my illness won't work on her. My mom would just get all tense that I've brought up the unspeakable.

Maybe I should let the dog sell herself. Who could look into those buggy eyes and then turn them away? It's impossible.

It's mostly impossible because you can't look into both eyes at once, but that's not the point here. Petunia stares up at me with snot coming out of her nose and her tongue hanging out the right side of her mouth with a string of saliva threatening to drip onto her paw. This might be harder than I thought.

New plan: My mom can't meet Petunia until she agrees that she can stay.

Petunia runs around in circles in the middle of my room. She burps, or maybe it was a hiccup. Finally she stops and squats.

"No!" I say, rushing over. "You don't pee in here!" She needs to get outside immediately. If my bedroom weren't on the second floor, I'd throw her out my window. Unfortunately, I have to pick her up and hold her out in front of me while hobbling down the stairs. She does an air-swim with her paws as if she's helping propel us forward. About halfway down, I hear the garage door opening. *Eeeeep!* Looks like we're headed back to my room. "Okay, maybe you can pee inside just this once." I drop her in the pile of dirty clothes, because those clothes are going to be washed anyway, right? One more practice smile in the mirror comes out looking kind of pained. Oh well. No opportunity to fix it now. Back downstairs I go.

"Hi, Mom!" Why didn't I think to bring home chocolates or something? Bribes, Natalie, bribes. They're a staple of dealing with moms.

"Hello, darling." She puts her purse down and takes off her coat. Her hair is perfectly tucked into a brunette bun at the nape of her neck, like it is every day.

"Did you have a good day at work? Was it, by any chance, the best day ever?"

"It was fine. I once again tried to convince Martha to wear something other than that bedazzled denim jacket, but she refuses. She says she hasn't changed jackets since 1987 and there's no reason to change now. I thought perhaps for her seventieth birthday she'd allow me to buy her something new, but no." She sighs and looks at the ceiling like she's asking the heavens how she ended up working with such a strange lady.

"She does *own* Runway Flair, so she kind of gets to do what she wants, right? Maybe that jacket was in style when she started the store."

My mom glares at me, and I realize I'm not helping my case.

"Natalie, I haven't missed a copy of *Vogue* since 1996. I know fashion. The consignment pieces she chooses never sell, which is why I'm practically running the place."

"I know, Mom. You're the best. She's so lucky to have you, and I'm sure you'll take over soon." I'm trying to recover, but I don't think she's falling for it. We both know she can't afford to buy Martha out.

"How was your first day back at school?" she asks.

"Great!"

"Is Brent home yet?"

"No. He has class until six-thirty."

There is a scratching noise on my bedroom door with an accompanying *charp*, and my heart sinks.

My mom drops her purse. Her eyebrows jump into her hairline. "What was *that*?"

For a moment I consider denying the whole thing and saying, "Wow, who put that dog in my room?"

My chipping nail polish suddenly seems very interesting. When my mom notices that I'm not that startled, she narrows her eyes. "Natalie, what's making that noise?"

"You see, Mom, the thing is—"

Petunia barks again. She's not making this easy.

My mom tucks a nonexistent loose strand of hair and smooths her already-unwrinkled slacks. "Is there a *dog* in our house?"

"Not exactly."

My mom's action reminds me to tuck in a couple of flyaway hairs, but mine are real.

"She's not a dog, per se. I mean, technically yes, she is a dog if you're thinking scientifically, but aesthetically she looks closer to, I don't know, a pig or something—"

"There's a *pig* in our house?"

"No! Of course not! She's not a pig, but she's not like other dogs." There's an awkward pause. "Am I in less trouble if she's more like a pig or more like a dog?"

My mom blinks at me. This conversation is not going how I imagined it. Then again, I didn't imagine it could go *well*, so perhaps it is going how I imagined it. I should have gotten Brent to pitch the idea to my mom. She always loves his ideas.

"I'll go get her. Hold on." It's nice to have an excuse to exit this conversation, even if only for a few seconds. I open my bedroom door and Petunia spills out into the hallway, jumping into my arms. "Be cute," I whisper. "Your life may depend on it."

When I get down to my mom I say, "I got her today." Do I sound chipper enough? Smile, Natalie. Be excited about this. Make your excitement contagious. "Look at how cute she is! Isn't she *great*?"

My mom squints at the dog, which I'm holding up under her front legs like Rafiki holds up Simba in *The Lion King*. Petunia loses all semblance of neck as her head sinks into the skin folds of her shoulders. Her legs stick out at odd angles, and then she starts wiggling around trying to escape. It's not as endearing as I anticipated.

My mom's mouth drops open. I've never seen that happen before. Whenever my mouth hangs open, she says, "Close your mouth, Natalie. Are you impersonating a fish?"

She finally says, "Uh . . ."

It's another thing she tells us never to do.

Oh boy.

"She was homeless," I offer. "And I'm really responsible." Petunia wiggles again, so I pull her close to me and realize I'm holding my breath.

My mom sighs. "Should I insinuate from this display that you're hoping to keep . . . it?"

"If you want to look at it as dog sitting for an undisclosed amount of time that might end up being a while, we could see it like that instead."

45

"Hmm . . . no." She gives a dismissive wave of her hand and goes to the kitchen. Her heels click on the tile floor, and she opens the refrigerator.

"Mom, all kids should have pets."

"You have Finny."

"Brent's fish doesn't count. He's not even mine!"

Also, we technically don't have Finny. But it's not like I'm about to bring that up.

"We don't need a dog." She closes the refrigerator and opens the freezer. "Shall I make lasagna for dinner?"

By *make lasagna*, she means "put the frozen lasagna in the oven." That's okay with me, because the one time she tried to make actual lasagna from scratch was a disaster. It was fun to see the inside of a fire truck, though.

Mom grabs some oregano from the spice rack that sits next to her pristine designer apron collection. She peels back the plastic from the top of the lasagna and sprinkles some oregano on it. She smells it, seems satisfied, and then puts it in the oven. Then she turns the oven on.

"Mom, look at her," I try again. "Look at her sad eyes."

Petunia is on the floor now, and she stares up longingly. She lets out a small whine. Nice.

My mom looks at her and then sinks into a chair at our kitchen table. "Why do you want a dog, Natalie? You've never wanted a dog before. I've done so much to give you a good life, and now you're saying it's not good enough?"

"Of course it's good enough. This isn't about that. It's that she was a sad, homeless dog, and I thought we could offer her a home. Our home is *so* happy and *so* full of love that I think we should share it with this creature in need."

That's not true, but I think I sold it well. It's what moms want to hear, right? Could she tell I was lying? There's a thick silence.

"Oh, and the Queen has dogs!" How did I forget about that argument before? "Queen Elizabeth has had dozens of Pembroke Welsh corgis, and you always say we should be proper like the Queen. I'm trying to be more Queen-like."

My mom does not look convinced. "That creature is nothing like a Welsh corgi, and you are not the Queen. When we move to Buckingham Palace, then you can have a dog."

We're quiet again. There aren't many arguments left.

"If you make me take her back to the pound, they might kill her."

"That's not really my problem, is it? You should have thought of that before you brought her home." She sounds determined. She watches Petunia for a moment and then shakes her head. "I'm getting a cup of tea."

I stand by the kitchen counter while she fumbles for a packet of Earl Grey. "Mom . . ." I hadn't considered the possibility, but my best argument might be the true one. "We have to keep her, because someone who knows about my secret asked me to."

She stops with the tea bag in hand and turns to me. "I beg your pardon?"

47

My mouth goes a bit dry. "There's a girl named Ella. She's a sophomore. She knows the truth about the accident, and she's blackmailed me into adopting this dog."

It's like a cloud covers my mom's face.

"After all of my warnings, you couldn't make it through one day of school without spilling the truth?"

"I tried! It's not my fault!"

"Nothing's ever your fault, is it?" Mom goes back to making her tea, but it's like she's stabbing the water with the tea bag.

I'm not going to cry. I hug my ribs. "Ella was there, Mom. She saw the whole thing. How is that my fault? I didn't know anyone was there."

Some water has splashed over the top of my mom's teacup. She stops bag-stabbing to grab a paper towel. She wipes up the spill, then crosses her arms and glares at me. "And she told you that you had to adopt this . . . creature, or she would what? Splash your news around school like a tabloid reporter? How much does she know?"

"I don't know." I hug my ribs tighter. "I think she definitely suspects the, um, suicide attempt—"

My mom's shoulders tense like I've said a horrible swear word.

"But I don't think she knows about, you know, the other thing." Mom's already so tightly wound that I don't dare say the words *bipolar disorder*. "I'm really sorry. She didn't make specific threats exactly, but I think they were implied. Why else would she have asked me to adopt her grandma's dog?

And homecoming elections are in only a few weeks. If too many people know the truth, they might start asking more questions. It could be bad for me."

I don't really care about being named homecoming queen. To my mom, though, it would be the completion of her American Dream: she's got the white picket fence and the son who got a baseball scholarship, so now it's like all she needs is the daughter who wins homecoming queen. Surely she won't let one measly dog ruin that.

"Natalie, I've warned you to be careful so many times. How far do you expect me to go to help you keep this secret?"

"This is the only thing, I promise. I'll be super careful."

It's like my secret is that we're Russian spies or something. In this case, though, her dedication to making sure our family looks perfect might work in my favor. I hold my breath. I don't have any arguments left. If this doesn't work, there actually is a good chance Petunia could die. Even though I've only known her for about an hour, I can't stomach that thought.

It's times like these that I wish my dad were alive. Maybe he would have been easier to convince. Mom and Brent are so close that sometimes I wonder if my dad was like me.

Petunia runs up to my mom and licks her shoe. My mom doesn't recoil.

"If she urinates on the floor or furniture, she is immediately gone."

"Absolutely." I nod. Mental note: Clean up that pee puddle in my room ASAP.

"Where will she sleep?"

I take this as a sign of my imminent success. "She has a crate. She can sleep in my room."

"Not on your bed. I will not have her drooling on your bedspread."

"Ew, gross. Obviously I wouldn't let her sleep in my bed." Mental note #2: Clean the spot she licked earlier.

My mom rubs her temples and sits down. "I think I'm getting a migraine." She's never had a migraine, but whenever she's stressed about something she says she thinks she's getting one.

"So, is that a yes?" There's another pause. All of this holding my breath has got to be bad for my lungs.

"One-week trial period. Don't get too attached. She's still probably going back." As she says it, she bends down to pet Petunia's head. "Does she have a name?"

"Petunia."

"That's dreadful."

"I didn't pick it."

My mom sighs and stands up. "I'm going to change out of my work clothes." She sweeps by me and heads upstairs.

Petunia looks at me, confused, and I smile back.

"Good girl." I pick her up. "Good, good girl."

Chapter 5

"I swear if we don't win this football game, I'm going to go jump off a bridge." Brynn is bouncing with nervous energy.

I wince at her insensitive remark and wonder if she'd still say things like that if she knew the truth.

It's Friday night, and we're at the football game before our postgame sleepover. It's usually at my place because of Cecily's crush on Brent. This week, both Brynn and Cecily are excited to meet my new "creature." I hope Petunia doesn't pee on anything while I'm gone. So far my mom hasn't thrown her out, but there's an incident with a potted plant and a lot of dirt that is now on my list of secrets.

The score is 21–21 at the end of the fourth quarter, and we have twelve seconds left on the clock to beat our crosstown rivals. It's the game people look forward to every year. Security guards are lurking around, ready if any of the screaming fans start fighting after the game like they did last year. One kid ended up in the hospital. The rivalry is pretty intense.

Our team is on fourth down and barely out of field goal range. Both teams are huddled in a time-out. The cheerleaders hop around in their maroon-and-gold uniforms. Cecily is captain of the cheer team. I used to be a cheerleader, too, before I dropped out last fall to run cross-country. Brynn has always said flying through the air looks terrifying, and she'd rather cheer from the sidelines. Cecily pulls out a giant cardboard key and waggles it in front of the student section, signaling that we should all shake our keys to hype everyone up for this "key play."

I shake my keys with the other upperclassmen. This always feels a bit ridiculous, but it would look far more ridiculous to leave them in my purse. The freshmen and sophomores are sitting higher up in the bleachers. Since most of them have no car keys, they shake their student IDs on their lanyards. Ella is up there, not shaking anything. She sees me looking and waves in a come-here motion. Almost everyone is on their feet, but she's sitting by herself to the right of the students. She has a notebook open in her lap and a textbook on the bench next to her. She can't be working on homework?

Everyone's cheering, so I can't hear what she's trying to say. She waves at me again to come up there. I point to the game. Can't she see this is important? She doesn't relent.

I hold up an open hand and mouth, "Five minutes."

She mouths back, "Now."

No way. Not now. Seconds later, my key shaking slows. Has she found out the full truth? I really might get homecoming queen this year. Homecoming at our school is based on a voting system. People are supposed to vote for which seniors they find "kind, studious, and exemplifying the best of our school community," but it usually just ends up being whoever has the most friends. It's not like I can tell exactly how many friends we have, but Cecily is captain of the cheer team, which makes her pretty popular. Brynn has over a thousand subscribers to her YouTube channel, and since the channel is mostly about what's going on around school, many of those subscribers are students. I used to be a pretty fast runner, I was class president last year, and I've won the art fair twice. Plus, I'm friends with Brynn and Cecily. My odds are pretty good, but if it gets around school that I deliberately drove my car into a tree, I can kiss that goodbye. Then what will my mom put on our Christmas letter?

Christmas letters are my nemesis. Mom sends one out every year, and it's like a résumé of how great our family is doing. Brent's Little League team won their tournament! Natalie made the B honor roll! (That year, by the way, was the first year I won the school art competition. I would have thought that would have made the letter.) One year, Mom made Brent take a picture of her tending a tomato plant to show that our garden had done great, though the "garden" was literally that one tomato plant. Bugs ate it a week later. Months in advance, she was already thinking about the freaking Christmas letter.

This year's is already written. It focuses on Brent getting his baseball scholarship and me winning homecoming queen. She even left a space where she's going to put in a picture of me wearing my crown. If I don't get it, what is she supposed to put there? A photo of my mangled car? Especially this year, she's militant about making us look picture-perfect. Since I'm the one who messed up the perfect picture, I feel like I have to put it back together.

My main competitors for homecoming queen are probably my two best friends, but we all say we don't care about it. Unfortunately, I think we all secretly do. Ella's not going to wreck my chances. I drop my keys in my purse.

"Where are you going?" Brynn yells over the cheers of the crowd.

"Bathroom," I yell, unsure of what other explanation to offer.

"Are you kidding me?! There are only ten seconds left in the time-out!" Brynn's eyes are huge, like I've announced I'm going to transfer to the school we're playing.

Cecily is still waving the giant cardboard key and yelling, "Go, Panthers!"

"I've really gotta go." I push past some other seniors and make it to the aisle. This had better be worth it.

"What?" I'm out of breath when I get up to Ella. "What do you want?"

"You haven't talked to me since you sent me the snap saying you picked Petunia up. How's she doing?"

I blink a few times. I turn to look at the field, and then I look back at Ella. Am I missing something? "Did you seriously just call me up here with twelve seconds left in the game to *ask me how your dog is doing*?"

"She was my grandma's dog, not mine. Also, you adopted her, so technically she's yours."

"I'm . . . I can't . . . *Are you serious?* This couldn't wait until the game was over?"

"Chloe always wants to leave right away. I wouldn't get a chance to find you after the game, and I've been trying to get your attention for fifteen minutes."

"I know, but . . ." Deep breath. Channel all my patience. "This is kind of a close game."

"Oh, right," Ella says, as if this just occurred to her. "But statistically, I'd expect them to run this play." She holds up her notebook. "And it's got a seventy-four percent success rate. We're probably going to win. Either way, you still have the dog. Who cares about a football game?"

"I do!" I sound a bit hysterical. "I really do. And these people do!" I motion to all the cheering fans. "I think you're the only one who doesn't!"

"Okay."

The players are crouched at the line of scrimmage, ready for action.

"Go ahead and watch the game. We can talk about Petunia in a minute." She pulls out her textbook and starts reading about the American Revolution.

People scream as the play begins. I yell, "Go, Panthers!" but it feels ridiculous to be yelling about a game when the person next to me is *reading*. Fine, I'll be quiet. I cross my fingers on both hands, willing the players to make the play.

The already-screaming fans get louder. First down! Also, now we're solidly in field goal range. There are five seconds left in the game, and it's all going to come down to our kicker. The other team calls a time-out.

Ella looks up from her book as the screaming quiets. "Did you know that the word *independence* never occurs anywhere in the Declaration of Independence? That's wild."

She shakes her head, and so do I. Except I'm shaking my head because she thinks the Revolutionary War is more exciting than this game.

"Uh, no, I didn't know that. Did *you* know that we're going to win or lose this game within the next minute or two?"

"What's going on?" She looks up from her book and squints at the scoreboard. "We're clearly in field goal range. Who's kicking?"

"Johnson."

"He's got good stats. We're fine." She goes back to reading.

"No, we're not fine! He could get tackled! He could miss the kick! There are a million ways that this could go wrong!"

"I know." She shrugs. "But probably we're going to win. That's all."

"What if we *lose*?"

"If we lose, then I have to find Chloe even faster because she'll be in a cranky mood, and I'll have even less time to talk to you about Petunia."

"That's all you care about here?"

Ella looks up from her book and stares straight ahead. "Yup, pretty much." She goes back to reading.

How can anyone be so cavalier about a game this close in a rivalry this intense?

"I'm going back with the seniors." I probably have enough time left in this time-out to get back to my friends.

"No, wait!" Ella says. "As soon as the game ends, I have to go out to Chloe's car. She'll be mad if I'm not ready when she gets there. If you go back, I'll lose you in the postgame mob."

"I'll tell Chloe she has to wait." I can appeal to Chloe since she's in my class.

"No way. She hates you."

My eyes are glued to the players, about to disperse from their time-out, but then her words register. "Wait, what?" I start to turn toward Ella, but then I turn away and face the game again. "Actually, you know what? Never mind. I don't care."

The players line up on the field again, and the time in which I can go back to the seniors has expired. Shoot. I drop my head in my hands.

"Crap, am I annoying you?" Ella shuts her book. "Hold on, I can pretend to be like the seniors." She flips her frizzy hair, made extra frizzy by tonight's humidity. She stands up and cheers. "Oh my *gosh*! Go, Panthers! Go, go, go, go! I hope we win so I can make out with you under the bleachers and pretend no one sees us!"

A few startled sophomores look over. My face flushes, but I snort in laughter.

Ella sits down and looks at me, completely serious. "How was that? Close? I think it was close."

"You are so . . ." I trail off, unable to think of a word to describe her.

She's opened her book again. The play begins, and everyone is on their feet screaming.

I jump up, too. "Go, Panthers!"

The ball's in the air.

"Go, go, go, go!"

The kick is good. I scream and look for someone to hug. Ella is calmly reading her history book. I hug a group of sophomores standing vaguely close to us. Finally I go back to Ella, and she closes her book.

"I have about three minutes." She checks her watch. "How's Petunia?"

As I sit down, something dawns on me. "You're *not* blackmailing me, are you? It's seriously just about the dog."

I went through all of that trouble for nothing? The whole argument with my mom was a waste? A streak of anger surges through me, but I'm not sure if I'm mad at Ella for unintentionally blackmailing me or at myself for being overprotective of my secret.

Then again, without the blackmail, Petunia would be sitting in one of those lonely shelter cells. Maybe worse. Thinking of her already-wrinkly face wrinkled in loneliness or fear makes my anger subside. No matter how she got to me, that little thing needed a home.

"Why would I be blackmailing you?" Ella looks confused. "What, because of the car accident?"

"Sh!" I look around to see if anyone heard.

"Natalie, everyone knows you got in a car accident."

Oh. Right. "Well, not about the accident, but . . . you know . . . the other thing."

Ella adjusts her glasses. "You told me not to tell anyone about that."

"I know. It's just some people say they won't tell secrets, but then they do. Or threaten to." Why am I giving her ideas? Coming up here was stupid.

"Threatening people sounds complicated." She puts her book away. "I said I wouldn't tell, so I won't. I don't *blackmail* people. Do I look like a mob boss to you?"

Any mob boss who dressed like Ella would get laughed off their turf. She's wearing an oversize gray sweatshirt over teal corduroy pants. She couldn't look less like a mob boss if she tried.

"I guess not. But thanks."

"You're *welcome*." Ella rolls her eyes. "I'm now down to one minute. Can we talk about Petunia?"

Chapter 6

Ella was right about the postgame mob being difficult to navigate. There are a lot of screaming fans, but I don't see any fights. Looks like the security guards have done their job. It takes me about fifteen minutes to find Brynn and Cecily.

"Bathroom, seriously?" Brynn asks. "We were two rows from the field. That ending was phenomenal."

"I know. I saw it from the upper bleachers." Cecily and Brynn wouldn't understand why I was hanging out with Ella, so I don't mention it. Maybe I won't talk to her anymore since it seems like she's not blackmailing me.

Oddly, the thought of having her totally out of my life feels more disappointing than I expected. There's something about the way she doesn't care about what people think of her. I've never met anyone like that before.

It takes us a while to leave. Cecily is surrounded by her usual fans, and Brynn is interviewing people for her YouTube channel's coverage of the game. I have a bunch more people come up and ask about the accident and my injuries. You'd think that would be old news by now, but it's becoming my claim to fame. I don't like it. If I win homecoming queen because of a car accident, that would be kind of sick. I don't want to win out of sympathy; I want to win because people like me.

When we get to my house, an unfamiliar car is parked out front. Mom is at the dining room table, working on her computer, when we walk in. She says the car belongs to Brent's friend from chemistry. "They're studying in the basement, so don't bother them. They have a big test coming up."

Cecily's face falls.

"We're spending the night," says Brynn. "You'll see him later."

Cecily feigns confusion. "What? Who cares? I don't care." She looks pointedly at Brynn and then shifts her eyes to my mom, as if to say, "Shut up, she's listening."

She's wrong, though. My mom's absorbed in whatever she's researching online.

In the living room, Cecily says, "Hey, can we see your dog?" If she can't see Brent, at least maybe the dog can provide entertainment.

Petunia's in my room. As soon as I walk in, she bounds toward me and jumps up to lick my face. Brent lets her out while I'm at school, but whenever I get home she always acts like it's been a million years since she's seen a human.

"Calm down, girl." I pet her, but it doesn't have the calming effect I'm going for. "We have to go meet some new friends." I carry her wiggly self downstairs. Once on the ground, she scampers to the living room, where she slides on the wood floor and smashes her face into the side of the couch. She bounces back, a little stunned, and then shakes it off, smiling up at everyone as if to say, "I'm good! Let's play!"

Cecily and Brynn raise their eyebrows.

"She's nuts, I know. I've started calling her 'Toons' instead of Petunia because she's so much like a cartoon dog."

"To clarify," says Brynn, "her face was that smashed in *before* she ran into the side of the couch, right?"

Petunia thinks this is great fun. She tries to jump on the couch to be with my friends, but she's not quite tall enough and tumbles to the ground.

"Poor baby!" says Cecily. She picks Petunia up.

"No, don't do that!" Did my mom see that? Phewf. Still on the computer. "Toons isn't allowed on the furniture," I whisper. "My mom would kill me. And possibly her."

Cecily sits on the floor so she can pet Petunia. Toons loves this attention and starts *charp*ing and licking Cecily's face. She's not supposed to bark or lick, but we're working on manners.

After the novelty of meeting my dog wears off, the three of us start talking about the usual postgame topics:

school, people at school, and what we're going to do when we're finally done with school. Brynn works on uploading some footage to her channel, and Cecily uses makeup wipes to scrub the temporary school spirit tattoos off her face. A few minutes later, we're knee-deep in a conversation about whether it would be more fun to live in France or Italy when we hear my mom say, "Oh, crap."

A second later, the smoke alarm goes off. *Screeeeee! Screeeeee! Screeeeee! Screeeeee!*

I slam my hands over my ears. Petunia howls, but it's a pug howl, so it's more of a strained, prolonged *charp* that sounds almost as annoying as the smoke alarm. We run to the kitchen, but we're hit by a wall of smoke. It burns my throat. I wave my hands, but now the alarm is assaulting my ears again. Argh!

"Mom? You okay?"

My mom waves an oven mitt at the smoke. "Open a window! Open a door!"

"I'm calling 911." Brynn whips out her phone.

"No! You're not going to call 911," my mom yells. Her arms flail around like that Crazy Daisy sprinkler we played in as kids. "I don't need the neighbors causing a fuss."

"The oven is on fire," Cecily says. "Shouldn't we do something?"

"I know the oven is on fire!" snaps my mom.

Petunia zooms into the smoky kitchen, and I run to catch her. My ankle complains, and I slow down. My mom turns on the faucet and grabs the sprayer nozzle. She shoots it in the general direction of the open oven, and water hits my face.

"Ack! Mom! You're spraying me!"

"Then get out of the way!"

I duck so she can shoot the water over my head. Oooh, there's less smoke by the floor. Elementary school Fire Safety Day wasn't worthless after all. I crawl around on the floor and yell for Petunia. Flames lick the inside of the oven, and my mom's water spraying doesn't do much good.

"I'm seriously calling 911," says Brynn.

Just then the oven door closes and a voice says, "Keep the door shut. The fire will burn out without oxygen. It's not nearly as bad as it looks. Oven fires are just smoky."

Wait a second. I know that voice.

Through the smoke, I see a guy take off his jacket and wave the smoke toward the window that Brent just opened. Down on the floor, it's easy to see his feet. He's wearing Birkenstocks.

Oh no! It's him.

Oh . . . yay?

Nope, I'm crawling on my kitchen floor like an infant. Back to *Oh no!* I look up, and through the smoke I can barely see his face. Is that a flash of recognition? This is not how I pictured us meeting again.

My mom grabs a broom and violently punches at the smoke detector with the broom handle until it finally stops.

"There," she says with a satisfied sigh. "Quiet."

The smoke alarm in the hallway starts screeching.

"You've got to be kidding me." She runs to the hallway to attack that smoke detector, too.

"Is the fire out?" Ty asks. He's still waving smoke toward the window. How is he so calm about this?

Toons thinks I'm playing with her and keeps dodging me. I give up trying to catch her.

"I'll check." I reach for the oven handle.

"Don't open it!"

Ty grabs my hand, and I swear his touch is even hotter than the oven. How is that possible?

"You want to keep the fire contained." He releases my hand and goes back to waving smoke.

Oh yeah. Oops. I squat to look in the oven window. There's no bright orange, so that's a good sign.

"I think it's out. I can't see a lot through the smoke, though."

Ty puts his green jacket on the floor and bends down next to me. We peer in together, which makes our faces awkwardly close.

"It looks out," he says. "I think we're good."

"Brent, are you okay?" Cecily calls through the smoke.

My mom is still smashing the hallway smoke detector, and the sound of splintering plastic mingles with the smoke alarm screeching.

"Mom!" calls Brent. "Stop smashing that!" He sighs. "Hold on, Ty. I'll be right back."

The smoke has cleared a bit, and I stand. Ty's green eyes are flecked with brown, like a leaf starting to change color.

"Hi again. I didn't expect to see you here. Natalie, right?"

"Yeah, I'm Brent's sister." There should be a rule against cute guys showing up unannounced. I'm lucky I haven't changed into my standard sleepover attire yet: sweats and no makeup. At least I'm still wearing a football jersey and skinny jeans.

Then again, my hair is dripping wet and my mascara has probably formed scary raccoon rings. It's not exactly my finest hour.

He takes off his baseball cap—Chicago Cubs today— and tries to wave away the smoke lingering between us. "I saw that winter scene you're painting at Soo's. You've got some serious skills."

"Thanks." I hear that every single time someone sees my paintings, but it means more coming from him. "Glad you like it."

Petunia runs in circles on Ty's jacket and then squats.

"No! Petunia!" I scoop her up and run toward the back door, trying to ignore the pain in my ankle. Ty laughs. Petunia pees the whole way, so by the time we're outside, she's already done. She sits in the grass and looks up at me, bewildered. Her pink tongue peeks out.

"You pee outside." This has got to be the millionth time this week I've said it. "*Outside.*"

"She was probably scared." Cecily walks up behind me. "That was freaky. I might have peed a little, too."

"I for real almost called 911," says Brynn. "Your mom is still on a murderous rampage against every smoke detector in the house, but everyone who isn't a smoke detector is safe."

"Toons peed on Ty's jacket." I frown at Toons again, but she's still smiling.

"Ty?" asks Brynn.

"The new guy. Brent's friend."

"Wow. Awkward."

Cecily rubs her arms. "If she's done peeing now, can we go inside? It's freezing."

We all look at Petunia, and she stares up at us like she's trying to figure out what's going on.

"I guess. It looks like she's done."

Petunia follows us inside. The house still smells smoky, but visibility has improved. The crisis appears to be over. My mom is fishing something out of the oven.

"What was it?" I ask.

"Pizza rolls. I was making a snack for Brent and his friend, but I forgot about them." She pulls out the pan with small charred chunks on it. "Do you think I could use these as charcoal next summer?" She gives a thin laugh.

Ty's jacket is gone, so he must have picked it up. Oh boy. Mom can't know that Petunia isn't quite as potty trained as I said. Hopefully she didn't see the wet spot.

Ty and Brent are in the living room discussing what movie to watch.

"That doesn't sound like studying for chemistry," Cecily teases.

"We've been studying for hours," Brent says. "We deserve a break, especially now that our snack is ashes."

I introduce Ty to my friends, and he asks if we want to watch the movie with them.

"Sure," says Brynn. She plops down on the couch before either of us can protest. Cecily sits on the love seat, resting her leg on the other half of it to save it for Brent.

"I'm really sorry about your jacket," I say to Ty. "Seriously. I'll have it cleaned."

"It's no big deal." He points to it, balled up on the floor. "Collateral damage from the September Pizza Roll Crisis. We're lucky it made it out with only minor wounds."

He's joking, but I'm hot with embarrassment. "No, for real." I grab the jacket. "Let me get it cleaned for you." I take it and go find a plastic bag to put it in before the dog pee can get on anything else.

By the time I get back, the movie is starting. Brynn and Ty sit on opposite sides of the couch, and Cecily has ended up by Brent. The only seat left is between Brynn and Ty. I don't want to sit by Ty. Every boyfriend I've ever had has ended in disaster, and I don't have the emotional bandwidth for more disasters at the moment. My mom has always said that dating in high school is a waste of time. So far she's been right, not that I'd ever admit it to her.

I grab the blanket from the back of the love seat and sit on the floor with my back against the couch.

"You can sit up here," Ty says. He points to the clearly available seat next to him.

"No, I'm good. I like the floor."

Brynn looks at me incredulously. "What?"

"The floor is way better for your back," I say a little defensively. For all I know, that could be true. I turn my attention to the TV and pretend I'm very comfortable.

I should be settling in for a couple hours of turning my brain off. Unfortunately, my brain is just getting warmed up. The scare from the fire, the embarrassment over the jacket . . . I can feel something happening. With the lights off and a boring movie rolling, my brain starts to run. That's bad. When my brain starts to run, it can be *very* hard to catch.

Chapter 7

Why didn't I let Petunia out before letting her run to the living room? It's fine, I tell myself. It's fine. It's *fine.* It's FINE. My heart races, and I'm not fine. I try breathing slowly to get my heart rate under control. Square-breathe, Natalie, like the therapist said: Breathe in four seconds, hold four seconds, breathe out four seconds, hold four seconds. Repeat.

Don't lose it, Natalie. Come on. Keep it together.

My friends have never seen me during a panic attack. Focus on the movie, I tell myself. Focus. This is a very interesting story. You are not going to panic.

My heart goes faster. My breathing for "four seconds" is probably only one second on each phase. What's even going on in this movie? No idea. Shoot. Forget the square thing. New plan. Crap. What's a new plan?

It's pretty dark in here, but I check that no one's watching me. My eyes dart around the room, bringing random details into sharp focus: the edge of the TV, the bricks on the fireplace, the crack in that brick, a book on the bookshelf, the last name of the author of that book—PERRIGO, PERRIGO, PERRIGO—the one piece of the carpet that's fraying, the zipper on Brent's backpack, back to the book. PERRIGO. Back to the cracked brick.

The blue light of the movie casts an eerie glow on the room. "I've gotta go," I mutter. "I've gotta do something. Be back in a little bit." Everyone in the room is glued to the movie, so they don't notice when I leave. Or maybe they do. Not sure.

I lock my bedroom door and run into my closet. With the door shut, I sit on a pile of shoes, my knees close to my chest. I press my eyes hard into the tops of my knees. I'm as small as I can possibly be.

"I'm fine," I whisper. "I'm fine, I'm fine, I'm fine." Maybe if I repeat it enough times, it will be true. "Everyone, calm down," I whisper. "Everything's fine. Everyone, *calm down*! It's *fine*!" Who am I talking to? My shoes? My clothes? The thoughts bouncing through my head like lottery balls?

Maybe my shoes are freaking out. I peek up from my knees and assure them that everything's fine. It's fine, it's fine, it's fine. Dr. VanderFleet said that when I start repeating words or doing irrational things, I should take my extra meds. Sometimes bipolar disorder is served with side dishes of anxiety and/or delusional panic, and my brain ordered the whole freaking platter. Does talking to my shoes qualify as "irrational"? No, I'm fine. It's not like I think they're listening. It's fine.

Waves of heat roll over my body, and my back feels damp. I keep my head buried in the darkness of my knees. I can tackle this on my own. It's fine. I don't need *more stupid* drugs. None of my friends need drugs. Brent doesn't need drugs. I can beat this on my own. I have to dig deep like they tell you to do at the end of track races. Dig deep, Natalie. It's fine.

Painting calms me downs sometimes. Paint—good idea. Paint. Okay, paint.

Where's the string for the closet light? There it is. The blue shoebox of paint is in its usual corner. My back is up against my clothes, and my knees practically touch the closed door.

I open the closet door a crack so the fumes can escape. My hands shake as they open the first color, glow purple. I love glow paints. All the glow paints. They're the only ones I use in here. Where's my shoebox lid? Oh, there it is. Oops, that might have been a bit too strong of a squirt, but I'll use it all. I'll paint big. My paintbrush aims at the back of my closet door.

IT'S FINE, I paint in block letters. Then smaller underneath it, *It's fine*. Then again on the side wall, in blue glow this time, *It's fine*. I don't wash my brush in between colors. I never do that while painting in my closet. There's a space in my room where I do my "real" painting, but closet painting is for times like now. The world's too much. It has to be smaller. My closet is where my world shrinks to only me and paints.

My breath still comes too fast. Why can't I hold my hand steady? The letters are wobbly and not in my normal handwriting. My clothes brush into the wet paint, but I don't care. I want to scream, but the people downstairs will hear. The scream explodes in my head, and I put my head between my knees again, gasping for breath. Okay, forget painting letters. "It's fine," I whisper again. I'll work on an abstract instead.

Miniature abstract paintings already glow on my closet walls. Every available surface is covered in paint. With my green glow paint, I work on a piece near the bottom of the door. It has sharp streaks of green sitting on purple circles. I add glow white to the edges, trying to make the green even sharper, even more distracting.

I'm obsessed with this white. It's bright like lightning. An MRI of my brain would show flashes of lightning right now. I'm sure of it. Most people don't have lightning in their brain, but I do. I let one of the paint streaks stray from the green and into the blue background of a painting I made weeks ago. Lightning isn't predictable.

My heart still races. I'm shaking. The painting isn't calming me down like it should. I drop the brush and paint splashes on the floor. That's okay—the floor has lots of paint on it.

I close the door all the way and turn off the light. In the darkness, the dim light from the glow paintings stares at me. The purple IT'S FINE is painted directly over one of my favorite abstracts. Oh no. Why did I do that? I try to wipe it off with my hand, but it only smears the *I*, *N*, and *E*. Now it looks ridiculous. The circles, the streaks, the lightning, all blur in front of me. I bury my head again. Tears silently race to my jeans.

What started this thing, anyway? It doesn't matter. It's a snowflake that's turned into an avalanche. It's going faster than I can keep up. Breathe, Natalie. Can I slow my heart down? I need to stop crying.

Oh no, I'm going to puke.

I burst out of my closet and race across the hall. The bathroom faucet is on barely in time to cover the sound of me over the toilet. Please don't let anyone hear.

When it's over, I wipe my mouth with toilet paper and sink against the bathroom wall. The faucet is still running. Sweat mixes with tears.

I should have taken my pills.

I pull myself off the floor and lean heavily on the bath-room counter. My head is down, but I make eye contact with myself in the mirror. Throwing up has forced my breathing back into a somewhat normal pattern. My mascara is smeared, and my face is flushed. There is fear, anger, and surrender in my eyes. I mouth to myself, "I'm sorry." My reflection is disrupted when I open the medicine cabinet. No hesitation this time. I'm taking the pills.

The garish orange of the pill bottle seems to mock me. Orange has become my least favorite color. My name marches across the front of the bottle, and the name of the drug is below it. I hate that the names are printed right next to each other like they go together. My name shouldn't go with any stupid drugs. I open the childproof cap and pour the pills into my hand. The little white ovals are so small, so light, that you wouldn't think they could have that big of an impact on a human body. Yet I know from experience that they do.

I turn the faucet on and put some water in the clear plastic cup I keep by the sink. I put all of the pills back into the bottle but one, and even that one I consider breaking in half. Would I feel less crazy if I only needed half a pill?

My breath is still steadying, and I know I need the full pill. I take a swig of water and put the pill in my mouth, trying to shove it in the middle of the water so it doesn't touch my tongue or the sides or roof of my mouth. Then I can pretend I'm just taking a big drink of water. I can almost pretend the pill isn't there. I swallow and put the pill bottle back in the medicine cabinet, promising myself that it will be a long time before I need it again.

Splashing water on my face cools me down, but does it make me look back to normal? I try out a smile in the mirror. It looks flat and forced. Maybe makeup will work. I put on fresh mascara with almost-steady hands. Toons is barking by the back door. How long has she been doing that?

When I let her in, Toons zooms by me to go rejoin the party.

"You okay?" calls Cecily from the living room.

"Yeah. Totally fine." My voice wavers, but no one is paying attention.

"You're missing all the good parts," says Brynn. "Hurry up."

Toons jumps into my lap when I retake my seat on the floor. I pull my knees to my chest and try to look very interested in *The Matrix*.

"Where'd you go?" Cecily asks.

"Bathroom." It's not a lie.

She buys it. Brynn is engrossed in the movie. Brent makes eye contact with me, and there's a brief flicker of sadness before he says he's going to go make popcorn.

Ty's foot nudges me, and I look up at him. He mouths, "You okay?" and I nod yes. He might be looking at the paint splotch on my jeans, but I can't be sure in the dark. I turn back to the TV before he can respond. My head faces the television, but my eyes watch Ty's foot. It hovers like he's thinking about nudging me again, but he decides to drop it.

Maybe Toons will fall asleep in my lap. I kiss her head and whisper, "It's fine."

Chapter 8

At school on Monday, everything seems normal. Does this mean I'm a good actress, or that my friends don't know me as well as I thought they did?

"I'm so sick of college applications," Brynn says after school. "If I have to write another essay about my 'future goals and ambitions,' I swear I'm going to abandon college and work at a McDonald's forever. Who doesn't like fries?" She takes a fry from Cecily, who's sitting next to her in the commons.

"Those fries are from lunch," I say. "They're disgusting by now."

"Never disgusting," says Cecily, "and I have to eat them before I get home. My dad hates fried food." She stuffs three in her mouth. "Colleges are going to like that I started the pre-nursing program here, right? That's got to be a plus."

"Not if they find out how much you love fried food," Brynn says. "You're promoting heart attacks."

Cecily eats another fry. "Job security."

My after-school Doritos bag crinkles as I open it. Cecily's going to get into a good college and probably get a scholarship. Me? Questionable at best. Especially if I can't keep it together for the Art Connect show. I think of Friday night's panic attack and cringe. By November 1, this all has to be under control. I look at my friends and wonder what would happen if I told them the truth. What if, instead of sitting here talking about fries and college applications, I could talk about the pills in my backpack and the real cause of the accident? Surely they would support me, right? I've known them since kindergarten. They're like my family.

Then again, my own family hasn't known how to handle my mental health issues. Brent walked into my bedroom during a bad panic attack once, and he still has a scar on his forehead from the high heel I threw at him. In my defense, he kept telling me to calm down, as if I hadn't thought of that, and when I kept getting more upset he finally said, "Nat, what the *heck* is wrong with you? You're a complete psycho."

He had never spoken to me that way before. Our biggest fights prior to that had been over pizza toppings or who got to use the car. I stopped crying for a second because I was so stunned, but then I cried even harder. I said he was the worst brother on earth, picked up a shoe from the floor, and threw it at him. That was admittedly immature, but I thought I was about to die at the time. Try being logical when you're positive that you're dying.

My mom thinks he hit his head on a cabinet door that day. I don't know why he never told, but we've never talked about it. Since then, if he ever hears me crying, he turns up the music in his room so he won't hear it. It is easier for both of us that way.

If my family can't support me, it's probably too much to expect that my friends could. Then again, it would be such a relief to share the secret, even with only two people. I wouldn't have to carry the weight alone. I take a deep breath, mentally weighing the pros and cons.

Cecily stands up and straightens her pink running shorts. "Do these make me look fat?"

I guess today's not the day for deep conversation. It's just as well. I wouldn't know where to begin with explaining everything.

I embrace the distraction and focus on the shorts in question. "Your butt's a piece of art. No shorts could make you look fat."

She seems unconvinced, as if I would say that no matter what shorts she's wearing (she's right). The shorts are short enough that people can see most of her perfectly toned legs. It's completely unfair that she eats the way she does and still has those legs. She stands in front of a trophy case in the commons and strains to see her reflection behind her.

"Is it cold out? Should I grab a jacket?" she asks.

"Oh my gosh," I say, suddenly remembering. "You're not going to believe what happened to Ty's jacket."

"What jacket?" asks Brynn.

"The one Petunia peed on." My stomach feels queasy at the memory, and even queasier at what I'm about to say next. "The cleaners put a hole in it."

"What?" Cecily sits down from admiring her butt. "You're joking."

"I wish." The cleaners told me that they had a new guy working on the jacket, and he used some upholstery setting when he should have used delicate. Or something. I was too horrified to really get the whole story.

"I've got the jacket in my car," I say. "What do I do? Do I give him the ruined jacket or throw it away and give him the money to replace it?"

"Was the jacket expensive? What if it was designer?" Brynn looks concerned, but a sparkle in her eye betrays the fact that she loves the drama.

"I hope not. They gave me fifty dollars to replace it, but I don't know how much it cost."

"Have you told him yet?" Cecily is putting her hair in a ponytail.

"No. I don't have his number. I'll see him at Soo's art studio today, and I'll do it then." My stomach churns again.

"Have you practiced what you're going to say?" asks Brynn.

"No, I haven't *practiced*. I've been trying not to think about it."

Crap, should I have practiced? Cecily and Brynn would have practiced. Shoot. I'll work on something while I drive to class.

"The jacket was kind of ugly anyway," says Cecily. "Maybe the cleaners did him a favor."

"Great idea," I say sarcastically. "Maybe I'll lead with that. 'Hey, remember your hideous jacket? It's destroyed. You're welcome.'"

Cecily flips her wrist over and checks the time on her FitBit.

"Three twenty-eight. I'd better head to cheer practice. Later. Good luck with Captain Fashionable." She jogs toward the front door and makes a long toss to throw the fry container in a trash can. Some guys turn to stare as she runs by. Brynn and I are still watching Cecily's silent fan club when Ella walks up.

"Hi." She plops her backpack down and sits. She's wearing black leggings with roses on them, a purple skirt, and a bright green polo. It's a very *loud* outfit. She has tried to tame her hair into a ponytail, but a lot of her curls have made a break for freedom.

"Oh, hey." I'm a bit startled.

Brynn looks confused. We have a fair number of people who come talk to us after school, but none dressed like Ella. I don't know if Brynn even knows her name.

"This is Ella," I say. "You know Ella, right? Chloe's sister?"

"Hi, Ella . . ." Brynn trails off, clearly hoping Ella is going to explain why she is sitting here.

Ella nods and salutes Brynn (did she really *salute*?), then turns to me. "Is it cool if I come over tonight? I don't have any homework."

"I have art lessons."

"Until what time?"

"Six o'clock."

She nods. "Cool, so I'll be there at, what, six-fifteen?"

Brynn coughs, but she's covering up a laugh. I shoot her a dirty look.

"Tonight isn't great, because after art I have dinner, then homework, and I'm supposed to be working on college apps."

Ella sighs like I am a huge inconvenience. "Tomorrow, then?"

"I have physical therapy tomorrow." It's taken two months, but all of my body parts are starting to get back to functioning effectively. Well, my brain's not, but it wasn't functioning before the accident, either. I've seen a string of therapists over the past year and a half or so, some more helpful than others. Therapy and I have a weird relationship. I hate that I need it, but I know that I do.

"When do *you* want me to come over?" Ella says. "You're one of those plan-aheaders, aren't you? Okay, fine." Ella takes out an assignment planner and flips to a random page. "Does October fourteenth work for you? I'm free then, see?"

She holds the planner up to show that October 14— more than four weeks away—is completely blank. Is she making fun of me?

"I could probably fit you in before *then*," I say. "How about Thursday?"

She flips through her assignment book to this Thursday. She scribbles something on the page before saying, "Nope, sorry, completely booked up on Thursday." She displays her book as proof. In scratchy capital letters, she has written *VERY IMPORTANT THINGS* in Thursday's entire block.

Brynn laughs.

"Just kidding," Ella says. "Thursday works. I'll be at your place at four. Can I also put you down for October fourteenth?"

"Sure." Every interaction I have with Ella is super weird but oddly refreshing. It's like there are no social rules.

"Perfect." She turns back to that date and writes, *Talk to Petunia about the current election season. Meet at Natalie's.*

"The current election season?"

"I'm not writing *Play with a dog* in my planner." Ella rolls her eyes. "That makes me sound like a five-year-old. Plus, I think I *will* talk to Petunia about the elections. I do every year. She always agrees with what I think."

Brynn leans over to see what Ella has written on other days that week. "October thirteenth is National Yorkshire Pudding Day?" she reads. It's written in neon-purple ink.

"Yeah. It's a great holiday. Think about it. How often do you take time to sit back and enjoy a good Yorkshire pudding?"

Brynn and I look at each other. Does Brynn know what a Yorkshire pudding is? I have no idea. She shrugs.

"What's a Yorkshire pudding?" I ask.

"You've *never* had a Yorkshire pudding?" Ella looks astonished. Then she drops the astonished face and says, "Me neither. No clue what it is. It was on a Google site of random holidays, and I'm celebrating it this year. It's going to be my cultural event for the month of October."

Brynn looks intrigued. "You do a cultural event every month?"

"Not sure yet, but I'm doing one in October. You're both invited if you want. BYOB, but by *B* I mean 'Yorkshire pudding.' Gotta go. See you Thursday, Natalie." She picks up her backpack and leaves as suddenly as she came.

"That girl is strange," Brynn says when Ella is out of earshot.

"I know, but she's also kinda awesome. I mean, Yorkshire Pudding Day? What's in *your* planner?" I grab Brynn's planner out of her open backpack and flip through a few pages. "All you have are a bunch of homework assignments and the homecoming game. Her life has spice. It has Yorkshire Pudding Day."

"My life has spice!" Brynn gets defensive and grabs her planner out of my hands. "Look. I'm collaborating with some guys from the football team for a YouTube vid next week. And"—she flips to a random page and starts scribbling—"I'm making February second, um, Pop Music Day."

"Party at your place? Sing into hairbrush microphones like old times?"

"Perfect. I'm putting that in there." Brynn starts scribbling in her planner again, and I shake Dorito crumbs into my mouth.

"I've gotta go to art. Time to face the music about this jacket."

My stomach feels jumbled—excitement about seeing Ty again is twisting around with the dread of telling him the truth. I'm not sure what he thought of me before this, but I hope any positive thoughts aren't ruined by what I'm about to tell him.

Chapter 9

My classmates are working when I walk into the studio. Ty is washing palettes by the sink. He nods hello—one of those upward chin jerks that guys do in the hallway.

I can't believe I have to admit the dry-cleaning fiasco. He probably thinks I have the jacket in my backpack. Maybe he's planning to wear it home today. Oh no. Can he see my face turning red? I'm not a cute blusher, like in movies where the main girl bats her eyelashes and her cheeks turn a pleasant shade of pink. No, I'm one of those blotchy, I-look-like-I-have-a-rash blushers.

This is ridiculous. I can't get one little bro-style nod from a cute guy without turning all scarlet fever-y?

I hide behind my canvas as quickly as possible.

Wait, did I nod back to him? I didn't even nod back to him. Now he thinks I'm ignoring him. I look up to fix it, but he's washing palettes again. Too late. I've missed my window of opportunity.

I wish I had scarlet fever.

The more I consider what Brynn said about the jacket, the more it freaks me out. What if it was one of a kind? My mom gets expensive designer pieces at her store every once in a while, and things that look like five-dollar clearance-rack specials have ended up selling for over a thousand dollars. I clearly have no clue how to judge these things. My mom is really good at it, but I didn't inherit her ability to identify name brands at a glance.

Well, the T-shirt he's wearing today is for a band I've never heard of, and the back shows concert tour dates from 1972. Vintage, sure, but probably not designer.

Then again, what if a designer designed that as a vintage concert shirt?

I'm screwed. Painting will stall this humiliation for a couple of hours, right? At least I'll have that. Maybe I can avoid him for the rest of my life. I ignored him once today, so that's going well so far.

I'm quiet as I take out a paper plate because I don't want to bother Jill while she paints her grasshopper. The studio has professional paint palettes, but I've always preferred paper plates. I've been using them in my closet since seventh grade.

Sunshine-yellow, vermillion, and ochre acrylics look great side by side. Before I use them on my canvas, I let them explore my plate. It will only take a few minutes. Soo won't mind.

Before I know it, half the plate is red; then I use gradation to fade the red into the orange. The orange eventually fades to white (the plate itself). I plop a few drops of yellow onto the red side. With a new paintbrush, I give the yellow drops tails, like they're comets streaking against the rest of the paint. The fading goes one way, but my yellows have their own ideas. I add watered-down yellow paint to the dots and hold the plate up so that the paint will drip.

This is taking forever. Should I have added more water? Hmm, where should the drips stop?

"What are you doing?" Soo whispers in my ear.

I jump and drop the plate. That's where the drips stop.

"Um, I was working on a, um, warm-up project? It's an abstract piece."

Soo looks at the red, orange, and yellow mash-up like she's missing what I'm trying to say. "It's on a paper plate."

"Right." It looks silly now. "Sorry, I'll get back to my painting."

"It's not a *bad* piece," she says, tilting her head, "but real art is not done on paper plates."

I want to protest that she never *lets* me do abstract pieces on canvas because I'm too busy doing these landscapes, but Soo knows what she's doing. I'll do whatever it takes to get into Kendall. Maybe when I'm an established artist, I'll do abstracts.

Abstract painting allows me to paint an *emotion*—other artists paint things we can see with our eyes. Some abstract painters, like Pablo Picasso or Cy Twombly, take something that occurs in the material world and warp it to be something

88

completely different. Colors dance on canvases in ways they usually can't. It's like abstract artists get to enter a different dimension. Instead of living here, they live "there." I like "there." Sometimes I think my brain has always been "there."

Before I start work on my canvas, I paint my initials in yellow next to one of the yellow streaks on the paper plate. This will go in the growing stack in my closet when I get home. It will be my eighteenth paper-plate abstract. I used to throw them all away, but I recently started saving them. Maybe one day I'll hang them up like wallpaper in my room.

Back to my winter scene. I've spent so many hours on it that it's like I'm a part of it. I can almost feel the biting chill and smell the smoke curling up from the cabin's chimney. About a half hour later, Soo comes to check on my progress.

"I like the evidence of wind." She points to the man pulling firewood toward the cabin. His scarf is blowing behind him, and he's leaning forward to block the wind from his face. "Great movement. The problem is your chimney smoke." I immediately see it. The smoke from my chimney is going almost straight up.

"Whoa, you're right. Thanks. I'll fix it." It's going to be way easier to fix the chimney smoke than it would be to redo the whole man. Plus, I *want* the wind and the movement. Making a 2D piece appear to be moving is like having the power to make magic.

Soo surveys the painting as a whole. "It's very good," she whispers. "Maybe this one would be a good piece to put in Art Connect."

By the end of class, the winter piece is almost finished. When I lay it on the counter to dry, Ty is working on a painting in the corner. How long has he been doing that? His baseball cap is backward, and he's leaning close to his canvas with his eyes narrowed. What is he painting? Almost as if he can feel my stare, he looks up.

"Oh, sorry," he says to the room in general. "I didn't realize you were done." He jumps out of his seat and runs over to get washrags. "Here, I'll take that." He takes a palette out of Karl's hand. "I've got it, man. This is what they pay me to do."

He rushes around helping people clean up. We've never had a studio aide before, but I'm not complaining.

I need to tell Ty about his jacket. I know this. Avoiding him forever isn't a good idea, right? But he's busy now. There are still a few minutes of dignity left.

While I wait for him, I sneak over to the corner of the room. His painting is—wow. It's a close-up of an eye, but the angle is from the side instead of straight on. The eyeball is turned to look at the painter. It's blurry in one area like he's going to paint a tear there. It seems deep. The eye is haunting. Tim and Karl are painting candy and fruit. Why this eye? Ty's busy wiping a table, and I get away from his painting before he can see me peeking at it.

Now I'm standing awkwardly in the middle of the studio with nothing to do. The other students are leaving. "You coming, Nat?" calls Jill. Starr is standing with Jill, readjusting her red-and-yellow scarf.

"Sure." I turn to Ty. "Are you coming out soon? I, um, need to mention something about your jacket."

Ty stops wiping the table and surveys how much he has left to do. "I can come out in about ten minutes? Are you in a hurry?"

"No. I'll be outside."

When Ty finally walks toward my car, I start talking before he says anything.

"Here's the thing. I don't have your jacket. Well, I guess that part was obvious since I'm standing here with no jacket. But I'm not *going* to have your jacket. Like, not next week, or ever, kind of." Brynn was right. I should have practiced.

"Kind of?"

"Well, no, not kind of. I don't know why I said kind of. The cleaners sort of put a hole it."

"Sort of?" Now he looks amused.

Oh shoot. I'm blushing. Fevering. Whatever you call it. I look ridiculous.

"Uh, no, they did put a hole in it. Something about upholstery mode instead of delicate? But they gave you fifty dollars to make up for it." I hold out the envelope that's now damp from my hand. "I don't know if that covers it, but if not, I can give you more. I'm really sorry." I wince. I wait for his face to fall in sadness or scrunch up in anger.

Please don't tell me the coat was Gucci. If he says it's Gucci, I'm going back to "avoiding him for the rest of my life" instead of paying the difference.

He drops his backpack on the ground and opens the envelope. "Are you kidding me? Fifty dollars?"

"Um, yeah." I can't read his face. "Is that a lot or a little?"

"Seriously?" He laughs. "I got that jacket at a garage sale for a dollar."

Now I laugh. "No way. For real? It's not . . . designer?" Phewf—dodged that bullet. I breathe for the first time since I started this conversation.

Ty motions to his ripped jeans and concert T-shirt. "Natalie, do I look like the type of guy who wears designer jackets?"

"I don't know! In fairness to me, ripped jeans and vintage T-shirts are made by lots of designers nowadays."

"That's valid." He takes off his baseball cap. "The only clothes I spend good money on are baseball caps. I got this one when the Giants won the World Series in 2014."

"Why baseball caps?"

He looks at the hat as if the answer is written on it. Then he shrugs. "Dunno. I love baseball. When I love something, I can't get enough of it. Last Christmas, my nosy great-aunt asked if I have a love life. I said yes, I have two great loves: baseball and acrylics."

I laugh. "Those don't usually go together."

He puts the hat back on. "Passion rarely makes a lot of sense."

That sounded almost poetic. Who is this guy? I have to keep him talking, because I don't want him to leave. "How many hats do you have?"

He laughs and looks toward the sky. "Well, there are thirty teams in the MLB. Each team has at least two hats. So I need twenty-nine times two. . . . Fifty-eight hats? I probably have around forty right now."

"Why only twenty-nine times two instead of thirty?"

He gives me a sly smile. "Can't stand the Yankees."

His smile is unreal. I smile just from seeing it. I look down to try to cover up the fact that I'm grinning like an idiot, but come on—I just found out that I don't have to buy an expensive jacket, and his smile is freaky contagious. This isn't my fault.

"So, you're not mad about the jacket?"

"Mad? You just made me forty-nine dollars. I should be thanking you."

I laugh and sit on my bumper. It feels like a huge weight has been taken off me. The wind rustles through the trees and carries some leaves to the ground. "By the way, your eye painting is really good."

He takes his hat off and puts it back on, readjusting it to the exact same angle as it was before. "You saw that, huh?" His smile fades (come back, smile!), and he looks over at the trees.

"Yeah. It's really good." Shouldn't that make him happy?

"Thanks."

It sounds like the conversation is closed, but I push further. "Why an eye?"

"Uh, no reason. I want to get better at eyes, I guess." He's looking at his shoes now.

Did I say something wrong? I pull my jacket closer because I'm suddenly chilled. Maybe that was a really personal question. I try something different. "How long have you been painting? Are you going to major in it?"

Ty laughs like I asked if he's the King of England. "What? Do an art major? No way. I wish." He sighs and meets my eyes for the first time since I mentioned his art. "I'm going for an associate's degree in accounting with a minor in chemistry."

"Ew," I say before I can help myself. "That's a long way from art."

"I'm aware." He rolls his eyes. "I hate it."

"Correct me if I'm wrong, but I thought that in college you got to pick your major?"

"Yeah, well, not when your parents are paying for it. They wanted me to play baseball, which I did from T-ball all the way through high school, but I didn't get any scholarships for it. So, my mom wants me to be an accountant, and my dad wants me to be a chemist like him. The agreement is that I major in one and minor in the other, and at the end I pick the one I like better for my career."

"That's a pretty short leash."

Ty shrugs. "It's free college."

"Don't they see that you're a good artist?" Even as I say this, I know I've had this battle with my mother enough times to get what he's going through.

"They say it was a fun hobby for high school. Now that I'm in college, it's time to 'buckle down' and focus on something that will put food on the table. Artists end up living in alleyways, surviving on moldy crusts, and begging for money to go buy drugs and paint."

I laugh, and Ty continues.

"Right, ha-ha. It's all very funny, except they said that exact quote."

"Come on," I say. "That's kind of hilarious."

Finally he laughs, too, but it's laced with disappointment. "Fine. My parents are special. They don't know I have this job at Soo's. They think I work part-time in a chemistry lab."

"Seriously?"

"Yeah. It's the only way I can do art. I work for Soo, and in exchange she lets me use her studio space. She's going to let me put some pieces in Art Connect, and she gives me painting tips, too, which are probably worth more than whatever I make while working. Lessons with her are not cheap."

"I know. I'm here on scholarship."

"Lucky you."

There's silence again. I wish I had something to say. I would stay here talking to him for as long as he'd stay talking to me. I fill the silence before things can get awkward. "I'd better get going. I need to make dinner."

"Are you as talented in the kitchen as your mom?"

"Even better. When I cook, the whole block burns down."

"Well then." He hoists his backpack onto his shoulder. "I'm glad I live across town." He smiles. (It's back!) His dimples make my heart do a weird flippy thing.

"You're lucky. Thanks again for being understanding about the jacket."

"Thanks for the fifty bucks. That will buy a lot of moldy bread crusts, drugs, and paint. See you next week."

He nods, and I don't forget to nod back this time.

He starts to walk away, but then he turns around. "By the way, a well-painted eye can tell a better story than an entire novel. Look at the *Mona Lisa*, *The Girl with the Pearl Earring*, any of Margaret Keane's paintings. Eyes are where art comes alive. I want to capture that."

I stop looking for my keys and stare at him. Is this one of those dreams where I think I've met a guy who understands me and my obsession with art, but then I realize it was my brain being stupid again? Brain, if I wake up in five minutes and this guy isn't real, you are going to be very sorry.

Ty pulls his keys from his pocket. "That's all. I don't usually tell people that. When I said that to my dad a few years ago, he said I was a 'wuss' and made me go chop wood with him all afternoon. You're an artist, so you might get it. Or not. Either way is fine." He turns and walks toward his car before I have a chance to say anything else.

Uh-oh. I think he's real. My brain isn't inventing him. That's simultaneously the most exciting and terrifying thought I've had all week.

Chapter 10

"You should go for it with Ty," Cecily says. **"The thing** about the eyes? That was him opening up to you. He was letting you into his *soul*."

"Oh my gosh. We've been over this," says Brynn.

It's Saturday morning, we've just woken up, and she's in her sleeping bag staring at my living room ceiling.

"He was not letting her into his soul," Brynn continues. "He was talking about his painting. It's a painting, not a marriage proposal."

"But it was more than that." Cecily runs her fingers through her hair. "He told her about the thing with his dad. That was vulnerable—like a cat rolling over so you can pet its belly."

"You're not seriously comparing a guy to a cat," says Brynn. "You're nuts. I have no clue how you get so many people to date you."

Cecily makes boys into a formula. If you enter values for x and y, then z is your result. For some reason, I don't think Ty is going to fit into her textbook situations. And he's nothing like a cat. I probably shouldn't have said anything to my friends. They're going to obsess over it, and I don't need that kind of drama in my life right now.

Toons starts *charp*ing in my bedroom. "Ugh, she needs to go out. I'll be right back." I haul myself out of the comfort of my sleeping bag and into the crisp air. My mom won't turn the heat on until the outside temperature goes below fifty degrees. Mid-September is cold, but not cold enough.

My pills are on my nightstand, so I decide to take them before letting the dog out of her crate. Petunia is so excited to see me that she barks louder.

"Quiet, girl. You'll wake everyone up."

She keeps barking. I swallow the pills quickly and toss the bottle on my bed. As soon as I let Petunia out, she tries to jump up and grab it.

"That's not a toy!" I grip her collar and head downstairs. "Stupid dog. Why can't you eat my homework like normal dogs do? You only eat shoes and hair-straightener cords and things I need."

Toons sprints into the backyard as soon as I put her down. The grass tips are blanketed in cold dew. The sky is blue with smudges of cloud, like someone tried to erase the sun and couldn't brush away the eraser marks. Toons dives headfirst into a pile of leaves that Brent raked yesterday. Then she pops out, happy as can be, and rolls around in them. She stops abruptly, realizes she has to pee, and runs over to a grassy patch. At least I'm not as crazy as my dog.

"What's for breakfast?" Cecily asks when I get back. She loves to eat at my house. Her usual breakfast is a protein shake and a handful of blueberries. In my family, we're strong believers in Froot Loops and doughnuts, unless Brent cooks.

"I can probably convince Brent to make omelets if you want to wait for him to wake up."

"That sounds awesome," says Cecily. "How long does he sleep in?"

"He usually gets up around ten."

Brynn checks her phone. It's 9:07. "Ugh, that's in forever. What else could we have?"

"I don't mind waiting," says Cecily. She's rolling her sleeping bag. No doubt she wants to go brush her hair and teeth before Brent comes down. She'll want to look "casual" and "natural," but like the kind of person who casually and naturally wakes up with nice hair, minty breath, and a cute shirt over a push-up bra. Brynn and I have tried to explain to her that this kind of person does not exist, but Cecily doesn't seem to care. We've also tried to explain that Brent has seen her in her actual state of bedhead and bad breath plenty of times because we've been having sleepovers since we were kids. That doesn't deter her, either.

Toons scratches at the back door, ready to come in again. It's clear why Ella's grandma thought this dog was high-maintenance. As soon as I open the door, she shoots past me into the living room, slipping on the wood floors and running into the side of the couch again.

"That could seriously be how her face got smashed in," says Brynn. "She has done that *so* many times. I bet she looked completely normal when Chloe's grandma got her."

"Maybe." How does this dog have so much energy? She runs around the room twice, smells the sleeping bags, decides there's nothing interesting in here, and sprints up the stairs.

"Good morning, ladies." My mom comes into the living room wearing her silk bathrobe over designer pajamas. "Natalie, you're not supposed to let your dog run wild in the house." My mom isn't Petunia's biggest fan, but she hasn't made me get rid of her yet. "Would you like me to make muffins?"

My mom calls muffins her "breakfast specialty," but all she does is combine a box of muffin mix with half a cup of milk. She pours them into muffin tins, bakes them for eight to eleven minutes, and—voilà!—Mom's home-made muffins. It's better, though, than if she tried to make muffins from scratch (which happened once, and trust me when I say that would have been a very opportune time to have a dog).

"Do you think Brent will make omelets?" I ask.

"You don't want muffins?" She looks a little hurt.

"Can we have both?" I try to look hopeful and also very hungry. "I'm starving."

"Of course. I'll get cooking."

At the mention of Brent, Cecily realizes that she's not in presentable condition. "I'm going to get ready." She grabs her overnight bag and heads upstairs. I roll my eyes at Brynn. A couple seconds later, Cecily comes down again. She pokes her head around the corner into the living room.

"Hey, Nat, I think Petunia's chewing on a pill bottle. Is that okay?"

"Argh! No!"

I bolt off the couch and sprint upstairs. Has Petunia eaten my pills? Are they going to kill her? I'm going to feel so bad if I kill that dog. How will I tell Ella?

"Toons! Bad dog!" I reach for the pill bottle, but Petunia growls and turns away. "No! Give that back!" I reach for it again, and she growls louder. The lid is still on the bottle, and she's chewing on the bottom of the orange tube.

"Here, I'll help," says Cecily. She comes up behind me and tries to grab Petunia. Petunia looks like she wants to bark, but if she barks she'll let go of her prize.

"Hold on. Let's get her treats." I call down the stairs, "Hey, Brynn, can you bring up the blue bag on the kitchen counter? It has a picture of a dog holding a piece of bacon."

A few seconds later, Brynn runs up the steps with the treat bag. "Is everything okay?"

"Yeah. Just need a distraction." I turn to Petunia. "Here, girl!" I shake the bag. "Do you want a treat? Do you want a *treat*?"

Her eyes widen and her tail wags, but she's reluctant to let go of the pill bottle.

101

"Come on, Toons. Come here." I open the bag and hold out the treat itself. That does the trick. She drops the bottle and runs over to me. Cecily scoops up the pill bottle.

"Rescued! I don't think she ate any." She studies the bottle, looking for holes or puncture marks. She reads the label. "Wait, these pills are yours? What are you on meds for?"

My relief at the dog's safety vanishes, and I feel like someone poured a bucket of cold water over my head. What am I going to say? Should I lie? What kind of lie can I even tell?

"They're, um, antibiotics, for strep throat. Which I had last week."

Cecily looks at the bottle again and then looks back at me. "Nat, I *started* the pre-nursing club. These aren't antibiotics. Also, you did *not* have strep throat last week." She goes from looking mildly curious to suspicious. "Why are you lying?"

Dang it. I forgot I was lying to a future nurse.

"Natalie?" Brynn walks over by Cecily so she can see the bottle. "What's going on?"

Their mouths are set in grim lines, and their eyes are wide. I have to say something.

"I, um, uh . . ." There are no good lies. Maybe it's time to tell the truth. Not because I want to, but because I'm out of options. Dr. VanderFleet's advice rings in my head: "Your true friends will accept you no matter what. You don't have to be ashamed of an illness." These are my *best friends*.

Surely they won't judge me half as much as I've already judged myself? My mom told me not to say anything, but her method of handling problems (aka not handling them) hasn't been going super well for me.

"Okay." I shut my door. "You're probably going to want to sit."

They look at each other, concerned. Brynn sits on the side of my bed, and Cecily sits in the pink bucket chair in the corner of my room. I'm jittery and hot. "The thing is . . . I mean, what I'm trying to say is . . ."

My friends sit in silence, waiting for me to go on.

"You know what? I'm just going to say it. Remember last spring, when I basically didn't hang out with you at all?"

Their faces are equal parts confused and concerned.

Brynn finally says, "Yes. You were grounded a lot."

"No, see, I wasn't grounded at all." My words start spilling out as fast as I can think them. "I was sleeping all the time. I'd go to school, go to practice or art class, then I'd come home and sleep. Or sometimes I'd skip practice to come home and sleep. Then my coach would say I couldn't run in meets because I wasn't at practice, and I'd think, 'Fine by me, because I don't want to run anyway.' So I'd sleep some more. Then I dropped out of track entirely, which made my mom super mad. I don't remember a lot about the end of the school year."

"So, you have memory issues?" Brynn's squinting like I'm one of those Magic Eye pictures where you try to get the image to come into focus.

"No. I mean, yes, but that's not the main thing." I start talking faster. "What I'm trying to say is, I was depressed, okay? I was depressed and no one knew, because I seemed all happy, right?"

Cecily starts to say something, but I hold up my hand.

"Wait, I'm almost done." Tears blur my vision. "So, I've taken all of these antidepressants over the last couple of years, and none of them worked, and I started believing that depression isn't even a real thing. That maybe people with depression just handle life worse than other people, and for some reason I couldn't handle life correctly."

Cecily is still holding the pill bottle. "So, these pills are for depression?"

"No, they're not for depression." This is frustrating. I'm revealing a huge secret, and I'm making it hard for them to follow along. Let's try another angle. "Remember when my aunts visited this summer?"

"Yes," says Brynn. "They made the best cookies I've ever had in my life."

"Right, okay." Perfect. We're all on the same page about something. "One night when I got up to get a drink of water, I snuck down the stairs so that I wouldn't wake anyone up. My aunts were still up, and they were whispering in our living room with my mom. They were talking about my dad and how he used to have panic attacks and was occasionally depressed. And do you know what? It turns out he was schizophrenic. So all these years when my mom wouldn't give me the details about how he died, that was why. I don't know if he killed himself or if he died in a psych hospital or what. My aunts asked if any of my symptoms might mean that I was sick like him, and I thought maybe I was crazy. And then my mom . . . Well, anyway, that's basically what happened."

Tears escape my eyes, and I stare at the floor. I can hear my mom getting out a pan downstairs while Brynn and Cecily sit speechless.

"It all started making sense, why I had these panic attacks and why I had times when I felt like I was losing it. But who wants to be insane?" My voice chokes off again. I rub my sleeve on my eyes and finish my confession. "The day after my aunts left, I drove my car into a tree because I wanted to die 'accidentally' instead of being like my dad."

A heavy silence blankets the room, and I'm scared to look up. When I do, Cecily has tears in her eyes and Brynn's mouth hangs open in shock.

"Why didn't you tell us? We could have helped!" Cecily sounds sincere.

I clear my throat. "It turns out I didn't have depression or schizophrenia. I have bipolar disorder, which is a totally different disease, and that's what those pills are for." My tears splash on the floor now, making an artistic arrangement. If I could cry paint, this would look awesome.

Brynn speaks first. "Are you *serious*?"

"I'm not explaining it again." I need to pull myself together. Why can't I be more like my mom? She'd never fall apart like this. It's like I'm standing naked in front of them.

No, it's worse than that. These two have seen me naked in locker rooms and in our bedrooms changing for gym classes and school dances plenty of times. This is way worse. It's like I'm naked from the inside.

"We didn't have any idea," Cecily says. "To think of what could have happened . . ." Her eyes are glassy.

Confession time is over. "It's really no big deal. It's something that happened. I'm on pills for it, so now I'm completely fine. I just thought you should know." Except no, I hadn't wanted them to know. I shoot another annoyed glance at Toons.

"So, can you tell when you're turning into another person?" Brynn looks alarmed but also morbidly interested. "Like, you suddenly think you're someone else?"

"What?" Now I'm confused.

"That's multiple personalities," says Cecily. "It's a completely different disorder."

"Oh, sorry."

When will Brent wake up? Come on, Brent. Bail me out here. Be useful to me for once in your life.

"So wait." Brynn is still trying to figure this out. "Is bipolar the one where you're super happy and then super sad? Like, your emotions jump around all the time?"

"No." I'm annoyed to still be discussing this. "I mean, yes, but no." I sigh. Why isn't there some handy information sheet that I could pass to my friends and say, "Here's everything you need to know"? I grab a pillow and hold it in front of my stomach.

"It's a chemical imbalance in the brain," I say. Brynn took chemistry. Maybe that will help her get this. "There are different types, so it's hard to generalize, but sometimes people with bipolar disorder go through periods of depression where they sleep all the time, have unhealthy eating habits, and don't want to do anything they usually like. It's strange, like moving through time without any attachment to what's going on in the world."

"That sucks," says Brynn. "Sounds bizarre."

"They may also have periods of hypomania or mania. They might never sleep, get super productive, and sometimes do things like gamble or go on huge shopping sprees. It feels great, like the world is perfect and nothing can touch you. One time I spent $600 on Amazon in a single night after I'd been up for a few days with very little sleep. I can't even tell you all the weird stuff I bought—did you know you can buy a giant body pillow that looks like a loaf of French bread? Because you can. My mom made me take it back. So yeah, I guess it's where people are super happy and then super sad, but it's usually over long periods rather than in the same day." Hopefully that's a good enough explanation. I pick at a thread on my pillowcase, but it won't come loose.

"What makes people become manic or depressed?" asks Cecily.

I've shifted the conversation from me to a more generalized "people," which makes things a little less awkward, but the only experience I can explain is my own.

"I don't know what the triggers are." It's not an exact science. "Maybe changes in sleep or seasons. Sometimes, it happens for no reason at all. That's the scary part."

Brynn looks at me like I'm a strange new form of bacteria. "So, you'll never know when you might snap?"

"*Snap* really isn't the right word. . . ." Ugh. This is frustrating. I had to work up a mountain of courage to share this secret, and now they want me to keep talking about it. I just want to move on and pretend it never happened. "Stop looking at me like that! I'm fine, okay? It's still me: Natalie. I'm taking some medicine, that's all. That's the only difference."

"Right. It's the same old you." Brynn tries to look like she believes it, but she's never been a great liar.

"We will fully support you," Cecily vows. She puts her hand over her heart like she's pledging allegiance and I'm the flag. "What can we do?"

"I'd rather you do nothing at all. Keep this a secret? Treat me like you always have?"

"But this is life-changing!" Brynn exclaims. "You can't pretend it never happened."

"I'm not. I'm taking medicine, going to therapy, whatever. It's fine." Maybe we should go out for breakfast. Anything to extricate me from this conversation.

"You shouldn't have to keep this a secret." Brynn puts her hand on my arm to comfort me. "Secrets will eat away at your heart. You have to let them free."

I rub the back of my neck. "That's, um, completely untrue. Lots of people keep secrets for years. Until they die, even."

"Yes, exactly." Brynn points at me like I've reinforced her argument. "They *die*."

Cecily should back me up here, but no help arrives. She's thinking hard about something, so I forge on. "Everyone dies, Brynn. That's why secret keepers die."

She doesn't appear convinced. "They would live longer if they didn't harbor so many secrets."

I put my fingers to my temples. "I'll take the hit. Just don't tell, okay?"

Brynn shifts to face Cecily, and now her back is to me. "We can't let her live like this. It's the twenty-first century. Why does there have to be a stigma surrounding mental illness? We need to start a campaign and fix it."

Cecily bites her lip, but then nods. "This could be like when Amira came out as gay last year. First she thought her parents were going to freak out, but they turned out to be super supportive and started the GSA chapter at school. Now she's a total advocate for change in our class."

"Yes, but I'm not Amira—" I try to cut in, but this conversation is quickly becoming a runaway train. My friends ignore me.

"That's a great idea!" Brynn says to Cecily. "We could start a mental illness support group at our school. Because it's probably not just Natalie, right?" Brynn is on a roll. "We could put up posters, and I bet we could meet in the choir room. . . . Hey! Let's start an Instagram campaign to drum up interest. Picture this." She forms a fake frame with her fingers as if it will help us envision her brilliant idea. "A black-and-white photo of Natalie. We put a yellow stripe across the middle with the words *Break the Stigma* on it. It goes school-viral, and people will be all, 'What stigma?' 'What's up with Natalie?' The caption will give the time and date of our first meeting. People will show up out of curiosity, and then we'll do a big reveal. I'll cover the whole thing on my YouTube channel, and it will definitely increase my subscriber count—"

"No." My voice is sharp.

Brynn and Cecily startle as if they had forgotten I was there. "I don't want a mental illness support group. I don't want an Instagram campaign or any YouTube coverage. My mom is not Amira's mom. All she wants is for this to go away. Can't say I blame her—I'd love that, too. All I want is for you to keep it a secret, okay? Are you capable of doing that for once in your life?" My face is hot, and my muscles are tense.

"We want what's best for you," says Cecily. "Do you want me to speak to your mom? After all, I'm in the pre-nursing club, so I could explain in medical terms—"

"No!" Now I'm getting mad. "You have completely lost sight of the point. I am not ready to be an advocate like Amira. And I'm not a medical specimen."

A photo on my dresser shows the three of us holding our Capri Suns after an AYSO soccer game from around second grade. I pick up the picture and toss it to Brynn.

"I'm Natalie, okay? Just Natalie. We're a team. Be on my team here. You're both being idiots."

"A team does what's best for all of the players," Cecily points out. "We're only trying to help. You don't have to throw stuff like a craz—" She stops.

I swear the temperature in the rooms drops five degrees.

My voice is low and quiet, just above a whisper. "If you are my friends, you will keep this secret."

Brynn and Cecily exchange a glance that I hate. They're deciding what to do about me, and I have no vote.

"We love you," is all Brynn finally says.

My hands are clenched at my sides. "We'll see."

Chapter 11

On Monday, Brynn and Cecily act like things are normal, but it feels a little forced—like they're actually acting. I try not to let it get to me. After all, maybe it's going to take them a day or two to get used to my news.

Luckily, my current predicament might get us back on track to our usual gossip—about *anything else* other than my brain. It's after art class, and my car is broken down on the side of the road. Ty's in my passenger seat. If that's not enough to steer Brynn and Cecily away from talking about mental health support groups, then I don't know what is.

We were headed to the Greater Falls Art Museum. Soo told the class that last year's Art Connect winners would be displayed there this week. Jill and I made plans to scope it out today, but at the last second she had to babysit her little brothers. Ty overheard and offered to ride along with me.

I tried to be super cool and nonchalant about saying yes, but my insides felt like jellyfish.

Jill raised her eyebrows from behind Ty's shoulder and mouthed, "You're welcome."

I was unsure if I wanted to punch her or hug her.

The drive was going quite well until now. Miles of cornfield and no help in sight have put a bit of a damper on things.

Cecily would say this is the perfect opportunity to launch a make-out session. Brynn would say I should impress him with my car knowledge and throw in a couple of potential mechanical issues. They're like the cartoon devil and angel characters on my shoulders, telling me what to do.

One problem is that I've never been the type of girl to make the first move, and another is that I know absolutely nothing about cars. *Poof.* Cartoons gone. I'm on my own.

"The car still won't start," I say. "I have no idea why."

"Here, let me try."

We get out of the car and switch seats. Unsurprisingly, it doesn't start for Ty, either.

I smile triumphantly. "See? I'm not an idiot."

"I never said you were." He studies the dials on my dashboard.

"I had the oil changed when my mom bought the car two months ago." I put my fingertips to my forehead. "Everything was working fine then. This makes no sense."

"When did you last put gas in it?"

"Right before the football game."

Wait a minute. Uh-oh. It wasn't this past weekend's football game, but the one before. Brent borrowed my car this weekend.

As if Ty can read my mind, he says, "Which football game?"

"Uh, right. There's a chance I might be out of gas." How did I forget to check the gas gauge? It has to be . . . Oh. It's on the right side, not the left side like my old car. My face flushes red in all its blotchy glory. "Ugh. I *am* an idiot!"

Ty laughs.

"It's not funny! What are we going to do?" I put my forearms on the dashboard and sink my head onto them. If it were possible to die of embarrassment, I'd be flatlined.

"If you're out of gas, it's an easy fix. This is a good thing."

"Oh really? A good thing?" I gesture to our surroundings. "Are you going to make some gas from the corn?"

"Isn't corn ethanol a real thing?" Ty looks pensive.

"Like you're really about to procure gas from this agricultural field?"

He should be stressed out with me. It's tough to be stressed when the person next to me is totally calm. I wish the ground would swallow me. I'm going to punch Jill. Not that my running out of gas is Jill's fault. But now I'm stranded with this really hot guy, and I'm so embarrassed that I have to spread the blame around. If not for Jill, I wouldn't be here with Ty. I wouldn't be feeling all fluttery inside and completely unsure about what to do with that.

"Chill out. We're fine." He pulls out his cell phone. "This is exactly why cell phones were invented."

How is he always so calm?

I snatch the phone. "Don't tell anyone I ran out of gas! That's so embarrassing!"

Ty gives me an are-you-kidding-me look. "You're right. Let's walk ten miles to the next gas station, then fill up"—he looks around the car and picks up my Nalgene—"this water bottle. Then we'll walk ten miles back to here, put the gas in the car, and run out again while trying to drive to the gas station. She's a genius, ladies and gentlemen!" He holds up the water bottle as he makes this announcement to the surrounding corn. Then he turns to me, one eyebrow raised. "I'll trade you this water bottle for my phone."

Should I cry or laugh? Both seem probable. I hand Ty his phone and take back my water bottle. "Don't call anyone yet. Give me a second to think."

Ty looks at me expectantly, a smile playing on his lips.

"I can't think of anything while you're pressuring me! Look somewhere else!"

"No problem. Take your time. Let me know when you come up with your brilliant plan. I don't have anywhere to be tonight." He pulls the lever by the side of the seat and leans it back. He puts his hands behind his head and tips his Phillies baseball cap forward like he's settling in for a nap. With the baseball cap covering his eyes, I take a second and stare at the view in front of me.

As he put his arms behind his head, his shirt pulled up above his waistband. I can see the smooth skin of his stomach pulled taut over the bottom of some abs. (Does he

115

have a six-pack? Couldn't he stretch his arms up a little more so I could find out?) He has a V-line at his hips, and a thin trail of hair starts below his shirt and then disappears under his waistband.

If he looks up and sees me staring, he'll think I'm a complete weirdo. Focus, Natalie.

I pull out my phone. How far away is the nearest gas station? Google Maps should tell me. Oh crap. My screen raises a new issue. "Uh, Ty? Do you have service?"

Ty pulls his phone out and uses it to push up the brim of his hat so he can see the screen. Apparently concerned by what he sees, he sits all the way up and puts his hat back on his head. He clicks a few things on his phone. "Um, no. No service."

"Ha, so your idea wasn't even good after all."

He stops looking concerned and smiles at me. "Really? We're stranded in the middle of nowhere, and you just want to be right?"

"I like being right. It's a good feeling."

"Is it a feeling that doesn't happen for you often?" Ty laughs and goes back to fiddling with his phone.

I try to put my hands on my hips, but it's tricky to do in a car. "*Excuse* me, I'm very intelligent!"

"Right, I know." He looks up. "Hey, why are we stuck here again? I forgot."

"Shut up." I start to laugh, but it comes out as a giggle. Ew, what? When did I develop a giggle? "I'm going to see if I get service outside."

"Good idea." Ty gets out of the driver's-side door, and we walk along the edge of the cornfield toward the intersection. We hold our phones up, hoping the magical satellites somewhere will find us. If an alien race studied us at this moment, I can only imagine what they'd say about humans: "They constantly reference tiny boxes and hold them up in the air as if making an offering to an invisible god." Come on, satellite gods. Smile on us.

When we get to the intersection, I look in all directions, because maybe a car will come along and help us. There are no cars to be seen.

"You're the one who said this was a shortcut," I say. "This is the worst shortcut I've ever been on. There is no one here. If we broke down on the highway, we'd have help by now."

"If I'd driven, we wouldn't have broken down at all."

"Touché." I point my phone at him to acknowledge his solid point.

We keep walking around in the intersection, phones up, when suddenly Ty cheers. "I have a bar!" He turns to face me. "Quick, who are we going to call?"

"Brent? I think he should be home."

Ty calls Brent and sends him a pin for where we're located. Brent says he'll be there with some gas in about forty-five minutes. Argh. Maybe we shouldn't have called Brent. I'm sure I'll hear about this as one more example of how he's more responsible than me even if he was the one who used up all my gas this weekend (which I will point out when he gets here, since I'm still spreading blame around). Whatever. I'll deal with that later. Assured of our impending rescue, Ty and I walk back to wait in the car.

We chat about Art Connect for a few minutes. There's a brief lull in the conversation, and I try to think of what to say next. If I don't say something soon, this is going to get awkward. Come on, Natalie. Say something.

"So, do you like the Phillies, or is that just another hat?" I point.

He takes off the hat to see which one he's wearing and then puts it back on. "My Uncle Gary got me this one. He lives in Philadelphia. He promised that next time I come out, he'll take me to a game. Gotta get the hat broken in so I'll be prepared." He bends the brim into the already-perfect curve.

Another silence. Oh no.

Ty turns to me like he's about speak. Phewf. I meet his eyes.

He opens his mouth, but then closes it again. Then he says, "Um, let's crack the doors to get some air in here." He looks out at the papery corn and readjusts his ball cap.

Oh great, his face looks kind of red. I should have thought of how hot it would get in my car. I'm roasting him. Could today possibly get more embarrassing?

I look out my own door at the corn. It's difficult to tell where one stalk ends and another begins. They'd be very difficult to draw.

"I have an idea." I reach behind the passenger seat and grab the sketch pad I keep in the pocket. There's also a mini sketch pad in my purse. It's filled with drawings done during tricky artistic situations like this one.

Ty looks intrigued. "What's up?"

"Let's have a draw-off." I open my center console and pull out a handful of pencils and pens. "We both draw the scene outside. When Brent gets here, time's up. We'll see whose is better, and if there's not a clear winner, we'll let Brent judge."

"He'll pick mine," Ty says. "Bro code."

"We won't tell him whose is whose. Plus, I'm confident that mine will be so exponentially better that, even with any bro-code bias, I'll kick your butt."

"Oh really?" Ty raises his eyebrows. "That's some big talk coming from a high school kid."

Ouch. Is that how he sees me? As a kid? Because I'll admit that the fact that he's a college guy and I'm still in high school might be a little strange if we were, you know, dating. (Oh no! My brain is going there.) But we're not dating.

Yet.

(Stop it, brain! Don't get your hopes up!)

Is our age difference really that much to overcome? Is high school graduation some glass wall, where we can see each other but have to stay on our respective sides? Hopefully not.

"I'm a high school kid who's better than you, and either you already know that, or you're about to." I hold up the two sketch pads. "You want the big one or the small one?"

Ty reaches into his backpack and pulls out a sketch pad the same size as my behind-the-seat one. "I've got my own, thank you very much. Because I am a *pro* at this. I'm better at drawing than I am at painting. You're going down."

We sit by the side of the car with our backs against the warm doors and our feet straight out in front of us on the asphalt. My feet are clad in old flip-flops. His are in new-looking tennis shoes.

I point with my pencil. "No Birkenstocks today?"

"My dad got these for me while I was training for fall ball," he says, "before I knew I didn't make the team. I tried to return them, but no luck. Figured I might as well use them."

Ty looks a little sad as he opens his sketch pad. I almost ask about the team, but I can't think of what to say.

As Ty flips to his nearest blank page, it's clear that he wasn't lying. He's very good at drawing. On one page he's drawn a tattered baseball that's so realistic I almost ask if that's a special ball to him for some reason. He's drawn a few pages of partial landscapes that look more like photographs. He has two whole pages of eyes: old-person eyes, baby eyes, laughing eyes, crying eyes. It would be creepy if it wasn't captivating. I want to tell him not to turn pages so quickly, but I don't need to sound like a fan when I'm trying to compete with him. I'm going to have my work cut out for me, but it just so happens that I'm also very good at drawing.

"Ready?" Ty says.

His sadness is gone, and his eyes sparkle with the excitement of a challenge. We're on blank pages. Our pencils are poised. Our eyes lock. How long can I keep staring at him before this gets weird?

"Ready, set, go," I say all in one breath. Our pencils fly across our pages.

Forty minutes later, my eyes hurt from looking at the same patch of corn for so long. Ty has turned his baseball cap around so that the shadow of the brim won't obstruct his view. He's leaning forward, his sketch pad on his knees, and he keeps looking up and down from the pad to the corn and then back again. I sneak a peek at his drawing. It's not the first time I've done this. Or the second. Or the fifth.

"Dang. You weren't lying. That's really good."

"Hey!" He grabs his sketch pad and holds it away from me. "No cheating!"

"Cheating?" I laugh. "Like I'm going to copy your answers? Spoiler alert—we're both drawing corn."

"Eh, fine." He puts the book back in his lap. "I already looked at yours, too. It's impressive."

"Whoa!" I snatch my book out of his view. "It's not done yet!"

"You looked at mine!"

"Fine." I put mine back in my lap, then hold it toward Ty. "Trade?" We trade books.

Ty's corn is amazing. He's gotten the shadows of the ears perfect, which is something I struggle to do. Shadows are hard. His thin lines show the veins of the husks so realistically that it looks as if the page is textured. I could learn a lot from this guy.

"This is good," I say. "Like, really, really good."

"I know. I told you I was good." He smiles.

The wind blows the curls peeking from the edges of his baseball cap. My stomach flips. I must be hungry.

"I didn't say you were better than me. I said you were good. Simply good." I try to snatch my pad from him, but he holds it out to the side.

"Hey! Give it back." I reach over him to get it, but he stretches it even farther away. I scooch closer and reach again, putting my hand on his shoulder for balance, almost on top of him now. Are all shoulders this solid? I think mine are kind of squishy. I need to start doing workouts for my shoulders. Ty manages to keep the sketch pad inches from my grasp.

I lunge for it. "Ha! Got it!"

Ty catches my wrist like he's going to take it from my hand again. I was not aware that my wrist had so many nerve endings. My entire arm is tingling. Make that both arms, because my other hand is still on his shoulder.

I look at him in mock indignation. He can't take the sketch pad again when I've won it fair and square. His eyes are laughing, but they slowly change to something else. It's more . . . serious. Questioning.

Crap. I'm practically on top of the guy. He must think I'm throwing myself at him.

"Sorry." I scurry off him and pull the sketch pad to my chest, holding it like a toddler clutching a teddy bear. "That was awkward, wasn't it? My bad."

"It wasn't awkward." We sit and stare at our respective sketch pads, but neither of us draws. The wind blows through the rustling corn. A flock of geese honks overhead. Geese are louder than I thought. I look up and try to find them interesting. Ty does, too. Then he gives a small laugh. I almost don't hear it.

"What's so funny?"

"*Now* things are awkward." He gives me that grin again, and things are not awkward after all.

There's no getting around it. I have a crush on this guy. It doesn't matter that dating in high school is a waste of time, and it doesn't matter that every time I've felt this way it's ended badly. A crush is like the flu. You can try to convince yourself you're not getting it, but you end up with stomach issues anyway.

I used to welcome crushes. It was part of growing up, and it made me fit in with my friends. It was a staple of our conversations from about sixth grade on. Who do you like? Does he like you back? But even when the guys did like me back, it was never the way I imagined it would be. I was underwhelmed by all the things Cecily and Brynn billed as "magical." My first kiss was behind the gym at the eighth-grade formal, and it was honestly kind of gross. The guy tasted like cheese.

The most recent guy I dated was a gorgeous blond tennis player. We went out for two months last fall. We got in a bad fight one night, and I felt awful about it. The next morning, I brought him brownies to make up for losing my temper. When I got to school and opened my locker, I found a bottle of Midol with a note on it. It said, *Sorry.*

You're too moody. Use this with your next guy, because I can't do this anymore. I ended up throwing the note, the Midol, and the brownies in the trash can at the end of the hall. I felt like I should put myself in the trash right along with them.

I've learned that if I don't pin my hopes high when it comes to guys, I don't have far to fall. I told my friends this past summer that I was going to have a guy-free senior year. In my book, *guy-free = drama-free.* All of my focus needs to be on getting into Kendall, and I don't need distractions.

Plus, there's another reason. I can't get super close with any guy this year because I might spill the truth about the car accident. If he knew the truth, he'd leave. And if I was close enough to a guy to tell him the truth in the first place, then his leaving would hurt. A lot. It would be way worse than when my ninth-grade boyfriend dumped me on Valentine's Day via text. There's also the chance that the guy might tell people why we broke up. Then I'd be heartbroken *and* mortified. The best way to avoid this is to stay away from all potential relationships for a while. I wish there were medication for crushes. I'd take two pills and be over this in the morning. Unfortunately, that's another similarity between a crush and the flu. Sometimes you just have to wait for it to go away.

"Your drawing is really good," Ty's voice breaks into my thoughts. "Seriously."

"Thanks." I nod with a tight-lipped smile. More geese fly overhead.

At the sound of a motor, we both look to our left. A cloud of dust in the distance promises an approaching vehicle. As the car gets closer, I see a familiar shade of forest green.

Brent's here—we're rescued.

When my brother puts the gas in my tank, the car starts with no trouble. We're almost to the gas station when I realize that Ty and I were so happy to be rescued we never decided who won the draw-off. Maybe it doesn't matter.

Chapter 12

"We're here to see the Art Connect display."

The woman at the counter frowns at us for inconveniencing her.

"The exhibit closes in ten minutes." Her frown wrinkles go deeper than the Grand Canyon.

I give Ty a look that asks if we should go in. We came all the way here. He shrugs. I turn back to Frowns. "We'd still like to come in."

Her frown turns into a scowl.

"All right." She takes our five dollars each and glares at the miniature Abraham Lincolns as she shoves them in the register. She hands us our tickets with a deep sigh and an eye roll.

"Thanks." I hand Ty his ticket.

We make eye contact but then immediately look away while trying not to laugh. Ty fake coughs. I pretend to hiccup.

The Art Connect winners are displayed in Exhibit Hall B. When we go in, a few people are reverently looking at the pieces. They whisper like we're in a library. There are paintings on the wall, sculptures on the floor, and a few benches for people to rest and take it all in. Or are those benches pieces of art? Tough to tell sometimes. Better play it safe and not sit on them.

"Where do you want to look first?" Ty whispers.

"I don't know. Maybe over there?" I point to an interesting sculpture of tied shoelaces. There is no shoe, just crisscrossed laces leading straight up into a bow. It is impossibly balanced on the steel frame below it. Sculptures that seem like they shouldn't work are the best kind.

"It looks like the wind is blowing it," whispers Ty.

His breath is warm and smells vaguely sweet. This is not helping me get over my crush any faster.

Ty takes a quick survey of the other pieces in the hall. "Whoa, look at that." He nods to a painting of a smashed goldfish bowl. "I'm gonna take a closer look."

Does he want me to follow him or not? Better do my own thing since the crush-y thing to do would be to follow him. I walk the opposite way and find some beautiful pieces. There are paintings in watercolors, acrylics, and oils. There are pencil drawings and sculptures that I couldn't dream up, let alone create.

Time goes by too quickly, and before I know it, there are only three minutes left. Ty is on the other side of the gallery with his back to me. I feel so stupid for running out of gas and cheating him out of gallery time. As I look at his shoulders, I remember what it felt like to have my hand on them. Ugh, I don't want to remember that. Why does everything have to be so complicated? Nothing's simple when it comes to relationships. I'm going to paint the most confusing abstract piece possible and title it *Dating*.

The oil piece in front of me is a tree-lined avenue in fall. It puts my landscapes to shame. For the first time, I worry that I'm not good enough to have my pieces in Soo's gallery display. I don't want to embarrass myself.

A chime rings, and a voice warns, "Two minutes till closing."

The piece after the fall scene is a watercolor depiction of two children at the beach. The boy, around three years old, is bent over the hole that he's been digging in the sand. His khaki bucket hat shades his face. The girl, a little younger, is standing with her back to the viewer and facing the water. Her hands are on her hips, and her pink swimsuit has yellow polka dots and a yellow ruffle near the bottom.

Huh. I used to have a swimsuit like that. I remember it because of a photo I keep in my bedroom of Brent and me as toddlers. We're in a blow-up pool in the backyard, and Brent is holding the green hose like he's about to spray me. I'm giving him a two-year-old's equivalent of a death glare, and my hands are on my hips like "I don't think so." My frilly swimsuit detracted from the intimidation, I'm sure, but it's a cute picture.

I need to find Ty, but I stop. Something about the watercolor painting is pulling me back. It looks vaguely familiar, but

I figure that's due to the similar swimsuit. The boy's swimsuit is blue with vague green splotches on the side. That's odd. That looks just like Brent's suit from the picture in my bedroom. When we were kids, my brother loved the Teenage Mutant Ninja Turtles. He always asked to wear "turtle clothes," but my mom preferred designer to Donatello. He had one TMNT shirt (which he still has in a box somewhere) and the matching swimsuit. My dad bought both for him.

The little girl's blonde hair is wet. I reach up to touch my own. The only other parts of the scene are a couple of seagulls and an abandoned sand castle.

I squint. What am I supposed to think here? Any two kids could have had those swimsuits, right? Not everything's about me, which my mom reminds me about a hundred times a week. Upon further inspection, I see that the little girl's thumbnails are painted lavender. I remember the three bottles of fingernail polish that I kept in my childhood dress-up box. The only three colors I had were pink, blue, and lavender. When I painted the refrigerator one day after kindergarten, my nail polish got taken away.

The artist statement next to the painting is minimal. It lists the artist's name as "Z." The medium is watercolor. It is dated last year. The statement next to the piece says simply, "Children at the beach, happy."

I look back and forth between the art piece and the artist statement as if some dots will connect, but the dots are farther apart than constellations. What is going on? Is this the world's biggest coincidence, or am I missing something?

"You about ready?"

I jump. Ty is standing next to me. How long has he been there?

"Sorry." He laughs quietly. "I didn't know you were so absorbed."

"Hold on. I need a picture." Everyone else has left the gallery. Frowns is standing by the door glaring at us. She looks at her watch.

With my phone, I snap a picture of the painting and one of the artist statement.

"Excuse me!" Frowns calls across the gallery. "There is no photography permitted here!"

"Oops, sorry."

I'm not sorry.

———

Petunia is whimpering to be let out as soon as I get home, so I do that before starting my homework. After Toons has been out for three minutes and I've done exactly one math problem, she starts barking urgently. Someone's obviously walking up to our front door.

"I'll get it!" I say before the doorbell rings. Perfect distraction from math.

"It's probably Ronny," Brent calls from the living room.

I open the door to see a shaggy-haired, pimply-faced guy wearing a shirt that says PIZZA PALACE and holding a pizza warmer.

"Hey, Ronny." He's the delivery guy on duty every Monday night.

"Hi, Natalie. Thank you for ordering from Pizza Palace, the king of pizza. One pepperoni, one supreme, and one order of breadsticks?"

"Yep." I pay him out of the pizza envelope that we keep in the mail holder by the front door. "Same as always."

"The store makes me say that before I hand over the pizza. I don't even look at yours anymore, so don't order anything different."

"We never do."

"Perf." He flips his hair. "See ya next Monday."

Petunia doesn't stop barking until Ronny's old beater pulls out of our driveway.

We sit at the dining room table for dinner every night, even when we're eating takeout pizza. We still use real plates, too, not paper plates, because even takeout pizza has to be treated as a "proper meal." Mom says dinnertime is family time. Usually Brent cooks on nights when he doesn't have class, but I think we all look forward to pizza Mondays. I'm jealous of friends who get to eat by the TV or even in their bedrooms. My mom says eating on a couch is "vulgar" and provides too many opportunities for messes. "How can we talk as a family," she asks, "if we're watching the Kardashians?"

She secretly watches the Kardashians when I'm not around, but it's not really a secret. I've seen it saved on TiVo.

"Brent, pass the pepperoni. Nat, how was Greater Falls?"

"Good. We saw some great art."

"I'm so glad Brent was able to bail you out during your gasoline mishap. I've told you and told you, Natalie. Don't let it get below a half tank. Then this wouldn't happen."

"It was no big deal," says Brent. He smiles modestly at his pizza. I want to smash his face in it, which really isn't fair. It was nice of him to help us out. But is it too much to ask for him to be the one who needs help? Just once?

"Can you beat the other art people?" He eats half a slice of supreme in a single bite.

"Uh, no." Clearly he doesn't understand Art Connect. "I'm not entering as a competitor. I'll have a few pieces under Soo's studio display."

"That's still pretty legit."

"Brent, careful not to talk with your mouth full. And, Natalie, why isn't your napkin in your lap?"

Brent and I roll our eyes at each other, and Mom pretends not to notice.

"It's a great opportunity," I say. "There should be some college scouts there."

"Solid," Brent says.

"What kinds of colleges?" Mom asks. "Ones with lots of different degree programs, I hope." She takes a dainty bite of pizza.

Ugh. I know what she's getting at, and I'm not in the mood to beat around the bush. "Yes, Mom. Kendall will be there."

"Mm." She nods, feigning enthusiasm, while she finishes chewing her minuscule bite. "That's very exciting for Soo,

I'm sure. Keep in mind, though, our conversations about looking into other options."

"I did look. Kendall's the best."

"Maybe it's the best for art, but I'm referencing when we discussed looking into other career options. Maybe a business degree? It's so versatile. If I had a business degree, I could own Runway Flair by now."

"Then go get a business degree, Mom. It sounds like you're the one who needs it."

"Nat, come on." Brent gives me a pleading look.

He doesn't want to hear Mom and me fight about this again. At this point, he could probably recite the whole argument by himself. Spoiler alert—it ends with Mom telling me not to be disrespectful and me agreeing to at least consider other options. I give in, but I don't mean it; I simply get bored with the fight.

As if on cue, Mom dabs the corners of her mouth with a napkin. "Natalie, don't be disrespectful. I'm only trying to help. Art is a wonderful hobby to pursue, but you also need to do something that will pay the bills."

"Fine, Mom. I'll think about it."

We skipped right to the end this time. Looks like we're both bored with the fight. Brent breathes a sigh of relief.

To keep Mom from pressing the issue further, I decide now is a good time to ask the million-dollar question. "Mom, do you know anything about an artist named Z?"

Mom pauses with her glass halfway to her mouth, thinks a moment, then takes a drink. "No, I've never heard of Z. It sounds like an odd name. Why?"

"I liked some art signed by someone named Z today, that's all." No need to tell her about the painting if she's never heard of the artist. She already has conspiracy theories about how the government is tracking our every move. I don't need her panicking about an artist who might have spied on our family at the beach fifteen years ago.

As if she can read my thoughts, she asks, "What was the art?"

"A scene at the beach. It was impressive. It was a picture of two kids, and they were wearing swimsuits just like the ones Brent and I used to have."

"I'm glad you saw things you liked."

Her voice is a pitch higher than it usually is. What does she know about this painting that I don't?

Wait a minute. All her late nights working at the store. What if . . . ?

What if my mom is Z?

Why wouldn't she tell me? I had to get my artistic skill from somewhere—what if it was genetic all along? I suddenly want to shake her shoulders and say, "Seriously, do you paint? You understand that part of me? All this time— why keep it a secret? Why couldn't I know?" I want to cry and laugh and—

Oh my gosh, I don't know my mom *at all*. A picture forms in my mind of us painting together, exchanging tips, and maybe even one day having a gallery show together. No Brent—just us.

Before I can ask more questions, Brent has hijacked the conversation to talk about his baseball practice and wonder why on earth the coach won't let him pitch. I tell him he should be happy that he made the team at all, and I think of Ty's new fall ball shoes that will never see a field.

As soon as dinner is over, I head to my room and start brainstorming how to best bring up this theory to my mom. After all, if she's kept it a secret this long, it's going to be quite a shock to her that I know. Toons takes her usual command post by my feet. She stands vigilantly for the first few minutes before deciding that no threats have been detected, at which point she curls up and goes to sleep.

I run a Google search on "Z." Sites about the alphabet pop up. "Z artist" gives me sites about Jay-Z and other musicians with Z names. "Z artist Art Connect Greater Falls" hits a bull's-eye. There's a page for an artist in Smithfield, about a half hour from Greater Falls. A home page showcases a few paintings, and the Art Connect piece is prominently displayed. Now, where's the "About the Artist" tab? Got it. There's a picture of Z sitting on a stool, facing away from the camera so we can see the brilliance of the sunset being painted on the canvas. Beneath the photo is this blurb:

> Z has been painting for over thirty years. He studied art at Michigan State University and the University of Oxford, England, and he has had paintings displayed in many national and international competitions. He is known for his expertise in landscapes and portraits. His inspiration comes from the beauty of nature, his family, and the pieces of life that make him smile. A

People's Choice winner in last year's Art Connect competition, he owns a small gallery in Smithfield that is open 12:00–5:00 on Mondays, Wednesdays, Fridays, and by appointment.

Oh.

Z is not my mother.

My heart sinks, and I feel stupid for thinking maybe my mom and I had something in common. My vision of us painting together slides into nothingness, like watercolors that have been drowned in too much water.

My dad was at Oxford for a semester when he was in college studying history, and that's where he met my mom. He often studied in a coffee shop where she worked as a barista to pay for her own study abroad. It was apparently love at first sight. They only dated for two months before they returned to the States and, in a rash and so-not-my-mom decision, got married. My grandparents on both sides were furious, claiming that my parents were too young to get married. After all, they were both only twenty. That sounded plenty old when I first heard it, but now that Brent will be twenty in a year, it actually sounds pretty young. Anyway, they set out to have the picture-perfect, American Dream life and prove their parents wrong.

So here we are, however many years later, eating pizza every Monday and letting our dog run around by our paint-chipped white picket fence. It's almost the dream, I guess. Sometimes I wonder how things would be different if my dad hadn't died. Surely this was not how my mom pictured her future back when she was in that coffee shop in Oxford. It makes me feel guilty. Now my illness is one more thing ruining her American Dream.

Other than that coffee-shop story, I don't know much about my dad. I would ask when I was younger, but my mom always started crying, which was scary because I'd never seen her cry about anything else.

I want to stop thinking about my parents' sad story, so I go back to clicking around Z's website. There's not much information about who he is, and nothing about the kids-on-the-beach painting. The address to his studio is there, but I can't very well show up and say, "Hi, were the kids in your Art Connect painting based on real kids? If so, were you maybe creeping on me and my brother on a beach fifteen years ago?"

I look again at his inspirations: "the beauty of nature, his family, and the pieces of life that make him smile." Maybe he has kids, and the picture is based on them. Maybe his son also likes Teenage Mutant Ninja Turtles. Maybe—

Wait a minute.

No.

No way.

Definitely not.

No. No, no, no, no. No.

My hands freeze over the keyboard. This is nuts. This is probably one of those irrational things that my brain comes up with, and this—this right here—is why I need to be on medication. Did I take my medication today? Hmm. Yes, I know I did.

My heart races. I look down at Petunia, and when her sleepy eyes meet mine she jumps up, alert. Can she tell I'm freaking out?

"It's fine," I say too loudly. "Go back to sleep."

I lie flat on my stomach so I can reach under my bed. I pull out some socks, an old hoodie, a half-chewed rawhide, and a fully chewed shoe. Dang. You wouldn't think such a small dog could do so much damage.

I reach back under and pull out a paintbrush and four issues of *Seventeen* before I finally find what I'm looking for—an old scrapbook. My mom doesn't know I have it, but I found it in the basement years ago. I brush off the dust and dog hair, and open its familiar pages.

There's a picture of my mom and dad standing by an old Hogwarts-looking building. My mom's hair is huge. She never wears it like that anymore. She's flashing her brilliant smile (she rarely wears that now, either), and my dad is looking at her like she's more beautiful than all the art in the world. It's my favorite picture. I'd frame it if I didn't think it would make my mom sad.

There are a few other pictures on the pages, and there's a hometown news clip about my dad, Henry Cordova, winning a scholarship to study at Oxford. There's a picture from my parents' wedding, birth announcements for Brent and me, and a handful of pictures of us as babies. In one of those, my dad is holding me all wrapped up in a little pink blanket. There are the obituaries for my dad's parents and programs from their funerals. There's a wedding announcement for my mom's sister. There's Brent's preschool graduation certificate. He graduated with honors. (Um, he was three. What does that even *mean*?) After that, blank pages.

There is space in the scrapbook for more, but Mom never added anything else. That fact didn't bother me until just now, when I realized something important was missing. There's something that should have been tucked in there years ago, and I can't believe it took me this long to wonder why it wasn't there. Surely, in a place where all important family notices are kept, she would have had it. If she had Brent's preschool graduation certificate, there's no way she forgot about *this*.

I spend a half hour online trying to find the document that should have been in the scrapbook. Maybe Mom never got around to scrapbooking it. Perhaps it was too painful, or maybe she has it hidden away somewhere special. But surely there'd be a record of it somewhere?

But there's nothing.

"Hey, Toons."

Petunia looks up, and I whisper the question I can't get out of my head.

"If my dad is dead, why isn't there an obituary?"

Chapter 13

The next day, I arrive at our lunch table before my friends. I'm mentally running though ways to tell them that I think my dead dad might be alive, but there's no way that doesn't make me sound like a weirdo. They'd chalk it up to me being crazy.

Brynn puts her tray on the table. "Have you heard the latest?" She sits and then takes a split second to appraise that, no, I have not heard the latest. She sighs like I've been living under a rock. "This is huge. Wait till you hear."

"What is it?"

The thing about Brynn is that everything is big news. This could be "Someone got expelled," or it could be "A freshman dropped a tampon in the hall, which was majorly embarrassing." I'm never sure what to expect, but that makes it kind of fun.

Brynn starts to speak but then closes her mouth. "Nope, I can't tell you."

"What?" This is new. "Why not? You tell me everything. Even stuff I don't want to know."

"Not this time. It's not my news to tell."

"Brynn, ninety percent of what comes out of your mouth is not your news to tell. That has never bothered you before now."

Brynn pauses. She looks at the turkey sub in front of her as if the answer to her moral quandary will be found in the lettuce shreds.

"I promise I won't tell a soul," I say. This is the gold standard when it comes to gossip. It used to include "cross my heart and hope to die," but that dropped off around fourth grade. I don't know why I'm pushing her to tell me. I think it's the fact that, for once, she doesn't want to.

Brynn looks around to make sure no one's listening. "Will you act surprised when you find out from someone else?"

"Uh, sure." Why is that important? We tell each other everything.

Cecily shows up behind Brynn. She puts her lunch on the table before sliding onto the bench next to her. "Did you tell?" she accuses.

"No!" Brynn looks so proud of herself. "I didn't. Seriously. Nat, tell her."

"Right." This is getting weird. "Whatever it is, she didn't tell me. So? *Someone* needs to tell me."

"You seriously didn't tell?" Cecily narrows her eyes at Brynn. Then she looks at me like she's trying to figure out whether or not I'm feigning ignorance.

"I don't know what's going on. If no one tells me in the next five seconds, I'm going to lose it."

"Okay." Cecily takes a deep breath, milking her dramatic pause. "Now, you can't freak out, okay?"

"I won't freak out." Why would I freak out? What is she about to tell me? It doesn't look like bad news. She's smiling so big I can see her molars.

"I . . . " She takes another breath.

What's with all these breaths? You'd think she's low on oxygen.

"Cecily. Spill." I'm losing patience.

"Okay." She takes one more breath (argh!), and then . . . , "I'mgoingoutwithBrentFridaynightpleasedon'tbemad."

"What?" I'm equal parts surprised and unsure I heard her accurately. She spoke at the speed of light.

She slows it down this time. "I'm going out with Brent Friday night. Please don't be mad. Okay? Because you know how much I like him, and if you get mad, it will ruin this whole thing. If you're okay with it, then Friday will literally be the best day of my life."

No pressure. I'm not going to ruin the best day of someone's life.

Cecily chews her lip and looks at me expectantly. Brynn looks ready to explode with cheers, but it all depends on my response. She's holding her breath.

I put on a smile that doesn't feel as forced as I thought it would be. "Cecily, that's so great!"

Cecily and Brynn erupt into squeals and give each other a hug. Cecily runs over and hugs me. Everyone around our lunch table looks at us, and I laugh awkwardly. My friends are acting like we just won the lottery.

Come to think of it, Cecily would probably rather have this than a million dollars.

"You're sure?" Cecily calms down enough to check with me again. "Are you positive? I don't want to do anything to make things weird between us." She suddenly looks scared again, as if maybe I lied the first time.

"It's no secret that you've liked him forever. I've had time to get used to the idea, I guess." I'm not squealy excited about it or anything, but it's great to see Cecily so happy. And Brent and I aren't that close, so it's not like I feel threatened by her being his number-one girl.

"Ah!" Cecily jumps up and down all the way back to her seat.

Is she going to cry? That's a bit much, even for her.

"I'm sorry," she says, wiping her eyes before any tears fall. "I'm just so happy!"

Brynn turns to me. "You are such a good friend."

"Yes." Cecily nods so enthusiastically that I'm worried her headband will fall into her eyes. "You are the best friend in the whole world. No offense, Brynn."

Brynn doesn't look the slightest bit offended, probably because she knows Cecily isn't serious.

Cecily puts her hand to her chest. "He's so gorgeous. I hope he uses that great-smelling mousse in his hair on Friday. Then again, messy hair might show he's truly comfortable with me, you know? And maybe he'll wear his green polo with his Adidas jacket. Ooh, no, I hope he wears his brown leather jacket. It brings out the brown in his eyes. I could drown in his eyes."

She's trying on his outfits like he's a mental paper doll. This is weird.

"I think you're supposed to say you'll drown in someone's eyes if they're blue," Brynn points out. "Because it's like water, and you could drown in water."

"Fine. I'll drown in chocolate, then." Nothing's going to kill Cecily's buzz. "What should I wear? Should I get new flavored lip gloss? I have to taste good, just in case."

"Ew." That's a little far. "Could we hit the brakes on this? He's still my brother. What if I said I wanted to kiss your brother?"

"I don't have a brother."

"Okay, how about your dad?"

"He's fifty. You wouldn't want to."

I hold my hands up in surrender. "Whatever. Just . . . You can go out with him, but it took me a year to get used to imagining that. It'll take me much longer to get used to your flavored-lip-gloss idea—maybe forever."

"No problem." Cecily momentarily comes out of la-la land. "I promise. No talk of all the things I want to do with your brother." Her eyes get hazy again. "Especially now that I might get to do some of them."

Ew. Gross. What have I done? "If you don't stop, I'll tell him embarrassing secrets about you."

"Okay, okay." She snaps out of it. "I promise. Sorry."

I roll my eyes. "I'm getting cheese sticks." I need to get away from this weirdness.

Brynn speaks up before I can leave, eager to share in at least part of spilling this story. "He texted her this morning. He said, 'Hey, do you have plans for Friday night?' To which Cecily said no, obviously."

"Even though I did," Cecily cuts in. "It's my Aunt Christy's birthday party. But—hello—she'll have another party next year, because she has a birthday party every year even though she's old." She motions at Brynn to go on, like she's entranced by listening to her own story.

"So, then Brent texted back with, 'I was thinking maybe we could hit up Olive Garden and then go see *Serial Stalker*?' And then Cecily, in a very good move to clarify the situation, said, 'Sounds fun. Who else is going?' And then Brent said, 'As many people as you want, I guess, but I was hoping for maybe just you and me.' And there was a smiley emoji."

"A *smiley emoji*," Cecily emphasizes, like that was a diamond ring's worth of commitment. "He's already comfortable enough to use emojis. And he left it open for me to invite more people if I wanted, which was super considerate of him."

Brynn takes over again. "But of course she responded back, 'The two of us sounds good.' And she included a winky emoji, so there has been an equal emoji exchange." Brynn says this with the authority of a notary authorizing a business transaction.

"Do you think that was too forward?" asks Cecily uncertainly. "The winky? Because I want to come off as flirty but not overly enthusiastic. Like, I don't want him to think I'm obsessed with him."

"But you are obsessed with him," I point out. "You stole one of his gym socks from my house."

"If you tell him that, I will kill you. I have to come off as aloof. Like I care but also like I totally don't."

The rules of dating are so bizarre.

Would it be like this if Ty asked me out? I try to picture it, but then I remind myself that I'm trying not to picture it. Even so, I can't picture us obsessing over an emoji exchange.

"Are you going to act scared during the movie?" Brynn asks. "So he'll put his arm around you? Because you already know all of the scary parts, so it might seem kind of forced."

"You saw it already?" I ask. According to the ads, it's a movie about a guy who connects with girls online, trails them for a long time without ever meeting them, and then kills them. Pretty morbid, but most horror movies are.

"Oh, um, yeah." Cecily suddenly gets very interested in her sandwich.

"When?"

"Saturday night." She doesn't look up.

"Who'd you go with?" That's odd. I'd mentioned last week that we should go see it together. It's perfect with Halloween coming up next month.

"Um, just some people." Cecily won't look at me.

Brynn pushes some crumbs together on her paper plate. Suddenly, the answer clicks into place.

"You two went without me?" That has to be wrong, but Cecily and Brynn exchange a look, and I know I'm right. "Why didn't you invite me?"

Brynn shifts uncomfortably in her seat. "Didn't you have plans? I thought you had plans."

Why aren't they being honest with me?

Brynn scratches her arm. Cecily takes a drink.

"Just *tell* me," I say. "You know I'll get it out of you eventually."

"We were, um, worried about you," Cecily finally says. Somehow the jubilant tone of this lunch has been completely zapped. Now I'm back to being confused.

"Worried about me?"

Cecily leans in close and lowers her voice to a whisper. "From, you know, *what you told us*. Your issue."

My issue?

I look at Brynn. She mouths, "Bipolar."

I look around to make sure no one saw Brynn and then cross my arms tightly to my chest. "Why would that stop me from going to see a movie?" I whisper.

It's the first mention of my illness since Saturday morning in my bedroom. I was hopeful that maybe my secret hadn't changed anything, that maybe my friends didn't think any differently of me. Now that hope lies shattered on the dirty cafeteria floor.

147

"We didn't want to, um, *trigger* anything," Cecily says.

She's talking quietly, but the words ring very loud. I'm different. I need to be cared for. I need to be sheltered.

"What would you trigger? I told you before, I'm fine."

"Right," says Brynn. "You're fine *now*, but that's how it all starts. Those people are fine one day, then suddenly they snap and go on killing sprees. I heard a case like that on a podcast once. We didn't think a violent movie was a good idea for you."

"*Those people*?" We are now whisper-shouting. I used to be a best friend, a trusted confidante, and now I'm one of "those people."

"No, I mean, *your* people, er, people like you, uh, come on, you know what I mean." Brynn scratches the back of her neck.

"Crazy people," I offer.

Brynn looks at Cecily nervously.

Cecily tries to smooth out Brynn's rough edges. "Not *crazy* people," she says. "People with mental illness. Mental illnesses are very real, and they're important to address. We're your best friends, so we're trying to help you."

"Well, this isn't helping." I roll up my sub wrapper angrily. "You're making me feel worse by leaving me out of stuff. The vast majority of 'my people' have no violent tendencies. That's not fair."

"I know. I'm sorry," says Cecily. She bites her lip.

"Me too," adds Brynn. "We weren't sure what to do."

"Here's what you do." I slam both hands on the table. Cecily and Brynn jump back, startled. "Treat me exactly the same way you've always treated me. I'm the same person.

Don't worry about sheltering me or making decisions for me. Just love me, okay? Be there for me like we were there when Brynn's parents forgot to tell her they went on vacation or when Cecily broke up with . . . I don't know . . . pick a guy."

"I feel like my parents' serial abandonment probably shouldn't be equated with Cecily's dating issues." Brynn's eyes narrow.

"I don't have dating issues." Now Cecily's offended, too.

I wave my hands in front of them. People are staring at us (again). "Hi, excuse me? Back to me. Friends are there for each other during hard times. *That's how friends work.* I'm simply asking for some support, and that means you pretend like everything's fine."

"Yeah, except that it's not fine." Brynn frowns.

"Right, I know. It *wasn't* fine, but it is *now.*"

Brynn and Cecily exchange another look.

"Hi, still here." I wave my hands again. I'm not usually such an attention monger, but I'm sick of feeling like a third wheel with my two best friends. "Stop looking at each other like I'm not here. I'm *right here.*"

They look at each other again, and I want to scream. I picture them at the movies, laughing and eating popcorn without me.

"Is this how it's going to be now? The two of you and then me, off to the side, as the crazy tagalong when I'm even invited at all?"

The Brent issue didn't make things awkward between us, but this certainly will.

Cecily speaks first. "We said we're sorry. We were only trying to help, not make you mad. From now on, we'll invite you to everything. Be patient with us, okay? This news has been hard for us to handle."

Because I want to keep it together and not act like a crazy person, I manage a nod and a tight smile. I'm sure this *is* hard for them. While nodding, however, I imagine a parallel universe where I jump up on my cafeteria bench, throw napkins into the air, and scream, "This is hard for *you*? You've got to be kidding me. No, wait. Allow me to be there for *you* during *your* time of need. It must be *so difficult* to have a mentally ill friend. Don't worry that it's completely destroyed everything I thought about myself. Really, I should be comforting you right now. Sorry for making my mental illness about me!"

Then, because I'd be yelling, everyone would stare. The whole cafeteria would be quiet. I'd look around and say, "Sorry, everyone. You're all going to school with a crazy person. I'm sure this is *very hard for you*." Then I'd storm out to the sound of my shoes on the cafeteria floor. Before I storm out, I'd grab some cheese sticks. Dramatically. Because I really want some cheese sticks. I'm trying to fit these in somehow when Cecily's voice breaks into my fantasy.

"Thanks. You understand, right? We're trying."

"Right." I nod. "You're doing the best you can."

Either they can't tell my smile is fake, or they choose not to notice. I feel like a shaken can of soda, but I keep myself from exploding.

I head to the cafeteria line to get cheese sticks. By the time I get back, the conversation will have moved on to something new. I guess bringing up my dad to them isn't a great idea until I have legitimate proof. It would only add to their suspicions that I'm completely nuts.

What does *crazy* mean, anyway? After all, I'm not locked up for trying to kill someone, and the differences between an anxiety attack, severe psychosis, and random homicide are huge. Where along the spectrum do I fit? I feel like I'm not insane, but at other times it feels like I'm dancing toward it, occasionally putting a toe over the line marked CRAZY. With this dad thing, maybe my whole foot has gone over. It's hard to tell.

Maybe I am crazy.

Chapter 14

"I'm going to promise you something right now."

Toons sits across from me on my bed looking me right in the eye. At least one eye. My wet hair drips on my purple yoga pants and the oversize Derek Jeter T-shirt I swiped from Brent.

"Are you listening?"

Toons pulls her tongue into her mouth and quits panting.

"I'll take that as a yes. Okay. Here is my promise: I'm never, ever telling anyone about my sickness again. Never."

Petunia nods.

"Okay, then. That's settled."

I lie down on my stomach. Her face is right in front of mine now, about a foot away. "No one else needs to know about the bipolar thing, okay, Toons? Just me and you." She jumps forward and licks my hair, which probably smells like my eucalyptus shampoo.

"Ack! Your breath is disgusting."

It's tough to have a heart-to-heart with a dog, but sometimes it's your best option. If only they'd brush their teeth.

I rest my chin on a pillow. "Telling anyone was a mistake. Now they think I'm all weird, but I'm not."

Toons keeps staring at me.

"My brain works a little differently, but that doesn't make me a freak. I can watch scary movies with my friends."

She tilts her head.

"Don't tilt your head at me. I can feel your judgment."

She tilts her head the other way.

"Did you have any friends at the pound who left you out of things?" I wait a few seconds as if she might answer me. "No? Well, then you're lucky. It sucks."

She licks my blanket.

"The worst part is that I don't know if they'll ever see me the same."

I roll onto my back. My view of the ceiling fan gets blocked by her curious squished face.

"If my best friends freak out, imagine how the other kids at school would react. Imagine how Ty would react. It's not worth the risk."

A drop of drool threatens to fall from Toons's tongue, so I roll over again and make her back away.

"It's just me and you, okay? Around everyone else, I'm the same old Natalie. I'm spunky. I'm fun. I'm *me*. I'm not bipolar. Got it? If you agree, don't say anything."

She stares at me blankly.

"Perfect."

Dr. VanderFleet told me it might not be so bad if some of my friends knew the truth about my bipolar disorder. She said true friends would stick with me no matter what. Well, what a grand idea that *wasn't*. My fists clench. Psychiatrists are supposed to be professionals. They're supposed to be able to predict how these things will turn out.

Well, I suppose they're not fortune-tellers. Just plain people. Maybe I shouldn't trust her quite as much as I thought I could. Maybe she doesn't know much about teenagers. But if she doesn't know much about teenagers, how is she supposed to help me? Am I supposed to help myself?

Toons crawls into my lap. She drools, and a small purple wet spot forms on the ankle of my yoga pants. I pet her and think back to lunchtime. I've become a liability and an inconvenience to my best friends. I pet Toons a little harder. She looks at me as if to say, "Um, why are you trying to squish me?"

There's a knock at my door. "Nat? You still up?" It's Brent.

"Yeah. Come in."

Brent sees Petunia and quickly looks into the hall to make sure Mom isn't coming. "Mom will kill you if she sees the dog on your bed."

"Then shut the door, nerd."

When the room is secure, Brent sits on the side of my bed. "Your dog isn't as obnoxious as I thought she'd be. Here, let me hold her." Toons wiggles in protest when I hand her over, but she soon settles down to take a nap.

"What's Mom doing?" I ask.

"Last I saw, she was watching the Kardashians. Or maybe it was *The Real Housewives of* . . . somewhere. I'm never sure. They all look like the same bunch of women yelling."

"Awesome. Then she won't come check on me."

"Yeah, you're probably fine." He pets Petunia, and soon she's snoring.

"I'm not sure if Cecily mentioned it to you, but I sort of have a date with her on Friday."

I recall the squealy jump-fest at lunch. "Yeah, she mentioned it."

"So . . ." He looks like he expected more of a response. "Are you cool with that?"

"I guess."

He lets out a deep breath. "Awesome. I didn't know if you would be weirded out or something."

"I really don't care." Which I don't. Losing my friends is bothering me, but losing one of them to Brent isn't the concern. "I mean, don't be a jerk or anything. If you guys have a messy breakup, it'll make things weird around here."

"Definitely." Brent is eager to agree. "It's not serious or anything. It's one date. Super chill."

Little does he know that Cecily spent the past hour texting Brynn and me pictures of various outfits for Friday.

"Right." I force a smile, trying to figure out how to extricate myself from this conversation for the second time today. At least I can be confident that he's not going to talk about flavored lip gloss.

My phone buzzes. It's a text from Cecily—probably a question about shoes or jewelry. I shove my phone under a pillow and change the subject. "Do you ever wonder about Dad?"

Brent stops petting Toons. "Wait. What does Dad have to do with Cecily?"

Oops, maybe that was a rough transition. "Um, nothing. But, speaking of Dad—"

"We weren't talking about Dad."

"Right. But now that you mention him, I can bring up something that's been bugging me."

Brent rolls his eyes. "Fine, Nat. What's up?"

Success.

"Did you ever read his obituary?"

Brent thinks about this for a second. "No, but I could barely read anything when he died. I was five. I'm sure Mom has it in a scrapbook somewhere."

"It should be available online, right?"

"I don't know." Brent gives me a where-are-you-going-with-this face. "Have you looked?"

I sit up on my knees and take a deep breath. "Yes, I did. I couldn't find one." I wait for the gravity of this situation to hit him. It doesn't. He and Petunia both stare at me blankly. I try again. "I couldn't find an obituary. Anywhere. There's no record of one."

He narrows his eyes and looks around like there's some joke he's not getting. "Okay . . ."

Ugh. This is exasperating. I'm just going to lay it all out there. "What if he's alive, Brent? He might be alive. That's what I mean." Now for sure he's going to gasp or recoil in surprise. I put one hand toward Toons in case he forgets he's holding her and drops her in his fit of shock.

Brent stares at me and then looks at my hand. "What are you doing?"

Oh. "Uh, petting Toons. In slow motion. Because she likes that."

I proceed to pet her in slow motion, and Brent looks at me like I've lost it. Then comprehension dawns on his face. Here it comes.

"Now I get it. Did you take your pills today?"

Seriously? He thinks this is all about me being under-medicated? I want to slap him upside his oh-so-sane head.

"Of course I took my pills, Brent. Just like I took them last night and yesterday afternoon and every freaking day of my life since they were prescribed to me."

"Then why do you think Dad is alive? He's dead, Nat."

"Maybe. Maybe not. Yesterday, when I went and saw last year's Art Connect winners, there was this piece by an artist named Z. It had two kids in it who looked like you and me at the beach. It was creepy. The kid even had Teenage Mutant Ninja Turtle shorts."

"A bunch of kids had those shorts."

"I'm telling you—it was us." I pull out my phone and show him the picture I took. I grab the framed picture of us in the blow-up pool and hold it next to the phone. "Look familiar?"

Brent looks at it and then up at me. He shakes his head and looks genuinely concerned, but not about our dad.

"Dude, those kids in the painting aren't even facing the camera. They could be literally anyone. I don't know what brought this on, but . . . he's dead, Nat."

"Is he?" I pull out the only other hard evidence I have—the scrapbook. I flip through the pages. "There's no obituary in here. There are obituaries for our grandparents. There's a wedding announcement for a wedding none of us even attended. All of our important life stuff is in here. Don't you think an obituary for our *father* should have made the cut? Or something from his funeral?"

Brent starts flipping the scrapbook's pages. "Dude, I graduated from preschool with honors? That's awesome."

I roll my eyes. "You're really missing the point here."

Brent continues looking through the scrapbook. "Don't get me wrong, Nat. I'd love to know more about Dad, too. But you know how Mom is about him. Maybe she didn't keep a copy of the obituary. Maybe no one even wrote one."

This isn't going well. Brent is my only shot at an ally, and I feel an irrational need to convince him that this makes sense. "I checked the county records. There's no death certificate either."

"Didn't he transfer hospitals at some point? Maybe he died in a different county."

"If I check every county in the state, then will you believe me?"

Brent shrugs. "Out of all the dead people in the world, it's possible they lost track of a death certificate from years ago."

"Really? Isn't it kind of their job to keep track of these things?" I ask.

Brent still looks unconvinced.

"Why haven't we ever visited his grave?"

He looks like I just asked why one plus one is two. "Seriously? Mom always said it was too hard for her, that there's no point in looking at a slab of stone that has nothing to do with the person we lost. We've both heard that, and it's made perfect sense until apparently today. What is your deal? Have you lost your mind?"

There's an uncomfortable silence.

"Sorry. I didn't mean—"

"Yeah, yeah, I know what you meant." I'm deflated. Brent's not going to be an ally. I'm on my own. Whatever. It's not the first time.

We're quiet again. Brent pets Toons. I will myself not to cry. The fan makes a small clicking noise as it spins.

"So, thanks for being cool about the Cecily thing. You sure we're good?"

"Just leave." I grab Petunia from his lap. "I don't want to talk anymore."

Brent looks like he wants to say something. He's quiet for a moment, then shakes his head. "Whatever you say." He walks out and closes the door behind him.

I pick up one of the pillows left on my bed and scream into it. This day is a hot mess. I'm not going to be able to sleep unless I de-stress a bit. My clock says 10:02. There's enough time before bed for a short closet painting, right? Sleep is overrated anyway.

My closet door is slightly open, and the jeans I wore yesterday are spilling from it. When I pull them out, I also pull out a few T-shirts, a skirt, and . . . Oh, *there* is my history textbook. With the closet emptied, I crawl in and pull out my shoebox of paints. I sigh when I look at my panicked wall paintings. My good paintings get so messed up when I paint like that.

The streaks of white that bolt like lightning around the circle painting aren't bad. I'll leave those. Both the large, jagged *IT'S FINE* and the smaller ones have got to go. I choose the large one and paint over it with my darkest purple.

As I'm painting over the shaky letters, Toons jumps off the bed and peers around the closet door. She walks in and tries to lick paint out of the shoebox lid. I put the lid on top of my shoe rack so that she can't reach it. Then I go back to painting while she looks longingly at the shoebox lid. She finally gives up and curls up in a ball next to me.

I paint the silhouette of a face. From the front of the silhouette, I use bright colors to streak back into tendrils that mix and run with one another. With the lights off, the glow of the paints is electric.

When I take a break to look at my clock, bright green digital numbers announce that it's 11:43. No wonder I'm tired. Time for bed.

Toons watches me while I get my pills from the nightstand and stare at them for a minute. As always, I decide to take them—at least for one more night. My therapist and psychiatrist have both highlighted the importance of taking my pills every night, but as I've recently established, medical professionals are wrong sometimes. What if they're wrong about this, too? What if I don't need these pills as much as they think I do? Petunia runs over and tries to lick my face.

"No, no, no." I pick her up and put her at the end of the bed. "Stay," I command. I get back into my spot and pull up the covers. "Lie down," I tell her, and she does. "Stay."

Hey, cool. Looks like we're getting better at *stay*.

As I pet Petunia and try to drift off to sleep, my mind keeps getting hung up on my dad. Why is there no record of his death? If he's alive, what does that mean to me? Where is he now?

My heart tightens with a feeling of longing, missing someone I barely remember.

Chapter 15

Ella is standing on my front porch. "I'm three minutes early. Is that acceptable?"

I open the door wider. "Yeah, no problem."

"Perfect." Ella walks in and shuts the door behind her. "Thank you for your flexibility."

Ella has started coming over every Thursday at 4:00 to see Toons, although she hates the nickname. She insists that the dog's name is Petunia, only Petunia.

She's my dog, though. I could call her Stupidhead for all Ella should care. Stupidhead might be a good name since she still runs into the couch at least twice a week.

"Outside today?" Ella asks.

As long as the weather is nice, we sit on the deck while the dog plays outside.

"Sure."

Is Ella going to want to do this in February? We're not hanging out on my deck in February.

"Great." She breezes past me. "Petunia! Let's go outside."

Petunia appears and bounds up to Ella. Ella sits on the floor to pet her, and it's easy to see how much she loves this dog.

"How are you doing, huh, girl? How was your week? Are you getting fat?" She flips Petunia onto her back and rubs her stomach. Petunia looks happy. Ella appraises her belly and then looks at me suspiciously. "How much are you feeding her?"

"The same amount I've been feeding her since I first got her. It's the recommended amount on the dog food bag."

"Hmm. Good. Okay, then." Ella lets Petunia flip back over and then opens the back door so she can run out.

It's become a bit of a routine for us. Ella first checks to see if Petunia is okay, then finds a nonexistent problem (Are her wrinkles dirty? Is she limping? Is she fat?), then decides that she's fine and lets her run outside. We usually talk, work on homework, and watch Petunia run around for a while until Ella suddenly decides it's time to go home.

Ella and I don't talk much at school. We say hi when we pass each other in the hall, and that's about it. Thursdays are when we catch up. It's quickly becoming my favorite day of the week. That was surprising when I first noticed the feeling, but I've accepted it. Ella is great. I haven't had a friend like her before. I hope she thinks we're friends; I think we're friends. We've never really talked about it.

"Do you want a drink?" I ask.

"Lemonade, please."

The backyard looks picturesque from the kitchen window. Ella heads out to play with Petunia while I make the lemonade. She starts by chasing Toons, then she stops, jumps side to side for a second, and runs away while Toons chases her. It looks like they're having tons of fun, and I feel a little bad that Ella couldn't keep Petunia herself.

When I bring out the lemonade, Ella is kneeling on the deck. Petunia lies on her back, panting happily as Ella pets her belly. Then she rolls over and licks Ella's combat boots.

"I think she's thirsty," says Ella. "Here." She takes the glass of lemonade and puts it on the ground. Toons eagerly laps up the sugary water, and Ella looks at me. "Could I please get another glass of that?"

I go to the kitchen and pour another glass. My mom would kill me if she knew that the dog is drinking out of our nice glasses.

Ella accepts the fresh glass and sits back in her chair. The dog is still drinking, but the lemonade level in the glass is almost too low for her tongue to reach. With no more distractions, it's time to start math homework. Ugh.

"My sister hates that I'm coming here." Ella takes a sip, like that was a totally normal thing to say.

"Chloe? Why?" I close my math book again. I know I'm not Chloe's favorite person, but trying to keep her sister from hanging out with me seems a bit harsh.

"She thinks you're stupid."

Now I'm glad I brought my math book out. "I'm in calculus. I'm not stupid."

"Not *that* kind of stupid." Ella sighs like I'm stupid for not understanding why I'm stupid. "I don't know. She thinks you're . . . Hmm, I believe her exact words were 'elitist and shallow.'"

That stings. Elitist and shallow? How so? My friends and I have lots of other friends. We're always talking in big groups of people before and after school. And okay, sure, we hang out just the three of us quite a bit, but that's because we've been friends for so long. Not because we're elitist. I hang out with other people, too. Obviously, I hang out with Ella. That's sort of because she invited herself over, but still. I could have said no.

And I'm not sure why Chloe would say I'm shallow. I like to dress fashionably, but who doesn't? Shopping is the social glue that holds high school girls together. It's not like I'm going to walk around in mismatched patterns, wild hair, and combat boots. That would be ridiculous.

Wait a second. Did I just describe Ella? Eeeep! That might have been a little shallow. But one shallow thought does not make me shallow *as a person*. It was a mistake, and it was only in my mind. I shoot Ella a guilty look. Did I used to judge people who dressed like her? Do I still? Note to self: Reflect on this later, because I am very deep and reflective.

"I'm not elitist." That one's easier to defend.

"*I* didn't say you were." Ella reaches into her bag and pulls out her American lit book, apparently ready to start homework.

Does she think she can end a conversation like that?

"Why does she think I'm elitist?"

"Because she's insecure."

Again, she says this with the confident authority that her one sentence should explain everything. She opens her lit book to a page bookmarked by a piece of notebook paper. She picks up her pencil, but I grab it out of her hand.

"Hold on. You can't say something like that and not expect to talk about it a little more than two sentences." Ella looks startled. It appears she hadn't considered that. I put the pencil down in the crease of her book. "That was kind of a mean thing for her to say."

Ella looks up and to the right. "Hmm, that wasn't supposed to hurt your feelings. Either it was insensitive for me to say, or you are overly sensitive. Never can tell in these situations." She picks up her pencil to start working, but then adds, "Like I said, I don't think you're elitist."

She doesn't add *or shallow*, but I let it go.

She bites her eraser before continuing. "I think Chloe is salty because she never gets invited to do stuff with you."

"She can hang out with us." This reminds me that even my own group left me out of a trip to the movies. I know what that feels like. "She should have said something."

"It's socially unacceptable to invite oneself to a party or other exclusive gathering," Ella says. "One should wait until receiving a formal or informal invitation from the host or hostess before presuming that one's presence is desired."

It sounds like she read that out of a textbook.

"It's in Chloe's book called *How to Survive High School*," Ella says in response to my questioning look. "I read it last year, but it's mostly fluff junk about how to get boys to like you and how to get invited to parties."

"You invited yourself over here, which would technically go against the book," I point out.

Ella looks thoughtful.

"I'm glad you did," I hurriedly add. "Seriously, it's fun having you over."

It really is. Ella tells it like it is, and there are no games around her. I don't have to guess what she's thinking, and that makes me feel free to be open. We're honest with each other in a way that I'm not with very many people.

"This isn't a party," she decides. "This is me and you and Petunia. I can invite myself to that."

She goes back to reading her textbook. Without any further distractions, I do a few math problems.

"Are we friends?" Ella suddenly asks.

She doesn't ask this in the insecure way that girls did back in junior high, when everyone had to have one half of a best-friends necklace to be cool. It's more like a scientific question.

"I'm wondering how to classify our relationship."

"Yeah, we're friends." Her question seems random, but I'm used to that by now. I go back to doing math.

"Hmm." Her elbow is on the table. She puts her chin in the palm of her hand and taps her nose with her fingers. "That's interesting."

"Why?"

"I don't usually do friends."

I put my pencil down. "What does that mean?"

She shrugs. "It's something I've always heard. It was on every report card: 'Ella struggles to make friends.' I had to see a counselor to learn social skills like introducing myself to new people or asking someone to sit with me at lunch. Everyone's always trying to make me do the 'friend' thing. Sometimes I think I have a friend, but then it turns out I don't. One time the teacher assigned someone to be my friend. I may not know a ton about friends, but I know that's not how it's supposed to work. I thought maybe you and I were friends, but Chloe said we aren't because I keep inviting myself over, and you're just being nice. So I was confused. But if we are friends, then I don't know how to do that." She stops a moment, thinking. "Hey, did a teacher assign you to be my friend?"

I raise my eyebrows. "No."

"My parents? Your mom? Anyone?"

"No."

"Hmm." She goes back to tapping her fingers. "Then how do you know we're friends?"

"Because . . ." I'm a bit stumped. "Because you come over to my house? Because I like hanging out with you?"

"Huh." Ella enters this into her mental database. "That's all it takes to be a friend? That doesn't sound complicated at all."

I think about Brynn and Cecily. "Sometimes it does get more complicated."

"This is my exact issue." Ella throws her hands up. "People want me to figure this crap out, and there are no formulas for it whatsoever. You know what's better than friends? Math."

"Wow, I wish I agreed." I nod to my math book. "This stuff sucks."

"Is that calculus? I'm pretty good at calculus. I took it last year. Want some help?"

She took calculus in ninth grade? Why am I not surprised?

"Sure."

We work on my homework for a few minutes, and Ella is a great teacher. She's patiently explaining how to type derivatives into my calculator, and I realize something.

"This is what friendship is. Here's a perfect example. I'm struggling with something, and you helped me. Even though it's not really benefiting you, you do it because you care about me and want me to succeed."

Ella keeps typing on the calculator. "Pretty sure I'm doing this because I like math."

"No, seriously." I pull the calculator out of her hands so she'll look at me. "This is you being a good friend. Own it."

Ella pauses. "All right. Is this like what your other friends do for you?"

"They do lots of stuff." I feel defensive, and I'm not sure why. "We talk about things, and we're there for each other when things are hard. Well, most of the time."

"Most of the time?" Ella's eyes narrow. "Is this another exception to the friend rules? There are too many exceptions. Maybe I don't want friends. It sounds tricky."

"No," I decide. "There aren't exceptions. If you're a real friend, you'll be there when your friends need you. Period."

"That sounds convenient." She appears to mull this over. "So, for example, if my grandma had another dog that I needed you to adopt, you'd do it? Even though you're not scared I'm going to blackmail you anymore?"

Oh shoot. I cannot take another dog. "Uh, does your grandma have another dog?"

"No. This is theoretical."

"Then yes."

Ella smiles. "Thanks. Even though I bet you said that because she doesn't have another dog."

"Maybe." I smile back. "But if you really needed it, I'd think about it. Or at least help you find somewhere for it to go. For real."

Ella nods once. "Good enough for me."

Suddenly there's a crash and the sound of glass clinking on the deck. Petunia jumps back in surprise. She bolts across the deck, almost trips as she races down the steps, and runs across the yard as fast as she can. Admittedly, it's not that fast. She looks like a fuzzy potato trying to run.

"Aw, man!" I start picking up pieces. The glass Toons was licking from has shattered, and a small puddle of lemonade reaches to touch as many of the bits as possible.

"I'll get the broom." Ella rushes inside.

I'm not sure how effective the broom will be, as many of the pieces will probably slip between the slats and fall under the deck. Also, how does she know where we keep our broom?

As if on cue, Ella sticks her head out of the kitchen window. "WHERE IS YOUR BROOM?" she yells, even though I'm only six feet away.

"The closet under the stairs." I respond in a normal volume.

"Harry Potter closet. Roger that."

She turns to go get the broom. I try to pick up the biggest pieces without cutting my fingers. By the time she comes out, most of the glass is cleared. She starts sweeping the remaining shards, but they make a screechy sound against the wet wood and, as predicted, fall through the slats. Ella stops sweeping.

"Does anyone in your family, human or animal, spend a significant amount of time under your patio?"

"Um, no." The deck is only two feet off the ground, and it's closed on the sides with latticework.

Ella nods and keeps sweeping until all the glass pieces have fallen through the slats. "Perfect. We didn't even need a dustpan."

Works for me. She leans the broom against the house and sits back down at the table. Toons has overcome her surprise and comes to investigate what we're doing. She starts licking the deck because it's now lemonade flavored, and I pick her up to keep her from finding any stray pieces of glass.

"I like the painting by the stairs closet," Ella says. "It reminds me of Crane Park."

"It is Crane Park." I've gone back to my homework, and the problem I'm doing is so complicated that I don't even look up. "It's a painting I did when I was bored on summer break two years ago."

"I took a picture of it. Is it okay if I took a picture of it?"

"Sure."

"Whew, that's good because I also took a picture of the beach scene in your bathroom and the woods scene in your living room and the other woods scene in your living room. Are those all okay, too?"

Well now, forget the problem. I look up from my book. "Um, sure. Why do you want all of those pictures?"

"Because I like taking pictures." Ella says this as if it's the most obvious thing in the world.

"Why do you like taking pictures?"

"Why do you paint?"

"Um, I guess because I like painting."

"Exactly." That's all the explanation I get. We work quietly for a while. Suddenly Ella jumps. "What time is it?"

My phone has the answer: 5:41.

"Ack!" Ella closes her book and frantically stuffs things in her backpack. "I have to go!"

"What's the big rush?" It's not like she has other friends to go see, especially not when she's wearing those horrible navy cargo pants. They zip off at the knee, which was cool back in the year she was born, maybe.

Oh crap. I *am* shallow, aren't I? Note to self: Fix this immediately.

"My pharmacy closes at six on Thursdays, and if I don't get my meds today, I am *screwed*."

There's a split second where I have to decide if I'm going to ask why type of medications she's on. It's an obviously inappropriate question, but social norms don't seem to matter to Ella. Curiosity overcomes decorum.

"Meds for what?" My mom would be appalled.

"ADHD. I have that, and I have autism. My brain's all sorts of fun."

She widens her eyes and moves her eyebrows up and down like a mad scientist. I half expect her to let out a *Muahahaha!*

"Oh." What am I supposed to say to that? This is like when I told my secret to Brynn and Cecily, but now I'm on the other side. In a perfect world, what would I have wanted them to say? Honestly, I don't even know.

While I'm busy trying to choose my next words, I notice that Ella doesn't seem nervous or uptight. Maybe it wasn't a big secret to her.

She drops the mad-scientist face. "Yeah, it's no big deal. My sister occasionally says I'm a weirdo, but she's the one who kisses her computer screen every night to say goodbye to her favorite YouTuber. Which one of us is the weirdo? Hmm? Exactly."

"I didn't answer your question."

"There was only one logical answer."

"Wait, so, um . . ." This is a thin-ice conversation. "It really doesn't bother you? Your autism?"

"It bothers me that it's now five forty-two and my mom is going to kill me if I don't get those meds by six, but other than that? No, it doesn't. Gotta go. Bye." She throws her backpack over her shoulder, unlocks the side gate, and rushes around the house toward the driveway.

How is it possible that she has two disorders and simply doesn't care? I tried to kill myself over having brain problems, and she can talk about her disorders over lemonade, like it's no big deal.

I take a drink of lemonade, but then choke on it when Ella bursts back through our gate and into the yard.

"I forgot to say goodbye to Petunia!" she calls over her shoulder. She runs up to Petunia, pats her on the head, and says, "Bye, girl." Then she turns and sprints wordlessly past me again.

"Bye," I say, but she's already gone.

As I watch Toons chase a quick-moving grasshopper, something earthshaking occurs to me: maybe my illness isn't that big of a deal. Is it possible that I almost died over something that isn't as monumental as it seemed to be? My stomach feels a little queasy at the thought. Maybe I'm really okay.

I shake the thought from my head as an impossibility, but it squirms its way back in.

Maybe it's not that big of a deal.

Chapter 16

After dinner, Ty comes over to study with Brent.
I'm finishing my homework in my bedroom and watch his Jeep park in our driveway. I want to go down and say hello, but I'm supposed to be getting over this crush. Recovering from a crush does not entail running down the stairs the second that the crush shows up at my house. Still, I can't help peeking out the window and watching him walk to the door. The top of his baseball cap is blue. He's wearing the Birkenstocks. Don't his feet get cold? He rings the doorbell and looks up toward my window.

I duck down. Did he see me? I smack my palm to my forehead. If he did see me, then he just saw me freak out and dive out of sight. It would have made way more sense to wave. My heart pounds. Why can't I act like a normal human being when he's around?

I hear Brent greeting Ty, and now I'm definitely not

going down there. My face flushes. We'll pretend that didn't happen. Back to studying.

I'm too distracted, so after a while I decide to study in the living room. Maybe a change of scenery will help. It's about the scenery. Not about the fact that Ty might take a study break and wander through the living room, where I could then have a nonchalant and totally suave interaction that might erase my previous idiocy.

Come to think of it, maybe it would be a good thing to run into him. Maybe this crush is like certain types of allergies, where repeated, limited exposure to the allergen can help you overcome the allergy entirely.

I've been studying on the couch for about twenty minutes before Ty comes upstairs. My stomach does its now-familiar flip. He looks surprised to see me, but almost too surprised. Like maybe he's faking it.

"Oh, sorry, Nat, I didn't know you were up here. I came to get a drink." He hurries to the kitchen.

The basement is right under the living room. He absolutely would have heard me come down here. Mom isn't home, so it had to be me.

He comes back in with his water and sits on the arm of the love seat. "What are you working on?"

"Literature homework."

"Fun."

"It's Shakespeare, so not really."

"Ah, but which Shakespeare? Because I agree with you if it's *Julius Caesar*, but *Twelfth Night* is freaking hilarious."

I hold up my book. "What are your thoughts on *Hamlet*?"

He holds out his cup of water and talks to it as if it's another character onstage. "'To thine own self be true.'" He takes a drink. "That was the best line in the whole thing, mainly because it's full of irony. The rest kind of sucked."

I'm impressed. "You know a lot about Shakespeare."

He smiles to himself. "Yeah. My dad hates Shakespeare. To be honest, it's probably the only reason I read it so much. I'm not proud of that, but there you go."

"Why does your dad hate Shakespeare? My mom practically worships him, even though I'm not sure she's ever read any of his stuff. But he's British and prestigious, so we have his complete works." I point to a matching set of volumes on our bookshelf.

"My dad says Shakespeare is too—and I quote—'artsy fartsy.' Also, Shakes says all kinds of odd stuff, like 'To thine own self be true,' and my parents think that's nonsense."

"You nicknamed him 'Shakes'?"

"We've spent enough hours together." Ty smiles. "A nickname seems logical once I feel like I know someone. I call you Nat. Does that bug you?"

"No." As a matter of fact, I love it. Especially now.

"There, see? So I bet Shakes wouldn't mind a nickname, either."

I laugh. "I guess not."

Ty takes off his baseball cap and puts it next to him. He tries to get rid of the hat hair, and it doesn't really work. Unfortunately, he looks good even with hat hair.

"How's your work for Art Connect going?" he asks.

"Slow. I put all this pressure on myself, you know? And then nothing seems right. It's like we have this one shot, and it's make-or-break."

"I feel you. It's like we're Little Leaguers in the World Series. I'm scared to look like an idiot. Plus, who knows? Maybe if someone offered me a scholarship, my parents would be more understanding about me studying art. Sometimes I think they like the idea of me as a son rather than the actual son that I am." He exhales and rubs his hands on the thighs of his jeans. "Sorry. Didn't mean to get personal."

"It's no problem. You're just being real." Except yes, it is a problem. Because it made my heart do that weird flippy thing again.

"We have a chance, right? Sometimes newcomers do great. There's a Rookie of the Year Award for a reason."

"Absolutely. We'll be all-star rookies." I smile. "Do you have any great ways to de-stress? Because I could use some tips." As in, I could use some tips right now. Because this situation is stressing me out. I'm supposed to be completely platonic with this guy, but I feel a little dizzy. And I'm looking at his shoulders and remembering what it felt like when I was leaning on them in the cornfield. My hand tingles at the memory. Are there platonic hand tingles? Can I pretend there are?

Ty looks thoughtful for a second. "Hanging with Shakes chills me out, I guess."

"Cool." Except now I'm going to think of him every time I read Shakespeare. He has ruined an entire literary canon for me. That is so unfair. I didn't like Shakespeare in the first place, but still.

He rubs the back of his neck and puts his hat back on. "Hey, I have kind of an out-there question."

He's going to ask why I ducked under the window. Quick, I need good reasons to duck under a window. I got tripped by the dog. I had to kill a spider. I had to shine my shoe. I thought I was going to throw up. (Nope, that's right now.) I was kneeling to pray. I dropped a pencil.

That's it. Dropped a pencil. That's completely normal. I was even working on homework at the time. Perfect. Dropped a pencil. Carry on.

"Yeah? What's up?"

"Have you heard of Crow's Nest?"

"No." Wait, this isn't about the window?

"It's a band. They're local, and they don't suck. One of my buddies is in it. Anyway, they've got a concert this weekend, and I didn't know if you were into indie music or anything...."

My face gets hot. He's asking me out. Red alert: He is *asking me out*. Right this second. This is not limited exposure to an allergen. This is a peanut allergy with a jar of peanut butter.

"Oh?" I try to sound noncommittal. It comes out kind of strangled. "I like some types of indie music."

Shoot, shoot, shoot. No, I don't. Right now, I need to hate all indie music. His eyes light up, hopeful about my response, and my heart tries to soar and thud at the same time. My chest hurts.

"They're good. I think you'd like them. Anyway, if you could take a break from Art Connect prep, I've got an extra ticket to their concert on Saturday."

"I see."

My answer hangs between us, meaning exactly nothing. His smile disappears, and he takes a drink of his water. I wish I had water. I wish he had asked about the window.

I want to go. I picture myself at a concert with Ty, pressed close together by a dense crowd. My skin feels warm just imagining it. Maybe our hands would be so close that our fingers would sort of mesh, and then we'd be holding hands. We'd smile at each other knowingly, because it would be an accident, but not really. I'd smell his fresh-woods cologne, not just briefly like when we talk after art class, but for hours. I'd try to talk to him, and he'd lean in close to hear me over the music. Then one time, he'd lean in like he's going to say something, but when I looked up at him, he'd kiss me instead.

Can he see my heart speeding up? I'm picturing the scene and it's perfect. Doesn't the world owe me this after all I've been through?

"I can't go."

Wait! What are these words coming out of me? I want to grab them and shove them back in my mouth.

Ty's face falls, and I feel even worse. It's not too late to say, "Ha-ha, just kidding. Of course I'll be there." A war wages between my heart and my brain. My body is completely agreeing with my heart. Just say yes, Natalie. Come on, change your answer.

"No prob. It was a silly idea." He rubs his forearm. "Figured I'd at least check."

I want to say yes. But if I'm this worked up thinking about going to the concert, imagine what a mess I'd be if I was there? I need the guy-free senior year.

Plus, a scary thought shadows his invitation: he only likes me because I seem normal. My blonde hair is pretty, but the brain under it isn't. If he knew the truth, I doubt he'd be inviting me. Who wants to date a crazy person? He doesn't really understand who he's inviting, so it wouldn't be fair to take him up on it. I'm 98 percent sure of that. After all, I hurt the people who love me.

———

The first thing I remember after waking up from the accident is an aggressively white hospital room. When I saw the white ceiling with the white light, I thought I'd gone to heaven. Then I took in my first breath, and the pain knocked away any conscious thought.

A large nurse wearing Sponge Bob scrubs hovered over me to take my vitals. She said, in a throaty smoker's voice, "She might be waking up."

Then it hit me: If I was here with Nurse Sponge Bob, then the plan didn't work. I was still alive.

"Crap" was the first word out of my mouth after a two-day coma.

"Oh, darling!" My mom was suddenly by my side, her face blocking my view of the ceiling. "Are you okay? Can you hear me? Do you know who I am?"

Her face was twisted in fear, and I'd never seen her look like that before. I'd closed my eyes to block it out.

"Ugh . . . Mom . . ." was all I could say. Everything hurt.

"Brent! She knows me!" My mom rushed to hug my brother. I winced in pain, and it wasn't only physical.

When I opened my eyes again, Brent was still hugging my mom. She was crying, and I wondered if it was from relief that I was alive or from pain at seeing me so messed up. It was the first time I felt guilty about wrecking the car she bought for me. Hopefully she wasn't crying about that. Brent looked up and made eye contact with me. His eyes were glassy, but he simply gave me a brief nod with a tight smile and went back to comforting my mom. You would have thought she was the injured one. I was the odd one out in my own hospital room.

The next few days were full of doctors, X-rays, and various treatment plans. Many of those moments blur together, but one stands out. It happened when my brother was watching a cooking show, my mom was reading a *Vogue*, and I was trying to sleep.

While I studied the blackness that is the backs of my eyelids, someone walked in to talk to my mom.

"Hello, Mrs. Cordova, I'm Dr. Iqbal, the psychiatrist assigned to Natalie's case." The doctor cleared her throat. "I see on Natalie's medical record that she's been treated with antidepressants and anti-anxiety medications in the past?"

Did she really have to say that with Brent in the room? Sure, Brent knew *something* was wrong with me, but I didn't need it announced.

"Yes, she's been on medications." My mom used her business voice. "She got them from her primary care provider. She's been doing better...."

"There's a chance that this crash was a suicide attempt," Dr. Iqbal said gently.

I expected a gasp or something, but there was only silence. I peeked through my eyelids. My mom took a stoic deep breath, and Brent looked panicked. He grabbed his phone and became fully absorbed in his screen. Shame settled over my whole body like one of those warm blankets the nurse put on me.

"I don't think so," my mom finally said. "I know she's struggled with depression in the past, but she said there was a deer. She swerved to miss a deer crossing the road. Car and deer accidents happen all the time." She didn't sound fully convinced.

I closed my eyes again, and my eyelashes felt wet. At that moment, I wished no one loved me. If no one loved me, I wouldn't have hurt anyone.

———

Now, in my living room, with Ty sitting on the arm of the love seat, my eyelashes are wet again. I scratch the back of my hand. "It wasn't silly. I just, uh, can't really date right now. It's not you, trust me. It's me."

I want to facepalm. Out of all the words in the universe, I had to string together the most overused line of all time?

Ty smiles ruefully, recognizing the blowoff. "No prob. It's cool. Good luck with *Hamlet*. I'll see you next week in Soo's class?"

"Yep." He needs to get out of here before I cry. "Next week. We'll get these projects done eventually."

We both laugh, but it isn't funny.

He leaves to go back downstairs, and I close my eyes. I can't believe that happened. Did I make the right decision?

"Hey, Nat?" My eyes snap open. Ty steps back into the living room.

"Yeah?"

"I just need to check—is this about Brent?"

"What do you mean?"

"He talked to me, so I figure he talked to you, too. He said it wasn't a good idea for us to, you know, be more than friends."

Hold up. Brent did *what*?

"He's my friend and your brother. I get how that might be strange, but I figured I had to at least give it a shot. I've never met any other girl who . . . Well, never mind. It doesn't matter."

Who what? What was he about to say? THIS DOES TOO MATTER.

"This has nothing to do with Brent," I say. "Brent does not control my life, and he doesn't get any say in who I date, especially considering . . . Well, let's just say he owes me. He had no right to say that to you."

"Oh, okay." Ty looks startled by my aggressive answer. "Sorry. No big deal." He practically runs out of the room.

Maybe I should have said I couldn't go out with him because of Brent. Then Ty wouldn't feel rejected. I was too distracted by anger to think of that, but now I feel guilty. There are a bunch of legitimate reasons to turn Ty down, and "I don't want to date him" is nowhere on that list.

But who does Brent think he is? I didn't freak out one iota when he asked one of my best friends in the whole world (at least I think she still is) to go on a date, but some guy from his chemistry class—who also happens to be in my art class—is off-limits? It's not even like he and Ty are close. They didn't know each other three months ago.

And yes, I realize that I'm not going to date Ty anyway because I promised myself I wouldn't, but that is beside the point. Brent is such a control freak. Why couldn't I have a supportive sibling? Or at least a neutral one? Why is Brent always trying to make my life difficult? I'm so sick of him making me feel small. I can feel however I want to about Ty, and he can't do anything about that. Also, I'm not stupid for wondering about our dad. He shouldn't have made me feel small about that, either. Looks like I can't rely on Brent for anything. Fine. I'll be fine by myself.

I need a distraction from Ty. If Brent's not going to consider that I might be right about our dad, maybe it's time to look for him on my own.

Chapter 17

The next day after school, I parallel park on a small street in Smithfield. At first I don't see anything that resembles an art gallery. Then I see it. Right next to the sign for Donut Dave's is a small black-and-white placard with an arrow pointing upward to the second floor. It says STUDIO Z.

The stairwell smells musty. On the second floor, there's a small hallway with doors on each side, but it's easy to find the studio door. It's painted with a tangle of black-and-white swirls that somehow form the words *Studio Z*. The rest of the hallway is completely undecorated. A plastic black-and-orange sign next to the door says, COME IN. WE'RE OPEN.

But maybe I don't want to go in. What if that guy isn't my dad? Worse, what if he is? What if he's my dad, but the reason he left is some terrible secret? He could have two families, and maybe his new wife doesn't know about me.

Maybe he's in a witness protection program, and finding him puts us both in danger. Maybe he faked his death because he committed some heinous crime, and the police were onto him. What if he has amnesia and doesn't remember that he has a family at all?

The sign says open, but the door is closed. Should I knock? I can't stand awkwardly in the hall forever. The stairway looks inviting. It's not too late to turn back. Before I can chicken out, I knock and hold my breath.

If no one answers this door soon, I will pass out. Still not breathing.

The door finally opens, and a man who looks exactly like a much-older Brent is standing there. The only part that doesn't look like Brent is his nose. It's totally different. Actually, it kind of looks like . . . mine.

He's the man from the scrapbook. I know it.

I suddenly want to cry.

His chin is up and his eyes are smiling. He looks relaxed, like people come to his door often. Maybe they do—he's a good artist. Why wouldn't people visit his studio? His relaxed posture takes an ounce of tension away from me, but only an ounce.

"Hi," I say after an awkward silence. "I'm Natalie. I'm wondering . . . "

Why didn't I prepare for this? What am I trying to say? "I'm wondering why you left?" "I'm wondering if that Art Connect picture is of me and my brother?" "I'm wondering if you can explain about mental illness to me?" My mouth goes dry. I'm about to say "Never mind" and run back to the stairs when he draws a sharp breath.

"Oh my gosh," he whispers. "It's you."

Maybe I don't have to explain. His face turns as white as the swirls on his door. Looks like he gets it. So it wasn't the amnesia thing.

He stares at me, his eyes squinting and then widening again, like he's studying me and surprised by what he sees. He blinks a few times. He opens his mouth as if to say something, then closes it again. I shift my weight from one foot to the other. I feel a little caught off guard by this reaction (though I'm not sure what I expected). My mom considers it rude to drop in unannounced, but it's not like I could have made an appointment for this. I hold his gaze for as long as I can. It feels like he's a scientist studying me, and I don't like feeling foreign in my own skin. I break the eye contact and stare at the floor. The floor is boring, but I still stare at it. For a while. When I look up again, his eyes are full of tears. They look to be a mix of relief and happiness.

"Natalie. Natalie, Natalie, Natalie."

He says it like he misses saying it, like the syllables taste sweet and he wants more of them on his tongue. His tone is varied in a way that makes my name sound pleasantly dramatic. Oh no, is he going to hug me? I take a step back. Please don't hug me, dude with my nose.

He realizes that he's left me standing in the hall and says, "Oh, come in!" He opens the door but looks like he's hiding behind it.

It's probably not smart to go into this room with a guy I just met, but he's an artist and he has my nose. Deep down, I know he's not a stranger. I remember the picture in the scrapbook where he's holding me in that small pink blanket, and I hug myself as I take a tentative step inside.

There are displays set up around the room, kind of like a tiny art museum. Paintings hang on freestanding gray walls in the middle, and on the outer walls as well. Tiny lights shine onto the paintings, and soft sunlight spills in from a window to my right. Near the window, an easel and a chair are set up. A half-finished painting of a ship is set up on the easel, and a clear piece of plastic below it protects the beautiful wood floors.

Some of the finest art I've ever seen hangs on his walls. The paintings look like photographs, but close inspection shows careful brushstrokes in acrylic and watercolor. One watercolor painting shows a cabin in the woods by a river. A teal porch swing looks as if it's swaying in an invisible breeze. It looks so real. I feel like I've been in that swing before. Have I? Did we go on vacation to that cabin when I was younger, or is this painting simply so good that I feel drawn into it? Are all his paintings based on memories, like the painting at Art Connect, or are some of these painted from his imagination? I aspire to be half the artist he is.

Well, technically, genetically I might *be* half the artist he is.

"These are amazing." I gesture to the paintings. "I mean . . . wow." It's not false admiration.

"Thanks."

He stares at me like I'm a ghost, which is quite unfair because he is the one who's supposed to be dead.

"Does your mother know you're here?"

"Not exactly . . ."

"Where's Brent?" He opens the door and looks in the hall again as if maybe he missed him the first time.

"He, uh, didn't come with me this time."

"Oh, I understand."

He looks down, dejected, and I'm not sure what it is that he understands.

"How long have you had this studio?" I ask.

"Ten years."

He's been around here for at least ten years, and I didn't even know he was alive? What is *wrong* with him? Or my mom? Or whoever's fault this is? *What the heck happened?*

There's so much to ask, but my mouth feels glued shut. He's quiet, too. He's waiting to take my lead. The silence is thick and heavy, and it's only getting heavier by the second.

Art seems like a safe topic. "Which painting is your favorite?"

He looks visibly relieved. "Come this way," he says, motioning. "My best paintings are in the back." He hurries toward an open door near the back of the studio.

My mouth drops open when I walk through the door. There's a small apartment back here. I'm facing a green plaid couch that's trying in vain to keep all its stuffing. A wooden coffee table holds art magazines opened to various pages. A single bed, unmade, is in the left corner of the room.

The deep green bedspread almost matches the green of the couch, but it's off by enough that it looks like that was an accident more than a purposeful choice. A wooden dresser against the wall next to the bed has one sleeve of a shirt hanging out of one of the drawers, but the rest of the area looks tidy. A kitchen area is to the right, and a takeout box sits on top of the stainless-steel microwave. The stovetop is very clean, which makes me wonder if he cleans his kitchen well or doesn't use it often.

"Take a look around," he says, as if I weren't already doing that. "It's not much, but it's enough for me." He surveys the room himself with a look of satisfaction.

A door to my right leads to the bathroom. I peek in. He keeps his comb behind the sink faucet handles like Brent does. There's one lonely toothbrush in an orange cup by the sink. The shower curtain is dyed with a bunch of different warm-colored pigments, and I bet he did that himself. The mirror above the sink looks like a medicine cabinet. Does he have pills in there? I wonder if he ever struggles to take pills like I do.

It would be a very plain apartment if it weren't for the walls. They are covered in paintings. They're eclectic and fun, where the ones out in the gallery look more professional and polished. The painting by the kitchen area shows pastel-colored children dressed in winter clothes. They're hiding behind piles of spaghetti and having a meatball fight. A clock above the door is painted as a pizza. The pizza is painted on the wall, and the clock hands are mounted in the middle. Every number is placed on a painted pepperoni. By the bathroom door, a bottle of Windex is locked in an epic battle with a toilet brush. The Windex is spraying, and the toilet brush is using a plunger for defense. It makes me laugh, and my laugh makes him laugh, too.

"I'm rather proud of that one," he says. "I was in a quirky mood that day."

There's a large window above the bed on the left wall. Abstract designs and tangles of black and white lines surround it. They look like a brilliant frame displaying the beauty outside. The view from the window is just a brick building's fire escape, but the frame makes it look exciting. My Aunt Kate once bought me a book on the Zentangle Method, and it looks like my dad has mastered the technique. The frame is divided into a couple dozen sections. One section of the frame is checked, another dotted, another striped, one with dotty stripes—they're all unique. The doodles remind me a little bit of what I do in my closet on paper plates, where I try to translate my thoughts into line and color. His are only black and white, but I love it. I feel inspired to try a black-and-white abstract when I get home.

The wall behind the couch is the centerpiece. There are frames painted all over it—elegant renaissance frames, modern sleek ones, wooden and metal frames, novelty frames. It's like nothing I've ever seen. It's the most beautiful conglomeration of frames, and none of them are real.

A painting lives in each one of them—my mom looking young and serving coffee, a building I don't recognize, our house, my brother hugging a Ninja Turtle toy, and me dressed as the Queen for Halloween. There's even one of him painting this wall. It's like the wall is a time capsule of his life, except none of these pictures show me, Brent, and Mom as we are now.

The only real frame in the room is on a small table by the couch. It's dimly lit by a lamp that matches the one in our living room. The frame is a pale yellow plastic that possibly used to be white. It's cheap and not nearly as beautiful as any of the painted ones. The picture inside is a photograph—the scene at the beach from Art Connect.

"I love that picture," he says.

"I saw your painting of it at Art Connect." This room is amazing. Not a square inch of the walls is white. It looks like my closet, and I've never felt so at home in a strange place.

"How did you find me?"

"When I saw your painting at the winners' gallery, I thought . . . I mean, I wondered . . ."

He finishes after I trail off. "You wondered if you were the girl in the picture?"

"Kind of. It was a beautiful painting, um, Z."

"Don't call me Z." He looks startled. "That's just my artist name. You can call me . . ." Now it's his turn to trail off.

What should I call him? I'm not calling him *Dad*. We look at each other, neither of us sure what to say.

"My name's Henry," he finally offers.

"I know."

"So you can call me Henry?"

"Okay." I don't like it, and it's obvious that he doesn't, either. It's weird to call your dad by his first name. Maybe I'll just never refer to him by name. That seems like the easiest solution.

"Do you want to sit down?" He motions to his couch.

We sit on the couch, and I notice there are no throw pillows. My mom has tons of throw pillows. If there was a throw pillow, I'd grab it and hold it in front of myself. Sitting here makes me feel exposed.

"Well," my dad says, as if he's going to start a conversation, but then he doesn't.

We both stare at the paintings on the walls.

I sneak a peek over to him, trying to take in more of how he looks, and at that moment he sneaks a peek to me, too. Ah! Awkward. We both turn back to staring at the walls.

He finally turns back to me. "Those are nice, um, earrings," he says.

I'm wearing my tiny paintbrush ones.

"Thanks." I survey him, looking for something to compliment in return. "I like your . . . shirt." It's a plain black T-shirt. You really think I could have come up with something better. "Because it's so dark," I add, trying to make it better. "My black shirts all end up looking like a kind of dirty gray after I wash them a few times." This is not making it better.

He smiles, like he realizes I'm trying. "Thanks. I use Tide Pods."

"I might have to get some of those."

I can't believe we have a lifetime of questions to answer, and we're talking about Tide Pods. What was I expecting to find? I think I wanted answers, but it's like all I discovered are more questions. Now I have a very alive dad, but he's a stranger. And there's no going back now that I'm here. There's no way to un-know this. Maybe it was a bad idea.

The awkward tension is cut by a loud voice in the gallery. "Z! 'Sup, bro? I've got your 'za."

He (Henry? Dad?) looks up at the clock. "Half past mushroom. Perfectly on time." He turns to me. "Hold on. I'll be right back." Once he goes into his gallery, I sneak to the door and peek out.

There's a tall man with blond curls that go almost to his shoulders. He's wearing a familiar red uniform and carrying a familiar red pizza-warmer box.

"Z-dawg. My man."

The pizza man and my dad do a complicated handshake.

Whoa, I just thought of him as my dad. This is bizarre.

"Thank you for ordering from the Pizza Palace, the king of pizza. One large supreme?" He takes the pizza out of the warmer.

"Maybe I'll pick something different next week," my dad says. He reaches behind one of his paintings, grabs an envelope, and pays the pizza man.

"Maybe you'll pick something different next week, and maybe I'll be the president. You never know, dude." The curly guy chuckles as he pockets the cash. "See you next week, bro."

"Take it easy, Blaine."

My dad turns toward the apartment door, and I hurry back to sit on the couch.

He smiles and takes a whiff of the supreme goodness. "Want some pizza?"

"Sure." I smile back. Pizza is a great tension defuser. If world leaders tried to settle issues in living rooms with pizza instead of in boardrooms with boring statistics, we'd have way fewer wars.

He grabs some paper plates from the kitchen, and we each take a slice of pizza.

"We get pizza every week, too," I say. "Also from Pizza Palace."

"Maggie still gets Monday pizzas?" He smiles as he remembers.

I've never heard anyone call my mom Maggie—she's either called Mrs. Cordova or Margaret. She doesn't seem like a Maggie. Did she used to be?

I take a bite of pizza and try to decide if I should bring up The Topic. By the time I swallow, I've decided this situation can't get much weirder. Might as well go for it.

"I thought you were dead." It's not accusatory or sad; it's just the truth. "This is good pizza," I add.

"It is good pizza." He takes another bite and then takes a drink from a water bottle. He starts to put the bottle down but changes his mind and drinks again. Then he puts it down. "I've wondered for a long time if it was the right choice." It almost seems like he's talking to himself. "I decided years ago that it wasn't, but by then it was too late."

"Does Mom know you're alive?"

"Of course!" He looks offended, then softens as he realizes it was a valid question. "Of course Maggie knows. We decided together that I should disappear."

"What?" That can't be true. Why would they do that? This is too much to process. I might throw up.

"The thing is, Natalie, that I'm, um . . ." He takes a deep breath. "I'm not a healthy man."

"I know. You have schizophrenia." I try to act like this is no big deal.

"You *know*?" He seems shocked.

"Yes. I found out this past summer."

"Then you know about the hospitals . . . about all of it?"

"Yep. I know all of that." That's a lie, but I've recently gotten quite good at lying.

My dad leans back on the couch, deflated. "I'm so sorry. I've thought about this day for years, and what I'd say, and what you and Brent would think, and . . . There's nothing to say except that I'm so, so sorry. Sorrier than you could ever know." Tears escape his eyes, but he doesn't reach for a tissue. He doesn't react at all. He looks past them. "We thought it would be for the best. I was too unstable—hallucinations, in and out of psychiatric hospitals all the time, couldn't hold down a job, so dysfunctional. And I was terrible to your mother." The tears come faster now. "It was awful. *I* was awful. We thought it would be best for the family if I . . . wasn't in it."

There's nothing to say to that, so I take another bite of pizza. It's like chewing cardboard now.

"We agreed that I shouldn't be a part of your lives anymore. Especially when I was refusing treatment. My inability to function in a healthy way would affect you and Brent, and Maggie thought she could raise you better by herself."

It's quiet for a minute. The thick silence is back. "You were still my dad," I finally say. "Maybe you were sick, but you were still my dad. Dads aren't supposed to just . . . leave."

"I *am* still your dad," he whispers, and hangs his head. "I shouldn't have left, and I'll never be able to make it up to you. What was I supposed to do—show up on your doorstep after all these years and announce I'm alive? I promised your mother I'd never do that. But I've missed you and your brother every single day since I left, I promise you that."

He looks so sad and so desperate. It's time for me to say something. What can I say? Come on, Natalie.

"Brent still has his Teenage Mutant Ninja Turtle shorts."

My dad looks stunned and then laughs a deep belly laugh. "He does, does he? He'd better not fit into them anymore."

I laugh, too, which kills the tension. "No, but my dog does. I tried them on her once, but Brent got mad."

"You have a dog?" He seems happy to have this tidbit of information, a piece of my life he didn't know about. "Tell me about her."

"Her name is Petunia. She's a pug. She's kind of ugly, but I like her."

"Does your mom like her?"

"No."

He laughs again. "Of course she doesn't."

I'm angry at him for leaving, and at my mom for keeping this from us. And I can't bring myself to tell him that Brent still thinks he's dead. But I'll worry about those things later. Right now I'm with a sad man that an earlier version of me loved, and all I want to do is make him feel better. We spend the rest of dinner talking about me and Mom and Brent. He has a million questions, and I answer them the best I can. When there's a pause, I tell him the news I've wanted to give him ever since I walked in here.

"I'm an artist. I paint my closet like you paint your walls. Your paintings are better, though."

"A chip off the old block, huh?" He looks around the room at his work. "I hope you're not too much like me."

There's an orange pill bottle on the floor peeking out from under his bed. We're more alike than he knows, but I'm not ready to talk about that yet.

"I'm going to have a display in Art Connect this year."

His eyes brighten, and there's a pride in them that my mom's eyes have never had. "Art Connect at age eighteen." He whistles. "You must be good."

"I didn't get in. My art teacher did. Her studio is going to be featured, so we get to display under her."

"What genre are you painting? What medium?" He squints at his own paintings like he's trying to decide which one might look closest to my artwork.

"I mostly do landscapes, but abstracts are my favorite. Usually acrylics, but some watercolor."

"You ever try oils?"

"I tried them. Didn't like them much."

His eyes sparkle again. "Would you believe I only ever did one oil painting? Oils are awful for cleanup and for mistakes. You can't make a mistake when you're painting with oils."

"I know! It gets smudged and smeared and makes a total mess. It also takes forever to dry." This guy gets me. My life would have been so different if I could have grown up with him. I'm not sure if this makes me happy or sad.

"It's easy to believe you're my daughter."

"Did you notice we have the same nose?" I'm starting to like this idea of having a dad—especially an artistic one.

"Do we? Come here, let's see." There's a full-length mirror on the side of his dresser. The mirror is small and thin, so we have to stand pretty close together to look in it. "Whaddaya know? We do have the same nose." He leans toward the mirror to take a closer look. "It looks better on you."

I grin. "Thanks."

We stand and look at the mirror, both mesmerized. I do look a lot like him. His eyes are teary again.

"I should get going." If he cries again then I might cry, and that would be embarrassing. When will I get to see him again? The picture in the yellow frame gives me an idea. "You should come see my art display at Art Connect. I'll be there on November first."

He walks away from the mirror and sits on his couch. "How do you think Maggie would feel about that?"

"She won't care."

My dad looks at me doubtfully. "You should tell her that you know the truth."

I nod. "Of course. I'm definitely going to."

Which I will, maybe. Someday. What if I tell her, and then she tries to keep me from seeing him again? She's done a pretty decent job at it for the last fourteen years, and I'm not ready to lose a dad I only just discovered.

He keeps thinking, then nods decisively. "If your mother knows that you met me, and if she doesn't mind, I'd love to come to the show."

"Great!"

How am I going to keep my parents apart for the whole show? I'll figure that out later.

He sighs. "Are you sure you have to go?"

"Yes." I need to straighten this all out in my head before I spend any more time with him. It's not every day that your dad comes back from the dead.

I don't know what I expected from a man who is affected by schizophrenia, but my dad's life doesn't seem so different from ours. I was nervous I would find someone who was falling apart, and maybe he did fall apart at some point in his life, but right now he seems to be functioning well. Maybe schizophrenia doesn't have to be as scary as it sounded at first.

As I put my coat on, he stands to walk me out. He fidgets nervously for a couple of seconds before saying, "Can I give you a hug before you go?" He doesn't wait for an answer before enveloping me in a bear hug. My mom doesn't really hug. Apparently my dad does. He smells of paint. He smells familiar, like a place I haven't visited in years.

For the first time in a long time, I feel safe.

Chapter 18

Now I have two secrets: bipolar disorder and my not-so-dead dad. Well, three secrets if you include the fact that Toons peed on the couch yesterday (again), but that one's not huge. If only all secrets could be hidden by a well-placed decorative pillow.

I wish I could tell Brent, but his loyalty to Mom outweighs his loyalty to me every day of the week. He'd tell her for sure. Luckily, he still thinks the whole idea was me being crazy. For once, this works to my advantage. Right now my only confidante is Toons. Who knew I'd end up with a best friend who is barely potty-trained?

It's not that Cecily and Brynn are my enemies or anything. After all, they listened when I nixed the idea of the mental illness support group and the Instagram campaign. Well, what they actually said was "We won't put the plan into action until you're ready." Which will be never. So, I guess we're still friends? Maybe? Things are weird.

——————

As I'm walking to history class Tuesday morning, my phone beeps with a text. I think maybe it's another consolation text from someone who thinks I should have been named homecoming queen. They announced the results this morning (even though the homecoming game and dance are still more than two weeks away), and Cecily won. My mom is going to kill me.

The two words on my screen make me stop in the middle of the hall. A few people run into me and give me odd looks, but I barely notice. The text is from Ella.

You're bipolar?

She gives nothing else away—how she knows or how she feels about it. I pull my phone to my chest so that no one else can read it, then out again to make sure I read it correctly. It's tough to misread two words.

Maybe she doesn't know. Maybe she just suspects? But that's impossible. No one has suspected the truth. All I've admitted to her is that there wasn't a deer involved in the accident. She's smart, but even Ella isn't going to make that kind of jump.

I don't text back. Should I acknowledge the truth? Deny it? *How does she know?*

When yet another person runs into me, I step to the side and put my phone in my backpack. My hands shake, and it takes a few tugs to get the zipper to work.

There is only one logical way that Ella could have found out. As soon as the answer forms, I start trying to figure out ways around it. There has to be another explanation. The one logical explanation can't be true, because the logical explanation is that she knows because *someone told her*. That someone isn't me. Brynn and Cecily were sworn to secrecy, and they don't talk to Ella.

My brain spins in all directions, trying to land on a logical explanation. I take my phone out and text Ella.

> Did someone say I am?

That's a good answer. It's noncommittal, but it could still procure critical information. I shove the phone in my pocket and run to history so I can beat the tardy bell. My phone buzzes right before I get to the door.

> Chloe told me.

Chloe knows? My heart beats faster and my brain finally finds a space to land—lots of people know, and that's why Ella does. Somehow the news got out (my money is on Brynn), and the lightning-speed gossip chain at my school has made it down to Ella. If it's made it to Ella, it's all over the place.

My phone vibrates again—another text from Ella.

So, are you?

I can't handle this. My phone's going to the bottom of my backpack—on silent—until after history. The tardy bell rings right as I slide into my seat, and I look around the room. Does the guy sitting next to me know? The girl sitting behind me? What about the exchange student in the corner who I've never spoken to?

Wait, do I care if he knows? What country is he even from?

Yes, I do care, because it's *my* secret, and nobody should know if I haven't told them. What have people heard? Do they know the truth about the car accident?

My reputation is shot. Also, my mom knows homecoming queen was going to be announced this morning. The thought of telling her that Cecily won makes me feel a bit ill. In addition, now my darkest secret has been sprinkled around the school like confetti. She warned me not to tell anyone. I thought it was safe to tell my best friends, but she was right all along. I can't believe I let her down again. Are moms right about everything? Is she right that I shouldn't be an artist? Everything's a mess, and it's all my fault.

If I bug my eyes out Petunia-style, maybe my tears won't fall. Look, I'll study that wall map of ancient Egypt. People in ancient Egypt didn't have these issues. If someone in Egypt had a secret, it was a secret. Their friends couldn't text a bunch of people at once and spread it like wildfire. Maybe they put it in hieroglyphics or whatever, but how many people looked at those?

My teacher starts class, my classmates take notes, and I stare at my empty desk. There is no way my brain can focus on ancient cultures at this moment. It won't focus on anything except the list of questions scrolling through my mind: Brynn? Who? How many? Why? When? Why? Did I already say *why*? WHY?

Don't be dramatic, Natalie. Breathe slowly. It's not that big of a deal.

What am I going to do?

What I'm not going to do is panic. Panicking has never solved anything. A panic attack during class would be the cherry on top of this disastrous day.

I need to talk to Brynn and Cecily. The second hand on the classroom clock crawls forward. I swear it goes backward twice. I can't sit still.

"Mr. Potter? Can I go to the bathroom?" I try to look ill. It doesn't take a lot of acting.

Empty halls are eerie. Most of the time halls are bustling with the hurried rush of students and teachers. As I walk to the bathroom, an open classroom door reveals students looking bored in a lab. A couple of them are whispering. Are they whispering about my secret? What are *their* secrets?

Bathroom stalls feel safe. They're like my closet at home. I sit on the toilet and pull my legs up so that my shoes are on the toilet as well. My knees are hugged to my chest. I wish I had my paints. Plenty of Sharpie graffiti peppers the stall dividers. Modern hieroglyphics.

I send a text to Brynn.

Senior hall bathroom, now.

The bathroom graffiti holds my attention until her response arrives.

Coming.

Strategy time. It has to be Brynn who told, but will she admit it to me? Should I get angry and cry, or should I keep things civil? After all, she's one of my best friends. Maybe she didn't tell anyone after all.

A call lights up my phone. It's my mom. I stare at the screen, unwilling to answer, unwilling to reject the call. Should I get this over with now? At least I won't be able to see her disappointed face. Then again, what do I say? I'm sorry? The call goes to voicemail before I decide.

Against my better judgment, I listen to the message. My mom has her fake happy voice on. I hate that voice.

"Natalie, darling, I just heard the news. Don't worry about it. We'll think of something for the Christmas card. After all, you must have done *something* this year." There's a pause. "Perhaps we can put in a picture of your dog and say you've volunteered at the humane society. Everyone loves a humanitarian. Bye. Study hard."

Fantastic. My greatest accomplishment this year is adopting a fuzzy potato. Art Connect is nothing to her. My eyes burn.

The bathroom door opens. "Nat?"

I'm still in the locked stall. Oops. It feels weird to leave a stall without flushing, so I flush.

"Hey." The bathroom feels big with only the two of us in here. "I, um . . . I got this text from Ella."

Brynn takes my phone. She reads my exchange with Ella and looks confused. "Chloe told Ella you're bipolar? How does Chloe know?"

"I was hoping you could explain that to me."

Brynn's face pales, and I know the truth before she says anything. "I didn't tell her. I swear."

"Maybe you didn't tell Chloe." I roll my eyes. "But who did you tell?"

Brynn looks at the wall tiles. She catches her reflection in the mirror and smooths her hair before taking a deep breath. My arms are crossed. My teeth are clenched tight to keep my tears from falling.

"I only told a select few people, and I told them in strictest confidence. They promised they wouldn't tell."

"*You* promised you wouldn't tell."

"Right, I know." She nods enthusiastically. "And I mostly didn't!"

She says this like it's a legitimate defense, and in her mind it is. If she told significantly fewer people than she usually would, maybe that's her version of loyalty. I could press her for who she told exactly, but at this point it doesn't matter. It's down to Ella, so it's everywhere.

"Why? Why did you tell anyone?" A tear escapes, and I smear it angrily across my cheek.

"I was worried about you. When they announced homecoming queen this morning, I was afraid that might send you into an episode or something. I wanted to make sure everyone treated you really nice so you'd know how valued you are."

"I don't *care* about homecoming queen. There are more important things in life than who wins stupid homecoming queen." I think of the hospital. I think of my dad. I think of Petunia, and paintings, and Ella, and Ty.

Brynn has tears in her eyes. "I was trying to help."

"You didn't help, okay?" I feel venomous. "Nothing you've done has helped. I just want to be normal, okay? I'm not a freak. This was not your secret to tell, and I trusted you. You're supposed to be my best friend. Instead, you're exploiting me so that you can be the first one to have the scoop. You're not my friend at all."

Brynn takes a step back as if I hit her. "I'm sorry," she finally offers. She tucks some hair behind her ears. "I'll go tell people you're *not* bipolar if you want me to."

An idea swirls in my head, like storm clouds rolling across the sky, dangerous but impossible to ignore. What if I simply decide not to be sick anymore? Sure, Dr. VanderFleet said bipolar disorder isn't something that goes away, but she also said that telling my friends was a good idea. She's wrong about a lot. I'm sick of feeling hurt and embarrassed. Look at my dad— he's been through so much because of his mental illness. I don't want to go down that road. I mean, who knows? He said he was terrible to my mom. Maybe they had good reason to decide he should leave. Better to choose a new path now.

I take a deep breath. "You probably should go tell them, since I don't even have bipolar disorder."

"You don't? But you said—"

"They got it wrong." I hate myself for the words coming out of my mouth, but that doesn't stop me. "I learned a lot about mental illnesses when I thought I had one. The truth of it is that they had it wrong. I'm fine."

"You are? Are you sure?" She bites her lip.

"Yes, I'm sure. I don't take any pills anymore, and I'm fine. You can stop treating me like a science experiment, and you can go ask Cecily if I'm upset about homecoming queen. I already asked her if she wants to celebrate after school."

"Oh."

"So yeah, you should probably go tell everyone you were wrong." I open the door and leave Brynn in the bathroom alone.

Tears sting my eyes. Adults always say you can achieve your dreams if you try hard enough, right? Well, my dream is to not have a mental illness. I'm going to work really hard, eat extra spinach or whatever foods are really good for you, and I'm going to beat this.

———

A gallon of white paint costs thirty-three dollars from Lowe's on my way home from school. When I get to my bedroom closet, I only feel a small pang of sadness as I open the paint can. Within twenty minutes, all of my closet paintings are covered in white. My blue shoebox of paints is in a trash bag. Finally—a white closet. A *normal* closet. There are so many paint spatters on the floor that I paint that, too. Everything is white. Blank. Perfect. My closet hasn't looked like this since elementary school.

Next step—pills. There are five orange bottles on my nightstand, and I grab them all. Petunia follows me into the bathroom and watches me empty each bottle into the toilet. This moment feels significant. "The Eye of the Tiger" should be playing in the background. I flush the toilet, and Toons gives a supportive *charp*. My therapist certainly wouldn't approve, but she doesn't know everything. She doesn't know how committed I am to making this work.

This is the beginning of my fight, and I. WILL. WIN.

Chapter 19

The next day at school is a total nightmare, starting immediately when I walk in the front door. Mrs. Hattan, the school guidance counselor, hovers in the entryway like she's waiting for someone. As soon as I see her face, I know that that someone is me.

"Natalie, honey, come here a minute." The students milling about in before-school boredom look at me curiously. My face flushes. Please, dear-God-that-I-mostly-believe-in, please let Mrs. Hattan be asking me about college applications.

"Natalie, I heard the news." Her eyes are full of pity. "You know, about your *illness*." She whispers the last part behind a cupped hand as if we're sharing a special secret. "Honey, I want you to know that I'm here for you. If you ever need to talk, if life feels overwhelming, I'm here to help. It's my job. Do you want me to set up an appointment for later today?"

"Um, no." Mrs. Hattan is nuts if she thinks I want to hang out in her office and talk about my feelings. "I'm fine. Really."

"Transitions are hard. My own dear mother had dementia before she passed, so I know that mental illnesses can be difficult on the entire family."

She's comparing me to her mother who had dementia and *died*? This is too much.

"No, really, Mrs. Hattan, I don't have a mental illness."

She frowns. "You don't? But I had several concerned students and even some parents call to tell me about—"

"No, I don't." There's no way I want to hear about the phone calls. "Someone was mad at me and started that rumor. I don't have any illnesses, mental or otherwise."

"Oh." Her chin lifts, and she huffs. "This school is ridiculous. You kids have got to stop spreading these poisonous lies about each other. Mental illnesses are not funny." She glares at me.

"I didn't start the rumor!" I hold my hands up. "This isn't my fault. I'm the one trying to fix it here."

"Right, right." She pats my arm absentmindedly. "It might be time to do another gossip workshop."

Is she looking for a response? "Sure, yeah. That'd be good."

She looks at the clock. "I've wasted enough time on this nonsense." She gives me a forced smile. "I'm sorry about all this, honey. Keep your chin up. People will move on. If gossip were food, this whole school would be fat."

I manage a thin laugh because she's trying to be funny.

———

Brynn and Cecily look repentant as I walk up to them. Neither one asks what Mrs. Hattan wanted to talk about.

"We're so, so sorry," Cecily says.

She apologized yesterday, and Brynn did again after school, but it's like being sorry for squeezing all the toothpaste out of a tube. They can be sorry all they want, but there's no way to put it back.

"Thanks." I want to add "It's fine," but it isn't. I'm still angry and hurt, but this can't ruin our friendship. Therefore, I will figure out a way to be fine.

Alyssa Jackson walks up to our group.

"I can't believe it," she says. "I cried all night. To think of you feeling that awful, that hopeless . . . it's so terrible. I'm sorry I wasn't there for you in your time of desperate need." She offers me an awkward hug.

I'm too stunned to speak. Luckily, Brynn jumps in.

"Alyssa, none of that is even true. It was a rumor started by who-knows-who, and it's completely false."

Alyssa looks confused. "Brynn, you're the one who told me."

"Oh, right." Brynn pauses. "I had faulty information."

Alyssa looks even more confused. "You said Natalie told you herself."

Now Brynn is really struggling for what to say. She looks to me for help, and I shrug. She's on her own. She made the mess; she has to clean it up.

"Okay, uh, I meant Natalie Smithson. She's the one who told me."

"Isn't she a sophomore?" Alyssa's eyes narrow. "Why would she know?"

"I have no idea." Brynn shakes her head and sighs. "She was probably jealous of how beautiful and smart Natalie is, and she wanted to bring her down. I never should have listened to her. But she seemed so sweet, you know? I didn't know she was a liar. I was trying to help my friend here."

She puts her arm around me, and she's lucky I don't shove it off.

"I was led astray, and in doing that, I hurt one of my best friends," Brynn continues to Alyssa, then turns to me. "I'm so sorry, Nat."

Alyssa balks like she wants to say something else, but she walks away. When she's out of eyesight, I do shove Brynn's arm off me. "What's wrong with you? Now you're spreading lies about a sophomore we don't even know."

Brynn puts her finger to her lips, like she honestly hadn't considered this. "She's never going to know I said that. I was covering for you. You want me to cover for you, right?"

"Yeah . . ."

"Then there's going to be a little collateral damage. That's how cover-ups work."

This seems to satisfy Brynn's conscience, but the whole thing feels wrong to me. It's not okay to pin this on some innocent sophomore.

me well, but I don't say things like that about people. You can ask any of my friends."

She looks distraught, and it feels like someone punched me. "I know you didn't start it."

"You do?" Natalie lets out the breath she was holding.

"Yes. I know exactly who started it. Don't worry. I think you're fabulous. The pottery you had in last year's art show was great." I am sure she had pottery in last year's art show because when I first saw the name *Natalie* by some pottery, I thought they had put my name by the wrong pieces.

"You liked my pottery?" Her eyes shine with hope and pride. Bull's-eye.

"Of course! Amazing technique."

"Wow, that means a lot coming from you. Thanks."

"No problem."

"Okay, well, I have to go. I'm glad you're not mad at me."

"Not mad at all." I smile. "See you around."

She practically runs out of the senior hall.

At lunch, I sit at my normal table. Brynn and Cecily look nervous. They're waiting for me to make the first move. Anger and loneliness fight for my top emotion: If I'm mostly angry, I'll yell at my friends. Mostly lonely? Try to force normalcy. After feeling like a freak all morning, I decide loneliness wins. I'll be angry later. I've become somewhat of a pro at pretending things are okay when they aren't, so here's hoping I can do it again.

"Nachos again?" I nod to my tray. "I for real want to see the ingredients list for this cheese, because I think there's plastic in it."

"Are you really okay?" Cecily asks. "Brynn said that the doctors got it wrong. Is that the truth, or is that what we're telling people?"

"No, it's true. I'm not taking meds anymore or anything." That feels great to say.

"That's awesome," Cecily says. "Obviously we would have been there for you no matter what—"

Doubtful.

"But it's so much easier this way. We don't have to be careful around you or anything."

"You weren't supposed to be careful around me in the first place. Remember? I told you to treat me like I was totally normal."

"Right." Cecily waves her hand dismissively. "And we were trying. But now we don't have to treat you *like* you're normal because you *are* normal, and that's so much easier."

She really doesn't get this, but whatever. It's easier for everyone if I simply stop being sick. I should have thought of this weeks ago.

"We're glad to have you back," says Brynn. She gives me a hug, and I try to feel happy. The bell rings, and we head to class.

On my way to English, Marcus Bisbane stops me. "Uh, this is awkward, but someone said you tried to kill yourself because I didn't ask you to prom last year? I'm sorry. I didn't know you liked me like that. I'd love to take you out sometime. You're, uh, super hot—I mean, pretty. I don't care that you're bipolar or whatever. It's cool, man." He's staring at my boobs, which is probably good because my face is a mix of intrigue and horror. How many permutations of this rumor are out there?

"No, thanks. That's not why I did it. Wait, actually, I didn't do it at all. There was a deer. The accident was me swerving to miss a deer. I never wanted to go to prom with you." That came out sounding kind of mean. "Not that you're not great. I had a mad crush on you in seventh grade." This part is true. "I'm over it now, because I'm sort of involved with someone else." This part is false, right? I'm losing track of what's true and what's false anymore.

"Man, that's a relief. I was feeling really guilty, you know, if I was the reason or whatever. That was rough." He shrugs to let his backpack hang lower on his back like he is literally shaking off the guilt. "See you around."

He leaves for class, and my face is hot.

It's difficult to focus during English. After class, my teacher asks me to stay for a minute. This day needs to end. How is it possible that it's only second hour?

"Natalie, I heard what happened," she says. "How are you doing?"

"I'm fine," I say for the millionth time today. "All of the rumors you heard were false. Someone was spreading stuff because they didn't want me to win homecoming queen."

"That's *awful.*" She seems to think this is almost as concerning as the actual rumor. "Are you okay? High school can be so hard. Do you want me to make you an appointment with Mrs. Hattan?"

"I already talked to her. I'm coping very well." [...] wants to believe that I'm fine, so "I'm coping," sound[...] priately dramatic but still safe.

"You are so brave." She's making me feel kind o[...] "Know that the staff is here for you. We were talkir[...] staff room before school about how glad we are that[...] here." She stands up and gives me an awkward teac[...]

She means the staff-room thing as comforting [...] super creepy. The teachers were standing around[...] about me? Don't they have better things to do?

In third-period Spanish, a kid I've never talked [...] me a note. She's quiet and only wears black. The n[...] *Thanks for being honest about your story—it inspir[...] get help for some of my issues. I made an appointm[...] Mrs. Hattan this morning.*

I don't know how to respond. Denying the rum[...] stop the girl from getting help, but acknowledging t[...] means that I need help. I simply smile and nod [...] smiles, too. She has a beautiful smile. I've never seen[...]

When I'm putting my books away in my lock[...] lunch, someone taps me on the shoulder. It's Natalie S[...] and she's tiny compared to the kids in the senior [...] clutching the strap of her backpack, and her face is [...]

"Hi, um, Natalie? I'm, uh, Natalie, and someone[...] you think I started the rumor that you tried to kil[...] and you're bipolar? I didn't start it, I swear." She ha[...] her eyes. "I voted for you for homecoming queen, a[...] still have the ballots, I can prove it. I know you d[...]

"Eh, they're better than quinoa," says Cecily. She and Brynn visibly relax, like they've been holding their breath. "That's what my mom packed for me." She crunches a chip. "How was your morning?"

"Fine. Marcus Bisbane asked me out."

"Ah! That's amazing!" says Brynn. "He's so hot. He made the conference all-star team in basketball last year."

"You've been waiting for this moment since seventh grade!" exclaims Cecily.

"I said no." I eat a chip and relish the looks of shock on my friends' faces.

"You said *no*?" asks Cecily. "Why?"

"I did like him in seventh grade, but I don't now."

"But if you start dating Marcus," says Brynn, "all of this other nonsense will disappear immediately. Everyone will talk about you as the new 'it' couple."

We're interrupted by a group of cheerleaders coming up to congratulate Cecily about homecoming queen. They ask what she'll wear when she gets her picture taken for the paper—and isn't it so exciting that she'll get to be on our school's parade float in the local holiday parade? Is it just me, or do they give me some weird looks? Has Cecily been talking about me to them? My insides feel crawly.

"I've had quite enough of people talking about me," I say when they finally walk away. We're a little too close to the topic that I'm trying to avoid. "Speaking of 'it' couples, Cecily, how are things going with Brent?"

Brent and Cecily went out again last night. The hot gossip until my story came around was that Cecily is dating a college guy. It probably gave her the needed boost to win homecoming queen.

"He's amazing," Cecily gushes. "So mature, you know? Not like high school guys."

"Great." I'm trying to be enthusiastic, but now I have to hear about how mature he is both when I'm at home and when I'm at school. Super.

"Did you kiss him yet?" asks Brynn.

"I need to respect Natalie," Cecily says stoically. "I am not at liberty to discuss any interactions that may have been perceived as sexual in nature."

"Can she please tell?" Brynn implores me. "I'm dying to know."

I know Cecily will tell Brynn behind my back if I don't let her say it now. I want to be included in their lives, so I guess I don't have a choice here. "Okay, fine. You can tell."

Cecily breathes a sigh of relief. "He did kiss me! And it was amazing. It was so much better than how high school guys kiss. Like, I think he learned stuff at college. He does this one thing with his tongue—"

"Ew, stop. Too much information." Never mind what I said earlier. I prefer if they talk about this behind my back. "Brynn, did you finish redecorating your room yet?"

"Almost. I need to go shopping for a few odds and ends, so maybe we could hit the mall this weekend?" A group of students walks by our table, and Brynn leans in close. "Maybe while we're there, we could buy a new jacket for Chloe. Did you see what she's wearing right now? It's out of control."

Chloe is wearing a jacket covered in fur.

My friends laugh.

I laugh.

There should be a rush of happiness because things are finally somewhat normal. We're talking about boys and fashion. This is what we do. This is what a normal life is like.

It feels different now.

"Maybe her jacket's not that bad," I say. If I want people to stop gossiping about me, it seems a little rude to say mean things about someone else.

"Uh, yes. It is that bad," says Brynn, and that's the end of that conversation.

Cecily starts discussing what she should wear on her next date with Brent—the yellow shirt with her red necklace, or the red shirt with the gold hoop earrings? That gets boring fast, so I look over at Chloe. A girl stops to compliment her jacket. Chloe smiles, and when she looks away the girl rolls her eyes and giggles with her friend. Ella is sitting at a far table working on some homework, and I can't help but think that she would never treat anyone like that. She's so nonjudgmental. Another group of people comes up to congratulate Cecily.

As I take another bite of stale nacho, I try to remember what about high school is supposed to be so awesome.

Chapter 20

I've been off my pills for four days, and it's going well. My paintings are coming along great, and I feel stable. The doctors had this wrong for sure. My therapist called today to see why I skipped my appointment, but I let the call go to voicemail.

A knock on the door interrupts a sketch I'm working on. We're not expecting pizza, and Brent is still at class.

"Can you get that, Nat?" Mom calls from the kitchen. "I'm chopping mangos for the lasagna."

My mom occasionally tries new recipes. Tonight's zucchini-mango lasagna—her first lasagna attempt since the fire-truck fiasco—will hopefully be better than last month's raspberry-pickle pork, but there is a secret stash of granola bars and beef jerky in my room for nights like this.

When I open the front door, Ella is on the porch.

"Hey, Ella. What's up? It's not Thursday."

"It's October fourteenth."

She says this as if the date has special significance. It's not my birthday, and I don't think it's her birthday. I'm lost.

"What's October fourteenth?"

Ella holds up her planner. "We made plans weeks ago. I brought leftover Yorkshire pudding from Yorkshire Pudding Day, so you're welcome."

"Oh, right." Should I pretend I remembered? Nah, Ella won't mind the truth. "I forgot, sorry."

"Good thing I didn't."

She walks straight to the kitchen carrying a container of what must be Yorkshire pudding, and before I can shut the door, Petunia zooms outside in hot pursuit of a squirrel.

"Toons!" I yell. "Get back here!"

My heart jumps to my throat. Our road isn't super busy, but it only takes one car. I start chasing her. I haven't run cross-country this season, but my ankle has mostly healed, so I figure I'm still fast enough to catch my dog. My stride is okay for a few steps, but then it turns into more of an aggressive hobble.

Ella hears the commotion and runs after me, her combat boots clunking on my front steps. "Her name is Petunia."

Toons races around the front yard, enjoying her newfound freedom. She runs along the side of the fence. When she gets to the walkway opening, she stops and stares at the world beyond. She looks back, sees me running, and thinks I'm trying to play chase. She smiles with her tongue

225

lolling out, curls up her tail, and sprints out of our yard. I can almost see the thought bubble over her head that says, "WHEEEEEEEE!"

"Petunia, get back here!" The situation is getting desperate. I stop trying to run so she'll know the "chase" is over. She realizes I'm not following her, and about sixty feet from me, she turns to see why I stopped. Time to muster up my best mom glare.

"Petunia May Cordova, you get back here this instant!" Pointing firmly to my toes adds a strict effect.

"Her middle name is May?" Ella catches up to me, a little out of breath. "Seriously?"

With my mom glare still firmly fixed on Toons, I whisper out the side of my mouth, "I made it up right now. I needed a middle name so she knows she's in trouble."

Ella raises one eyebrow. "She's a dog. She doesn't understand you. And it's weird that you gave her a middle name. *Petunia May* makes her sound like an old Southern church lady."

"An old Southern church lady?" I momentarily forget to glare at Petunia, take my hands off my hips, and turn to Ella. "How do you even think of things like that?"

Ella shrugs, then looks alarmed. "Petunia!"

Toons is running again. She runs into our cranky neighbor's yard, and Ella and I chase on tiptoe to avoid drawing the neighbor's attention. She reaches the next yard over, and we're gaining on her. She ignores my repeated calls. Freedom is way too much fun. She jumps over a stick and keeps going.

"Get her treats!" I call over my shoulder to Ella. "They're on the kitchen counter!" Ella turns back to the house. I'm almost to Petunia when she cuts right and heads into the road. My breath catches. Please don't let there be a car.

We get lucky this time.

She reaches the other side and runs around a minivan parked in someone's driveway. She scoots under it and waits for me. When I get to the van, my breath is embarrassingly heavy. I drop to the concrete and find myself face-to-face with her, but she's still out of reach.

"Come here, girl." I use my sweetest I-love-you voice. "Do you want a belly rub? How about a belly rub?" She pants happily. If I lunge for her, she might run. Hurry up, Ella! We need those treats.

"Here, Tooner. Want a *treat*?" She knows that word. She cocks her head and looks at me as if she's trying to call my bluff. She's been tricked before.

Just then, the door of the minivan's house opens, and a woman calls out, "Are you okay out there?" It must look strange for a teenage girl to be sprawled in her driveway.

"Yep." I wave as if this is totally normal. "Trying to get my dog."

The woman comes closer. "Do you need help?"

Her presence startles Toons, who sprints out from under the van and into the road. Unfortunately, we're not as lucky this time. A pickup truck is speeding right toward her.

I scramble up to run, but it's easy to see that the truck will beat me there. I scream. Ella comes out of my house just in time to see the situation. She drops the bag of treats and covers her face. The truck comes closer. It's fifteen feet away. Ten. Five.

I look up to the sky. I can't watch. The woman behind me gasps. Tires squeal.

When the street is finally quiet again, I race toward the stopped truck. (Why couldn't I move that fast earlier?) Tears blur my vision. Ella meets me there, the treat bag left on the lawn. We don't need it now.

Someone has to look under the truck. "You do it," I tell Ella. "I can't."

"No way. I'm going to be even more traumatized than when I watched your accident. At least you made it out."

A scream is exploding somewhere in my chest. I'm in a nightmare. This can't be happening.

Near the back-left tire, Toons creeps out from under the truck and whimpers.

"TOONS!" I yell. "You're alive!"

She runs toward me, and I bend down to let her jump into my arms. She's shaking.

"Did I miss that dog?" A man in a trucker hat climbs out of the pickup. "I'm awful sorry. It jumped out so quick. I tried to turn."

"You missed her," I confirm. That will go down in history as my favorite three-word sentence.

"Thank you for the impressive maneuvering of your vehicle." Ella shakes the man's hand. "Your driver's ed teacher would be very proud."

The man was probably in driver's ed about twenty years ago, but he smiles.

I kiss the top of Toons's head. She's breathing fast from running and probably from adrenaline. "She needs some water." I need some water, too. All of my bones have turned to soup, and my nerves are on fire.

"I'll take her," says Ella.

Letting her go is difficult, but the only person in the world who might love this dog more than me is Ella.

Ella pets her back and turns toward our house. "Don't run in front of cars," she says to Petunia. "That's how you get killed. It's like running with scissors or fighting a bear or dabbling in the South American drug trade."

I say goodbye to the man, wave to the minivan neighbor, and follow Ella. She's in the kitchen filling up my mom's decorative china bowl with water. Mom's lasagna is in the oven.

"That was too close." I pour glasses of water for both of us.

We watch Petunia eagerly lap water out of a bowl that has been in my family for three generations. Good thing my mom doesn't frequently check on her cooking.

I'm shaky, and focusing on my glass is difficult. Ella says something about Petunia, but she sounds far away.

The water in my glass is shaking. That's interesting. The water is shaking. How strange. My eyes dart around the kitchen. Look at the stove. The stove dial. The little tick mark right after HI and below HI/MED. The next tick mark over. No, the first one. No, the next one.

"Hi, Toons," I say to the dog while staring at my glass. My voice sounds a little weird. Everyone knows that petting dogs releases tension, so I pet her two times.

Three.

Four.

Five.

Wait, no four and half because I didn't go all the way down her back that time. I rub my hand over her fur to erase that pet and try another one that goes all the way to her tail. There. That one's five. But was the other one fully erased? I rub again to erase the whole thing. My dog's an Etch A Sketch.

"What are you doing?" asks Ella.

She still sounds far away. This feels familiar.

"I, um, I gotta go." My heart picks up its pace. The starting gun sounds, and my blood races through me, trying to set a new record. Breathe how you're supposed to, Natalie. In for four seconds, hold for four seconds, out for four seconds, in for . . . Wait, *in*, is that right? . . . In, out, in, out, out, out, out. Forget it. This is too hard.

I grab Petunia and head to the nearest safe place. If I can get away from everything, then maybe I'll be okay. There's a tiny bathroom down the hall from our kitchen, so I go in there. It's almost like my closet—dark, closed-in, and small. I huddle in a corner, as far as possible from the danger lurking everywhere. It's hard to get away from everywhere, but that doesn't stop me from trying.

Toons cuddles close, like a warm teddy bear. If I hold her really tight, she'll be safe from the danger. She squirms.

Is that her heartbeat I feel in my stomach? I loosen my grip a bit so she can breathe, but then I realize I'm not breathing. Oops. In out, in out, in out.

Tentacles of light slither into my darkness from under the bathroom door. That crack in the door is bad. Who knows what could come through that crack? There's all sorts of danger out there. An octopus could slide its tentacles in and reach me.

That's it. I know it. An octopus is going to slide its tentacles under there. It will grab Petunia and take her away. I have to stop the octopus.

I grab some hand towels and shove them into the crack. Petunia is firmly gripped under my arm so that the octopus can't take her. Even with the towels shoved in as tightly as possible, pinpricks of light seep through the sides. If the light can get through, so can the octopus. What else can block the deadly openings? I open the medicine cabinet, but the darkness keeps me from seeing anything. Hopefully my rescue wasn't in there. What else could work? Aha! Toilet paper.

Toilet paper stuffs well into the cracks. The octopus had better not attack before I'm ready. What if it grabs my hand while I'm trying to barricade my fort? After quickly shoving the last of the toilet paper into place, I go back to my corner and wrap my arms around Petunia. The octopus isn't going to take her unless it takes me, too.

A knock on the door startles me. I bury my head in Petunia. This is it.

"Uh, Natalie? Are you okay in there?"

It's Ella.

"I'm fine!" I call back. "I'm staying safe from the danger."

"There's no danger," she says. "The truck is gone."

"Not the truck." How can she be thinking about the truck at a time like this? "Do you see an octopus out there?"

"A what?"

"An octopus."

"The sea creature?"

"Yeah."

"In your hallway?"

"Yeah."

There's a pause. "Um, no, there is no octopus."

I ask her if she's looked. She takes a moment and then assures me that, no, there is no octopus in my hallway. We are quiet for another minute. Petunia is breathing, so if I match it, then I can probably remember how breathing goes.

Ella knocks again. "Natalie? Why is there toilet paper under your door? Can I come in?"

"No." It's dark in here. Darkness is good. It's safe. I can't notice everything.

"Please, Nat? I think I need to come in."

Ella has never called me Nat.

Maybe it would be a good idea to let her in. Good friends wouldn't leave friends in danger. Also, there's something about an octopus attacking me that doesn't make total sense. I can't put my finger on it, but something seems off. I open the door a crack.

"Nat?" Ella looks concerned. "Can you come out here? There's no octopus. I promise."

The hall looks like my normal old hallway.

The sliver of light hits the open medicine cabinet. Our downstairs cabinet hardly ever has anything in it, but there is a lonely orange pill bottle on the right side of the bottom shelf. That's right, I put a bottle of anxiety meds down here weeks ago just in case. Not sure what "just in case" was for, but this seems like it.

It's an anxiety medication, and this seems anxiety-ish. Do I need it now? If I take it, is that admitting there's a problem? I'm *not* sick. I need to rally at the moment, but overall I'm fine. Definitely not bipolar, in case anyone was wondering. But this medication isn't for bipolar disorder. It's for anxiety. Which I might be. Anxious, I mean. Or maybe I should take it to calm me down because if I'm going to get dragged down to the depths by an octopus, I might as well drug myself up for it.

Wait a minute, what "depths"? There is no ocean here. This is very strange.

"Should you maybe take those?" asks Ella. She motions to the pill bottle in my hand.

How did this get in my hand?

"Maybe." There can't be an octopus here. This is the Midwest. The word *delusional* comes to mind, but I had delusional panic attacks when they thought I was bipolar. Not now. At least I'm not hallucinating. It's not like I actually *see* an impossible octopus—it just feels like one is there. I'm totally fine.

"Here you go," says Ella. She hands me my glass of water. "Maybe we should go sit down."

She puts her arm around me and coaxes me out of the bathroom. I swallow my pill before I can change my mind. One pill for anxiety does not make me bipolar.

"I want to watch TV," Ella says as soon as we sit down in the living room. "Let's watch TV." She grabs the remote and turns it on. MTV shows people screaming at each other about who has the best hair. We watch in silence for a few moments.

"These people are really crazy," she says. "In case you were wondering what crazy looks like."

Her subtext is appreciated.

It's two episodes later of whatever-this-is before I'm completely calmed down. The oven timer has dinged, and my mom must have gone into the kitchen because I hear her exclaim, "Yorkshire pudding! Where did this come from?" Fear has turned to embarrassment. An *octopus*? What was I thinking? How did that even enter my brain? Ella seems completely unfazed.

"Sorry. I know that was weird. I, um . . . I get freaked out sometimes."

"It's no problem. I read some books on abnormal psych last year."

"I'm not bipolar." Am I trying to convince Ella or myself?

"Really?" She looks curious. "It was going around school that you are."

"Well, I'm not." That comes out sounding pouty. How is it that she heard the rumor but not the rumor retraction? Stupid gossip chain.

"It doesn't matter if you are or not." She stops watching TV to face me. "You get that, right? I thought you were, and I'm still here. It makes no difference to me if your brain works differently than other people's. You're my friend. Friends don't care about that kind of thing."

It's embarrassing that I'm the one who tried to teach her about friendship, when she's sitting on my couch, completely chill about the fact that I just tried to rescue us from a stray octopus. If that's not a good friend, I don't know what is.

In fact, she might be the best friend I have.

"Thanks," I say. I start to add, "But I'm not bipolar," but then I stop.

Strangely, I believe that it really doesn't matter to her.

Chapter 21

School is a weird place to be lately. Teachers are awkwardly nice, and students stare at me like I'm a giant walking question mark. Is she bipolar? Or isn't she? Which rumors are true?

Did my dad go through this when he was diagnosed? He wasn't in high school, but maybe adults do the creepy wonder-stare, too. Did he feel defined by his sickness? Do I, even though I chose not to have it anymore?

I walk into the cafeteria on Monday and find Brynn and Cecily staring at Chloe. Today she's wearing a 1980s-style bedazzled denim jacket that looks like she stole it from Martha, the owner of the store where my mom works. My friends are giggling again, but I don't find it funny.

In a move that is true high school insanity, I head for an open spot at Chloe's table. "Can I sit here?"

Chloe looks surprised and a little suspicious. "Um, sure," she says after an awkward pause. She moves her backpack to make room.

"Hi, everyone," I say to the table.

There's Chloe and her friends Ruth, Jenny, and the Riley twins. Ruth was on the track team with me, but she wasn't very fast. She once mentioned she thought she might have the school record for the slowest mile run, but no one knows if that's true. Jenny is the QuizBowl captain and has hair that would be beautiful if she took a little better care of it. The Riley twins both look like the *Mona Lisa*: thin smiles, light eyebrows—it's uncanny.

They all say hello back, and then no one says anything. It seems they're waiting for me to announce why I'm there.

"I, uh, I don't know you very well, and that's too bad," I say. "I thought I'd come say hello, that's all."

I take a bite of my pizza. They also take bites of their lunches.

"You adopted my grandma's dog, right?" Chloe says to break the silence. "How's she doing?"

"Really well." Phewf. A conversation topic.

"She's so weird-looking," says Chloe.

I laugh. "Right? Like a baby alien."

"Your dog looks like a baby alien?" asks Ruth. "Can I see a picture?"

"Sure." While the girls pass my phone around, I look over at my usual table. Brynn and Cecily stare at me like *I'm* a baby alien.

Ruth and the Riley twins say that Toons is cute, but Jenny says she looks freakish. All of them are right. When

I ask Jenny how the QuizBowl team is doing this year, she tells me that they've qualified for the state finals. Why didn't I know this? If an athletic team makes it to state, the whole school freaks out. If QuizBowl makes it, no one cares? The other girls at the table are going to the finals to cheer Jenny on, and they say I can sit with them if I want to go.

Within about ten minutes, I've learned a lot about the people at this table. They're really funny—why have I never talked to them before? They ask about me, and Ruth admits that she had a crush on Brent last year. (Did everyone have a crush on Brent last year?) I mention that he's dating Cecily now, and they all already knew that. Ruth blushes, and it's clear that "last year's" crush isn't totally dead.

Chloe says she needs to go shopping after school to find something to wear to the golf banquet. I didn't know she played golf.

Inspiration strikes, and I reach for my backpack. "Here." I pull some cards from the side pocket. "These are discount vouchers for my mom's store."

"Doesn't she own Runway Flair?" asks Jenny.

"No. I wish. But she's the manager there, and she's great at putting outfits together. Ask for Margaret Cordova, and these will give you forty percent off anything you buy." Coupons for clothes are the high school equivalent of an olive branch. As I hoped, all the girls are excited and thank me. They say they'll go right after school, and they ask if I want to come. Unfortunately, I need to get home and start studying for midterms, which are starting tomorrow and which I've totally neglected. They look sympathetic but also a bit appalled that I haven't started studying yet.

The clock says there are only ten minutes left in lunch, so I head back to my normal table.

"What was that about?" asks Brynn.

"I don't know them well, so I wanted to say hi." I shrug like this is no big deal.

"Not knowing them well has never bothered you before," Cecily points out.

"It does now." Why do I have to explain sitting at another table for a few minutes?

Brynn and Cecily exchange an odd look. "Is this because of your secret?" Brynn asks. "We already said sorry. You've been acting so weird."

Have I?

"I don't think it's that weird to sit at another table for ten minutes."

"It's not just that," says Cecily. "You seem different. I can't put my finger on exactly what it is."

Brynn nods in agreement.

"Is it a bad kind of different?" I ask.

"No, I don't think so," Cecily says. She's less than convincing.

Our conversation is interrupted when Ella drops her backpack next to me and sits at our table.

This is surprising, but also vindicating. See? People switch tables. Ella usually sits alone in the back of the lunchroom with her pile of books, and now she's sitting with us.

"I noticed you switched tables," says Ella, "so I took that as a sign that it is now socially acceptable. Chloe has told me in the past that it is not socially acceptable."

Blast. Maybe it was a little weirder than I thought.

When no one immediately says anything, Ella fills the silence. "Or is it only today? Is it a holiday or something? Is this like in elementary school when we had Meet a New Friend Day and read with new reading buddies?"

"No," I say. "It's completely okay to switch tables whenever you want."

I smile confidently, and Brynn rolls her eyes. Ella starts scanning the room.

"Hmm, okay. Then I think I will start sitting with the football players."

The football players are having an armpit-farting contest.

"Joking," Ella says when Cecily looks at her in horror. "That was a joke. I'm occasionally hilarious." She takes a bite of her sandwich and talks with her mouth open. "How's everyone's day going?"

Brynn's face makes me almost laugh out loud. She looks stunned, like everything she knows about the high school lunchroom has been thrown in a lunch lady's blender. Some people at other tables have started pointing and whispering, too.

"I'm having a good day," Cecily jumps in. "The pre-nursing club got approved for our meetup with the college group from Greater Falls."

"That's great!" I say. Cecily has been working on that for a while.

"You'll be a good nurse," says Ella. "You have that calming demeanor about you, and you're clearly smart, because you're in AP Biology."

"Thanks, Ella. That's really nice of you."

"And you"—Ella turns to Brynn—"have very nice hair."

"Thanks."

A compliment about Brynn's appearance is a great way to warm her up. Her hair is in a fishtail braid today.

"I could do your hair like this if you want. It's super easy."

"Really? Awesome." Ella gets up from her seat and walks over to Brynn. She sits down with the back of her head facing Brynn and says, "I'm ready." Brynn looks a little startled at first, but then shrugs as if to say, "Well, I guess now is as good a time as any." She starts working on Ella's hair.

"I'm getting pie," Cecily says.

I go with her. While we're in line, I look back at our table and see Brynn doing Ella's hair. Ella is saying something, and Brynn laughs. It looks like they're having fun. The inside-out form of the fishtail braid is starting to take shape. They make an odd pair, but I love it. Sometimes odd can be fun. Look at Petunia.

When lunch ends, Brynn and Cecily walk out ahead of me. Ella walks next to me and says, "How are you feeling today?"

"Better. Thanks for helping me out last week."

"No problem. Take care of yourself, okay? You have to be okay to care for Petunia."

"I know. I've got it under control."

"Good." She adjusts her backpack strap. "Also, let me know if you ever need any help. You're my best friend, and I've never had a best friend. Well, you're my best friend that's not a dog."

Before I have a chance to respond, she throws her braid over her shoulder and hurries to her fifth-hour class.

I'm her best friend?

Wait a minute. Who's *my* best friend? I used to think it was a tie between Brynn and Cecily, but now things feel off with them. After the incident on October 14, it feels more like that might be Ella.

It's like I'm standing here with half of a best-friends heart charm, wondering who deserves the other half. Brynn or Cecily? Ella?

No one?

Chapter 22

I haven't slept more than two hours a night for the past three nights. Or four, if you count so far tonight. My therapist would say it's evidence of a manic episode, but hey—it's midterm week. Everyone stays up all night studying.

Maybe three or four all-nighters in a row is a little strange, but I have a heavy course load this year. My calculus, physics, and literature midterms were three days in a row, but the studying paid off because I'm very smart. Ace, ace, and ace on those tests. Probably. That's how smart I am.

Now I'm sitting in my bedroom, painting an abstract piece on a large canvas. I am an extremely talented abstract artist. It has recently occurred to me that perhaps Soo wants me to stick to landscapes because she herself is not very good at abstract art. Landscapes are easy to judge. Abstracts take a special kind of mind.

My mind is special, but not bipolar.

Brilliant, not crazy.

The abstract is a copy of the silhouette I did in my closet and covered with the white paint. It will look great in my Art Connect display. Soo can't *force* me to choose landscapes, right? My artist's instinct tells me to paint abstracts, and everyone says to trust your instincts.

It's great to have a break from studying. During my all-nighters, I memorized my notes from each class verbatim. There was no way the teachers were going to trick me on anything. My memory is fantastic.

The clock on my nightstand says 2:12 a.m. My favorite time to paint is after midnight. It feels like the entire world is asleep. Think of half the globe shrouded in darkness, with only one light showing a pinprick of brilliance. That light is from my bedroom window.

Soo will like this painting. She has to. It's amazing. I add another stroke of purple and then sit back and look at it. This is probably the best painting I've ever done. Abstracts are my true calling. I should spend every day painting instead of wasting meaningless nights memorizing notes for exams.

That gives me an idea.

I should be an artist instead of a student. College would be fun, I guess, but I already have the skills I need. Look at this painting. Is this the painting of someone who needs college? No, it isn't.

What a great idea. Why wait years for my life to start? My life can start now. I put down my paintbrush and grab some clothes from my closet. This is a phenomenal idea. I'm going to be an artist in Paris. Everyone knows that the best artists live in Paris. I picture myself on a grassy lawn in front of the Eiffel Tower, wearing a beret and eating a croissant. The sunlight will hit the metal and I'll think, "This inspires me to interpret life in a whole new way." And then I will. The Louvre will have a display room on me one day—The Girl Who Ran to Paris. People will study my life and say, "Wow, she was only eighteen when she started her international art career?" Parents will warn their children that I'm the exception, not the rule, and that good kids should stay in school and not assume their stories will be as successful as mine.

Where's my duffel bag? There it is, under my bed. After I shake the dust off, I choose which clothes to bring. I don't take much—I'll have a small studio apartment like my dad, and I can wear clothes two days in a row. Possibly three. No one knows me, so no one will judge.

Thunder rolls in the distance.

Before long, my bag is full of mostly socks (because I won't wear socks two days in a row—that's disgusting). Toons stares at me from her perch on my bed. Her head is cocked. The thunder must have woken her up.

Hmm. What can I do with Petunia? No problem. She can come with me. She's easy. I only have to pack a leash and some snacks.

"Wanna go to Paris?" I whisper.

She smiles and wags her tail.

After five minutes, clothes packing is finished. Next up is painting supplies. Too bad I threw away my shoebox paints. It's also a bummer that I can't take the abstract I just finished. I'll leave it for my mom, who will no doubt be very proud of me but might also miss me a little. Where will she put the painting?

With fresh inspiration, I sneak downstairs and replace the landscape above the fireplace with my new piece. Hopefully it's dry. It looks much better in this room than that ridiculous landscape did.

This gives me another great idea. (Tonight is full of great ideas!)

I go around the house and take down all of my landscape paintings. There were two in the living room, one in the hallway, two in the dining room, and one in the bathroom. The one in my mom's room is impossible to get because she might wake up, but that's okay. She can keep that one.

The pile of paintings is assembled on the dining room table. Wait, was that a noise upstairs? I freeze. Is someone waking up? After a full three minutes of standing perfectly still, I move stealthier than I did before. There's the thunder again, closer this time. A flash of lightning makes my dining room momentarily bright as day.

I tiptoe up the stairs and grab the duffel bag in one hand and Petunia in the other. The only thing standing between me and freedom is getting the car out of the driveway unnoticed. Good thing my mom's room is on the opposite side of the house.

With Petunia and my duffel bag safely stowed in my back seat, I close the car door. Petunia hops up to put her two front paws on the window. She gives a *charp*, and I put my finger to my lips.

"Shh," I whisper. "Be right back."

There's one more thing I need—my paintings from the dining room table. These are the paintings from when I was part of the establishment, the ones made when I used to let authority figures stifle my creative genius. They've gotta go.

Before I leave, I take one last look at my dining room. Who knows if I will ever eat there again? Lightning flashes and makes the room an eerie blue-white.

Time to go.

A few houses away, I stop to look back at my house. Do any lights come on? Five minutes. No lights. My mom must have taken an Ambien or something, and Brent can sleep through an apocalypse. Looks like I'm good.

I put my car into drive and rev the engine. Here we go— Paris or bust.

The nearest airport is an hour away, so it's a good thing I'm not tired. There are a few things I need to do before I leave town.

The first is at the bridge over the Vicksburg River. I park my car in the middle of the bridge. No reason to pull over, because the road is empty. Also, I won't be here long.

I peer over the edge. The rushing water is even farther away than I imagined. What would it be like to jump? Would that have been a better plan than crashing my car? It would have been less messy, and it might have worked. Then again, how far can a human fall without dying?

No matter. I'm alive and on the brink of something awesome.

I leave the side of the bridge and grab my landscape paintings.

Rain starts to fall. An umbrella would have been a smart thing to pack. Oh well. It's not raining too hard. Plus, if my feet get wet, I can always change my socks.

The paintings and I are at the edge of the bridge now. This is the moment of truth. Should I throw them all at once or one at a time? It's more dramatic to throw them one at a time, like I'm throwing away all the parts of me that I hate. Then again, this trip to Paris was a sudden decision. It hasn't included a lot of flair so far, so there's no reason to start now.

The stack rests on the ledge. So many hours of my life went into these. It's a shame to throw them away. I look through them—the woods, the beach, the ocean, the farmhouse. They'll all be ruined as soon as they hit the water. Soo will have nothing to display from me. She says landscapes are my best work? All of my "best" work is about to be gone forever.

Don't care.

I push the paintings off the edge, handing them over to gravity. I grip the railing and lean far over to watch them hit the water.

Splash. It's done. No more landscapes. I'm an abstract artist now.

A satisfied nod marks the end of this errand. Is it my imagination, or is the rain coming down harder? I jump in my car and turn it on. Now to find a gas station. The corn-field taught me to always watch the gas gauge.

While I pump gas, I think of Ty and our draw-off. Who won that, anyway? I think he did.

Will I marry an artist one day? Maybe I'll meet him in Paris. He won't speak English, and I won't speak French, but we'll have our art and that will be enough.

Wait. That won't work. How will I ask him to pick up milk on his way home? Maybe I'll be better off with someone who speaks English. I wish Ty could go with me to Paris.

Whoa, did a literal lightbulb just go on above my head? No, it was one of those aggressively fluorescent lights flick-ering above the gas pumps. Close enough.

I'll bring Ty. This is genius. Why didn't I think of this before? He loves art, I love art. We're perfect for each other. Now that I'm not bipolar, there's nothing keeping us from being together. Yes. This is perfect. Brent will hate it, but screw Brent.

I grab my phone from my jacket pocket and text Ty.

You up?

The gas pump clicks—my tank is full. Would I like a receipt? Press yes or no. No.

He doesn't need to text back, because I'm going to his house anyway. My engine revs again as I speed out of the gas station. At a red light, I check my phone.

I'm up now. Sup?

Everything. Coming over.

Okay . . . ?

Wait, where do you live?

He sends me a pin to his address. Great.

Green light.

Eighty miles an hour might not be the best idea when driving a winding road with a speed limit of twenty-five, but this is Vicksburg. No cops will be out.

The rain comes down hard. My windshield wipers flap furiously. It only takes minutes to get to Ty's house, and I text him again.

Here. At the road.

No reason to drive up his driveway. Maybe his parents don't take Ambien. My heart flips while viewing his house. Ty is in there, somewhere behind the dark shutters and two-story brick. A light goes on in the lower right side of the house.

A minute later, a shadowy figure comes toward me from Ty's driveway. It's him. I wave, but he doesn't see it.

Ty gets in the passenger side and shuts the door. He wears sweatpants that he probably wasn't wearing two minutes ago and a wrinkled shirt. He's not wearing a baseball cap, which feels intimate. He always wears a baseball cap. His curly brown hair is sort of sticking up at odd angles, like he didn't even take the time to run his fingers through it, but the rain has matted it down a bit. He looks half-asleep.

"What's going on? Are you okay?"

"I'm great. I'm on my way to Paris."

He blinks at me.

"Like, France."

"I know where Paris is." He rubs his eyes. "I don't know why you're going there at three o'clock in the morning."

Petunia pops up on the center console and tries to hop to the front seat.

"No, girl. Stay there." I throw a treat to the back seat before turning to Ty. "I'm going because I had a brilliant idea, and there's no reason to wait. Are you coming with me or what?"

"What?" Ty shakes his head as if trying to wake himself up from a dream. Rainwater jumps from the ends of his curls. "I'm not going to Paris at three in the morning. Are you okay? Have you been drinking?"

"I haven't been drinking. I've never been better." How can he not *see* this? I put my elbows on the steering wheel and my face in my hands. How do I explain this? Aha. Got it. I sit up again. "Have you ever had that moment in life where everything makes sense, like a puzzle where all of the pieces suddenly fall into place? That is my life right now."

He looks completely baffled. "Puzzles don't do that—"

"Argh!" I hit my forehead with my palm. "It's a rough metaphor, but you have to see past it. You have to see the deeper meaning! I'm going to be an abstract artist."

"In Paris?"

Rain pelts the windshield, and I have to raise my voice to be heard. "In Paris. Are you in?"

"No. I'm not. You shouldn't go, either. At least sleep on it and decide in the morning."

"Haven't slept all week. I'll sleep when I'm dead."

"You should probably sleep before that." He laughs nervously. "You must be sleep-deprived. You're not thinking clearly. Go home, Nat. Get some sleep. Let's talk about Paris after art class next week."

"No, I don't think—"

Ty puts his hands on my shoulders, cutting me off. Mm, I wish he'd let those hands slide over my shoulders and down my back. I want him to pull me close and whisper that he'd love to go to Paris with me.

His hands stay on my shoulders. "Natalie. Look at me."

I stare into his eyes. They're mesmerizing.

"You need to go home. I'm worried about you."

"You know who you should be worried about? People in the establishment. You should be worried about people who are never going to be strong enough to go after what they want. Come on, Ty. You want to be an artist, right?"

"Of course, but—"

"But nothing. This is your chance. This is *our* chance. Can't you see it? The Eiffel Tower and the baguettes and the berets?"

Ty clears his throat. "Are you sure you're okay?"

"For the first time in such a long time, yes. I'm sure. I'm great." Toons starts scratching at my back door. "Shoot, she probably has to pee. Hold on. I have to let her out."

Ty almost yells over the rain. "You can't let her out right now. It's awful out there."

"What, you think I can tell a dog to hold it? She's not peeing in my car, Ty." I roll my eyes and reach for the leash. Before he can protest, I'm out of the car and opening the back door. "Here, girl." I hook up the leash and set her on the pavement. She blinks a few times and backs up, trying to get out of the rain.

"No, no, you can't go under my car. Come on, Tooner." I pull on her leash and practically drag her to the middle of the cul-de-sac. "There. Now you can go."

She tries to look up at me, but she gets rain in her eyes and looks back down. She seems to have lost interest in going to the bathroom. Her tail is down, she starts to shiver, and little drops of rain drip from her ears.

Ty gets out of the car. "Natalie. This is insane. Come on, get back in the car."

"You don't understand insane," I yell. "This is the sanest I have ever been. Everything is so clear to me, Ty. It could be so great."

He jogs over and doesn't speak until he's standing a foot away from me. "I already tried to be with you, remember?"

"I know, I'm sorry. There were complications back then, but they're gone now. So you'll come to Paris?"

"I asked you to a concert. Paris seems like a pretty big jump. Could we maybe start with the concert?" He tries to do his trademark grin, but the concern on his face makes it look distorted. His curly hair is plastered to his forehead now, and his shirt sticks to his chest. My hair is heavy with water, and I wish I hadn't worn jeans. It's like we're taking a shower with our clothes on.

Then it hits me like the lightning forking above us—he's not coming with me. I'll probably never see him again after tonight. I've never been great with goodbyes, so I say, "Sure, a concert sounds fine."

Ty stares at me. It's a deep stare that makes the lie feel naked.

I can't look at him anymore. "Toons, go potty." Toons looks up and whimpers. She takes a tentative step toward the car. "I'd better, uh, go."

"Are you good to drive?" He takes a step toward me. "Something's up."

"I'm great to drive. Never been better." That's almost true. He didn't have to complicate this perfect night by not going to Paris with me. How selfish.

I slosh back to my car in soaking tennis shoes, and Ty follows close behind. I put Toons in the back seat and slam the door. I'm about to open my own door, but then I turn around. If I'm never going to see Ty again, I'd better make the most of tonight.

I step closer to him, but he doesn't step back. My eyes lock on his, and his concern mixes with something new. Surprise, maybe? Anticipation?

I put my hands on his waist and slide them around to his back. His wet shirt is warm from body heat. I pull him closer, stand on my tiptoes, and turn my face to his—but then he stops me. He pushes me back a little but leaves his hands on my waist.

"Nat, come on. What are you doing? Talk to me? Please? You can trust me." He brushes strands of wet hair from my face. "What's wrong?"

"Does something have to be wrong?" I pull him in again, slipping my fingertips into the waistband of his sweats to keep them warm. "Me standing here, this close to kissing you, is not something wrong. It's something that's finally right. You can't tell me you don't feel it, too."

The concern in his eyes is battling the whatever-else-that-is.

My breath catches. "What you said about eyes, the other day—how they tell stories better than entire novels? I get it now."

He nods, not bothering with words when his eyes are saying plenty.

I run my hands up his chest and around his neck before I kiss him. It's not a light good-night kiss—it's a hold-him-close, goodbye-forever kiss.

It's an I've-wanted-to-do-this-for-a-long-time kiss.

It's a please-remember-me kiss.

It's an I'm-sorry kiss.

His hands find my neck, his thumbs on my jaw, and he pulls me close with the perfect combination of softness and urgency. The smell of the rain mixes with his woodsy scent. He returns my kiss, and my tears mix with raindrops. Why couldn't this have happened before? Why now, when I'm leaving? Why won't he go to Paris?

This should be the perfect movie moment. We're kissing in the rain, finally acknowledging what we've been feeling for weeks. But if this were a movie, we would see each other again after tonight. I wouldn't be leaving, and he wouldn't be letting me go.

Life, I have learned, is very rarely like a movie.

"I have to go." I can't keep kissing him. I might stay—and if I stay, it will ruin everything. There's a flight somewhere waiting for me. I try to mentally bottle everything about this moment so I can revisit it later: the water clinging to his eyelashes, the way his hands feel on the small of my back, the fireworks going off inside me.

His rubs my waist like he's tracing the curve of my body. "Don't go. Not yet."

He tries to kiss me again, but I push him away. I open the door and get in my car, shutting the door even as he tries to convince me not to. He tries to open it, but I've already locked it. He knocks on the window and motions for me to roll it down.

I start the car, eager to get the heat blasting to dry off my clothes. The air smells like wet dog. I open the window.

"Where are you going? Can I give you a ride? We could go somewhere and talk. Don't leave without explaining . . . all of this."

He gestures to the blank night around him like I crafted a movie set and dragged him into it without telling him the plot or any of his lines. He looks so confused, I can't take it anymore.

"Look me up if you're ever in Paris, okay?" I roll up the window, put the car in gear, and hit the gas.

Ty jumps clear of my tires.

I keep my eyes on the road and tell myself not to look back. I don't need to look back. My future is ahead of me.

But I can still taste him on my lips, and before I'm out of sight, I sneak one look in the rearview mirror. He's got one hand on his head, and I watch him kick the curb. Then, when I turn the corner, he's gone.

Chapter 23

The black-and-orange plastic sign has been turned from OPEN to CLOSED. I knock on the door anyway. My dad doesn't answer, so I pound harder. There's rustling from within. The door opens about a centimeter, and the light from the hall spills into the darkened gallery.

My dad squints, and he startles when he sees me. "Natalie? What are you doing here? Are you okay?"

My dripping hair, my smeared makeup, and the puddle of water forming at my feet don't exactly scream, "I stopped by for a casual chat."

He opens the door wider.

"I'm okay." I walk into the studio, and my dad flips the light on. Seeing the art makes me excited about my new life. "Just saying goodbye. I thought I should say goodbye to someone, but Mom and Brent wouldn't understand at all.

You will. I'm headed to Paris to be like you. Only, you know, in Paris instead of here."

His eyes widen and he says softly, "Natalie, don't be just like me."

"It'll be great. I'm going to start my own gallery, and everyone's going to love me. My friend Ty was going to go, too, but he's not now." Do I always talk this fast? "I'm leaving tonight, which is too bad because I just met you and found out that you're alive. Maybe you can visit me in Paris? You can come now if you want, but you've got this whole gallery and everything here." I gesture toward the pictures on the wall. Blast. My hands haven't stopped moving since I started talking. That might look a little wild. I put them down and mentally glue them to my soaking jeans.

He gives me a blank stare, not unlike Ty's when I told him my news.

"Dad—" That doesn't sound right. "Can I call you Dad?"

He smiles, which means yes.

"Dad, you'd be so proud of me. I'm a good artist. Like, really good. Everyone said I was best at landscapes, but I threw all of them off the bridge. Now I'm only going to paint abstracts, because those are way better. Also, in Europe people appreciate art more than they do here. I think they do anyway. I've never been there, but when I get there I'll find out. Hey! Maybe I'll study art at Oxford. That would be cool, huh? Family tradition and all." Shoot. Talking with my hands again. Whatever.

My dad's face isn't beaming with pride like I expected. It's a bit cloudy. "Have a seat. Can I get you a drink? Maybe a juice or a cup of tea?"

"No thanks." Should I sit on the wooden bench? My butt might leave a water stain. They should make coasters for wet jeans. Oh well. He said sit, so I sit.

"Good, because I don't have any." He gives a thin smile and sits next to me. We stare at the gallery together. "I've put a lot of work into this gallery," he says. "A lot. A lifetime. But I would trade every bit of it for a chance to redo what I had with you kids and your mother."

How could he possibly want something different from this fantastic gallery where he can paint all day long?

"I would have gotten help sooner and done what the doctors said. I wouldn't have let anyone convince me that I should give up my family."

"Doctors are stupid." I don't care that I sound childish. "They give you diseases that you don't want and slap labels on you that you don't need. Then they give you all these medications. My doctor had me on meds for bipolar disorder, and all the meds did was keep me down. Once you get off them—*boom!*—everything's great."

The gallery lights reflect off my dad's concerned eyes. "You have bipolar disorder?"

I shake my head. "No, you're not listening. I *don't* have bipolar disorder. That's the whole point. They thought I did, but I don't. I know it."

"Are you supposed to be on medication?"

"Dad." Saying *Dad* is fun. I'll overuse this to make up for lost time. "Dad, I am not sick. Medications are for sick people. If I was sick, would I be flying to Paris and opening my own art gallery? No, I would not."

He whispers softly, and I don't know if he's talking to me or to himself. "Oh no, you *are* just like me." He stands and paces in front of the bench. He's thinking very hard about something. His hair is sticking out at odd angles, and his faded black T-shirt and plaid pajama pants look like they've been clothing his familiar bones for years. His hair used to be black, but it's fading like everything else about him.

"Listen." He's composed now. He stops and faces me. Then he changes his mind and sits again. He takes my hands in his. "I missed out on your life, and that's my biggest regret. I forfeited the authority to say anything about your life or to tell you what to do, but—" He breaks off here. He takes a deep breath and looks at me with glistening eyes. "Natalie, if you're supposed to be taking pills, take them."

"I'm not—"

He cuts me off. "You were two the first time I went to the hospital. Doctors told me I had schizophrenia, but I wouldn't listen. I said I was fine. I would try harder and do better. I could be strong on my own. That was the first of multiple hospital visits." He looks up at the light and then back at me. His tears threaten to spill onto his cheeks. "It was the worst mistake I ever made. Without help, I kept having symptoms. I thought the FBI was trying to take your mother. I tried to keep her locked up so they wouldn't find her. Another time I forgot that I took you and Brent to the mall, and I left you in a toy store. When your mom and I went to get you, you were crying and scared. I've never forgiven myself for that."

One of his tears escapes.

"I couldn't be in a family. Whenever I was well enough to see the things I'd done, I knew I didn't deserve to stay. I was ruining everything, and I was afraid for you kids and for your mother. Your mother tried to get me help, but I didn't want the doctors and the drugs and the labels. In the end, she asked that if I wouldn't help myself, would I at least do what was right for my family and leave you all alone. I agreed.

"When I finally faced the fact that my brain had problems and I needed help, it was too late for me. You already thought I was dead. What was I supposed to do, pop up out of nowhere and promise to be different? How many times had your mother heard that from me?"

He holds my hands even tighter and looks into my eyes like he's trying to see into my brain itself.

"Natalie, mental illness doesn't have to ruin your life. The sooner you realize that, the better off you'll be. You can have a good, productive life. You can have all of this." He gestures to his gallery, then laughs to himself. "Not that it's much, but you say you want it. You can have it. Your mother and brother love you. I love you. If I can make one wish, one request, it's this: Please don't make the mistakes I did. They are not worth it. If the doctors say you need help, take it."

He may not feel like my dad yet, but if nothing else, I do look up to him as an artist. What he's saying is respectable, but he's living with an illness and I'm not. Well, I don't think I am. Maybe I could be. Perhaps a little. Probably not enough to need medications. I study my fingernails.

"Let me take you home."

"You don't think I should go to Paris?"

"Maybe another day, but not today."

A rebellious streak in me says that he can't tell me what to do, but it's difficult to argue with him. It wouldn't kill me to wait and leave for Paris once it's light out.

"I'll go home. Thanks for the offer, but I can drive myself."

"Let me give you a ride." He stands up and reaches for his keys. "I'd like to go for a drive. It's beautiful out right now."

Does he know how dangerously fast I drove to get here? Has he done that, too? It's not beautiful out at all. Maybe he thinks I'll still drive to the airport. He's probably right.

He holds his hand out. "Let's see those keys. I'll drop your car off tomorrow. You got any cool keychains?"

"A paint palette." I show him the silver palette charm. I'm hesitant to hand over the entire key ring, but I do. "Fine. But you have to give my dog a ride, too."

———

When we get to my house, the lights are on. Mom's up. This is going to be an issue.

My dad notices the same problem because he says, "Um, how about I drop you at the end of the driveway?"

As soon as I get out of the car, he disappears into the night. Right as he drives off, I see familiar headlights round the corner. Uh-oh. I'd better get inside.

I don't want to face my mom. This will be the biggest trouble I've ever been in. I've never snuck out before, but I feel like coming home at four in the morning would be in the handbook titled *Top Ten Ways to Tick Off Your Parents*. Will I be grounded for the rest of my life? Will she take away my dog? I hug Petunia closer.

Suddenly, I realize that I have the perfect way to distract my mom.

The door creaks as I open it. My mom runs from the kitchen and breathes a huge sigh of relief. She says, "Thank goodness, it's her," into her cell phone and hangs up without waiting for a response from whoever was on the other end. She shoves the phone into the pocket of her silk robe. Her relief turns to anger.

"Where on earth have you been?" Her face is red. "What is so important that you had to go out at this ungodly hour without the courtesy to leave so much as a note? A text? A carrier pigeon? I had absolutely no idea where you were, and the nerve of you to—"

"I was visiting my dad."

I try to keep my voice cold and steady, but I can already feel a fire burning in my chest. I hold Toons—my canine shield—even more tightly as the words hit my mom. Her face changes from red to white. Crap, is she going to faint?

She shakes her head like she must have misunderstood. "You were where?"

I say it slowly this time so there is no misunderstanding. "I was visiting . . . my . . . dad."

She holds on to the stair railing for support. She breathes in a few times as if she's going to start talking, but nothing comes out.

The back door opens. Brent is soaked, and his face is as stormy as the weather. "Who just left our driveway? Is Nat back?" He rounds the corner and sees me. He shoulders sag in relief. "Dude. Where have you been?"

I don't answer because I'm still staring at my mom.

Then he sees her, too. "Whoa, Mom, are you okay?"

She jumps when he speaks to her. "I'm, um . . ." She shakes her head, putting her fingertips to the bridge of her nose and closing her eyes.

Brent turns to me. "What did you say to her? What did you do?"

"Me? What did *I* do?" The fire is building. "What did I *do*? Really? You're assuming this is all my fault. Everything's always my fault."

You know what? I don't need the canine shield. I put Toons down, and she scurries away.

Brent holds up his hands. "Whoa. You're the one who left tonight. I have no idea what's going on."

"Do you want to know what's going on? I can tell you exactly what's going on." The fire inside me burns my eyes. My fists clench. I look over to my mom to see if she has anything to say. Should I spill the secret right now? Is this how Brent is going to find out?

Her face is still white. Her eyes widen, and she shakes her head no in a barely perceptible movement.

"No?" I feel myself growing a bit hysterical. "No? No *what*? Don't tell Brent? Or no, you can't believe I found out the truth? Which is it?"

She takes a breath, and it sounds like it's the first one she's taken since this conversation started. "Natalie . . ." Her voice shakes. "There's no need to be rash about this."

Is she joking? If there's no need to be rash about *this*, then there's nothing in life to ever be rash about.

"What's going on?" Brent looks from me to my mom. He frowns, and his muscles tense. His voice rises. "Will someone please fill me in?"

I narrow my eyes at my mom, and then turn to Brent. "Dad's alive." The two small words pierce the air, changing Brent's life forever. Changing all of us.

"Oh crap." Mom puts her hand to her head, stumbles into the living room, and sinks onto the couch.

"Oh, that again?" Brent rolls his eyes but looks relieved. He follows Mom into the living room. "Don't worry about it. Natalie's got this idea that Dad is alive, but it's just one of her brain things. She's not thinking straight."

"I'm not thinking straight?" I'm yelling now as I storm into the living room. Tears spill from my eyes. I know I should stay composed, but I'm sick of being composed. "If I'm not thinking straight, then who just dropped me off here? Some random guy with an art gallery and my nose? Some random guy?"

Brent's eyes widen, and his mouth presses into a grim line. "Mom, should we call a doctor?"

"I'm right here! I can hear you!" I am so sick of feeling like a specimen in a Petri dish. "Mom, tell him. You know I have all the proof in the world to show him if you deny it. Don't even try." I'm hot all over. If she denies this, I don't know what I'll do.

Her elbows are on her knees, and her silk robe hangs open to reveal her worn-out designer pajamas. Her head sags into her hands. "She's right," she says to her knees. I can barely hear it.

"What?" Brent leans closer.

Good. Now she has to say it again.

"She's right." She raises her head and looks at Brent. "We thought it was the right thing."

"Thought what was the right thing?" Brent looks between us again, like maybe both of us have lost our minds.

"Mom and Dad thought lying to us would be the right thing, Brent," I say. For some reason, having Mom confirm it makes it more real. I thought it would be a relief, but I'm even angrier. "Dad's alive. He owns his own art gallery and everything. Mom's been lying to us for fourteen years."

"Mom?" Brent's voice sounds tight. "What?" He takes a step back from her.

Now her eyes are filled with tears, too. "I'm so sorry," she whispers.

"You're sorry?" My heart pounds, and there's a rush of blood to my head. The fire inside me has scorched any chance I had at staying controlled. "You don't get to take away our dad for fourteen years and then simply say sorry. You wrecked our entire family. You ruined everything."

"You are so young," Mom says. A little color returns to her face. "You don't know what you're talking about. It wasn't going to work."

"What wasn't going to work?" Brent looks desperately lost in his ratty T-shirt and gray sweats. I'd feel bad for him if I had the emotional capacity to feel anything besides anger.

"Dad has schizophrenia," I say by way of explanation. "And Mom decided it would be better for us to grow up without a dad than to grow up with a crazy one."

"You don't understand." My mom's spine stiffens, and her eyes flash. "It was impossible to continue like it was. It's beyond difficult to deal with someone who . . ." She trails off.

I don't give her the chance to choose her next words. "With someone who what, Mom? Someone who's mentally ill? Is that what you were going to say? How do you think it feels to *be* mentally ill? I didn't ask for this. Dad didn't ask for this."

I'm yelling so loud that my mom looks nervously toward the window.

"Are you worried the neighbors are going to hear me? Are they going to hear how you married a crazy person and gave birth to a crazy person, and together we have *completely ruined your life?"* I'm out of breath, but I'm far from being out of rage. I'm shaky. My hands are tingling.

"I didn't say anyone ruined my life." The words are condescending instead of sympathetic. "Don't twist my words."

"I'm not twisting them! I know *exactly* what you said: 'If she's like him, then her whole life is ruined. My life is ruined. I can't handle this again.' That's what you said."

She looks like I slapped her. "I would never say that."

"But you did! You were sitting right here." I point to the leather chair. "Aunt Grace and Aunt Kate were sitting here and here." I point to the sofa.

Comprehension slowly dawns on her face.

"You remember now, don't you?"

"I'm sure that's not exactly what I—"

"It is, Mom. It's exactly what you said. Those aren't the kind of words that a kid forgets, okay? I have nightmares about those words. I tried to kill myself over those words."

"No." She puts her hands over her mouth and shakes her head. Finally, she whispers, "Say that's not true." Her eyes fill. "I've only ever wanted you to be happy. My worst fear has been to lose you or Brent. I couldn't handle it."

I'm sick of secrets. "It's true, okay? Because clearly you'd rather have dead family members than mentally ill ones. I've spent my whole life trying to make you proud. But I couldn't ever be like Brent. I didn't win homecoming queen, and I'm sick of working so hard for nothing." I dissolve into sobs. "You're a terrible mother. I'm not the one who ruined everything. Dad's not the one who ruined everything. You are."

"I . . ." Her hand flies to her chest. "I've always been proud of you, Natalie. You're an amazing artist, and—"

"I *am* an amazing artist, you know that? And I'm probably going to move to Paris and never see you again, but in the event that I decide to stay here, I don't want you to come to my show at Art Connect. You've never supported my art, and now I know where I got all of my talent. I'm an amazing artist in spite of you, not because of you."

Mom blinks back her tears. "You have no clue what we went through to try to give you a happy childhood. I did everything I could to support your dad—everything—and he didn't want the support. Wouldn't accept it. I put up with so much pain. In the end, when he decided to go, I had to let him. I loved him, you know that? A lot. And to watch him suffer the way he did broke my heart."

Her words seem to snuff out the fire that had been raging in me. I'd never really considered my mom's role in all of this. She'd basically seemed like the evil villain who sent my dad away. But what if she really had tried to help, and he hadn't accepted it? Her side of the story, the one she gave me just now, fits with what my dad told me in his studio half an hour ago.

Mom's elbows are back on her knees. Now she's crying, too.

Brent, who has been silent almost this whole time, walks toward Mom, and I sink my head into my hands. This is the way it's been for my whole life: those two against the world, and me over in the corner figuring things out on my own.

Suddenly, Brent's strong arms pull me into a hug. I look up, surprised. What's he doing over here? He holds me tight, and I bury my head into his shoulder. It feels good to be held. Someone is protecting me.

"I'm sorry," he says into my hair.

I don't know exactly what he's apologizing for. Maybe it's for not believing me about our dad. Maybe it's for not ever taking my side before this moment or not being there when I needed him. It feels like he's squeezing this apology into my very core, willing me to believe it. I do.

I cry harder. Any mascara left on my lashes is going to stain his shirt. Neither one of us cares. When he pulls out of the hug, he goes to the kitchen. I sniff and look at my mom. We're both confused.

He comes back with a Kleenex box and his keys. He sets the Kleenex box on the couch by my mom.

"We'll be back later," he says, then turns to me. "Come on, Nat. We're going for a drive."

Chapter 24

It's still raining as Brent and I sit in the Steak 'n Shake parking lot, but the rain doesn't sound angry anymore. Instead of pounding on the windshield, it's simply washing it for us. I'm not hungry, but I wasn't willing to pass up a cookie dough shake—the ones that are so thick you need to eat them with a spoon. That's probably why Brent drove us here. Well, that and the fact that the only other place open at four-thirty in the morning is Bowl-O-Rama.

Brent sits next to me with his strawberry shake. After we left the drive-through, we parked, and the restaurant's orange-and-blue OPEN sign flickers in front of us. Brent didn't say anything the whole way here. If you could hear brains whirring now, our car would be louder than a full-blast stereo. I don't think I've ever seen Brent so focused.

Brent shouldn't have had to find out this way. To be fair, I did try to tell him, but I should have tried harder. I should have told him when I knew for sure, after the first time I went to our dad's studio. I should have told him before I told Mom, and we could have confronted her together. Pretty much any way of finding out would have been better than this. Guilt overtakes me.

"I can't believe this is happening." It looks like Brent is talking to his cup. "I have a dad."

"I'm sorry, Brent. I should have told you sooner."

He's quiet again, and I don't know if he's refusing to accept my apology or if he's too deep in his head to have noticed I gave it.

"I barely remember him. I remember the smell of his flannel jacket and the way he pushed us on the swing set. He pushed us a lot higher than Mom ever did."

I smile. "He always said that if I kicked a cloud, a rainbow would come out."

Brent shakes his head. "I thought for an embarrassingly long time that that was how rainbows were made. I would get so mad that I couldn't swing high enough to make one. When he died . . . I mean, when he left, I went and cried on that swing set for a really long time. Without his pushes, I was never going to be able to make a rainbow."

Brent sighs and takes another bite of ice cream. I'm not sure if I'm supposed to say more or wait for him to ask something else. I wait.

"What's he like now?"

"He's really cool, Brent. Amazing. You're gonna love him." I tell him about going to Dad's gallery and his artsy apartment. I tell him about the framed picture of us at the beach. I even tell him about my nose matching our dad's. "But you have his eyes," I add.

"Really?" Brent looks up from his ice cream for the first time.

"Yep. Looking at you is like looking at a younger version of him." I hope Brent will see this as a good thing.

His lips turn up in a small smile as he takes another bite of his shake. Then the smile fades. He pauses like he's about to say something, but he stops. Then he decides to say it after all.

"Do you think he'll like me?" He takes two bites of shake in quick succession and seems very focused on his spoon again.

"What kind of question is that? Of course he'll like you. You're his kid." I expected that Brent would have a lot of questions, but that wasn't one of them.

"I don't know. I'm not the one who found him. I never even looked. And you guys have so much in common, you know, with your art and stuff. I'm the odd one out."

"*You're* the odd one out?" I give a strangled laugh. "For real, right now? I would love if you'd be the odd one out. Welcome to the last fourteen years of my life."

Brent looks confused. "What are you talking about?"

Is he serious?

"Dude, you and Mom are like this." I twist my pointer and middle fingers together. Then I put on my best Mom-voice. "Brent, darling, thank you for making dinner. You're such a good man of the house. Brent, I'm so proud of you for being captain of the baseball team. Brent, isn't it lovely that you won another award? Natalie, why don't you get better grades like Brent? Natalie, why aren't you responsible like Brent?" I stop and look out my window because I don't want to cry again. I think I'm cried-out for the night.

"Nat? Really?" When I see his face, he looks stunned. Even hurt. "You think you're the odd one out?"

"No. I know I am."

He's quiet, and then he takes a deep breath. "Have you ever considered what it's been like for me?"

Is the reflection of the light hitting his eyes weird, or is he tearing up? I haven't seen Brent cry in at least ten years. I'm a little freaked out by the prospect of it. My whole family is crying tonight. It's like a parallel universe.

"What was *what* like for you?" I ask. I put my spoon down.

He puts his cup in the cup holder. "I had to be the man of the house at age five. Five, Natalie. Do you know what kind of pressure that is to put on a kid? She's been calling me 'the man of the house' since I could barely tie my freaking shoes. When my friends were out riding scooters in the neighborhood, I was learning how to cook so that Mom wouldn't burn the house down. I watch the Food Network instead of ESPN. How many teenage guys do that?"

"But you like the Food Network."

"Because it makes my job easier. I learn how to cook stuff, and Mom's so proud of the crap I cook. That's the only reason I watch it."

"What about when you said that one chef on Food Network is hot?" I don't know why I'm bringing this up. I guess I've never considered that he'd rather watch something other than the Food Network.

Brent glares at me. "You know who's hotter than her? Every single one of the NFL cheerleaders. But I'm stuck partying with the Food Network." He picks up his cup and stabs his spoon angrily into it.

Before I can think of what to say, he continues. "And you want to know what the worst part is? No matter how hard I tried to take care of you and Mom, I couldn't. You almost died in that accident." A tear spills onto his cheek, and he jerks his head like he can shake it off his face. "I should have been there."

"You couldn't have been there." Does he really blame himself for this? "That was my fault, Brent. I've got . . . you know."

"I should have been there," he says again. "I should have been there for you that day, and before that day, and lots of days. . . . But I never knew how. I couldn't figure you out." He gives me a sad but confused look, like I am a jigsaw puzzle that is forever missing one piece. "When I heard you crying in your room, it hurt so bad. I would have done anything to be able to help. But when I tried, you'd shut me out or throw your stilettos at me."

"I only did that once." It's a weak defense.

"I still have the scar." He pulls his hair up to show me. "It's enough to make a guy think twice about going in there again. So I didn't try anymore."

"I know. You'd just turn up your music so you didn't have to deal with me."

"What? Natalie, that's not . . . Are you serious? You thought . . . ? Ugh." He leans back and bangs his head against the headrest. He takes a couple of deep breaths and angrily wipes tears from his face. "When you would cry in your room, I did turn up the music in mine. But it wasn't to drown you out, Nat. I would never do that. It was . . ." His voice catches. "It was so that you wouldn't hear *me* crying."

What?

"I couldn't handle the helplessness." He stares straight through the windshield now. "I knew you weren't okay, and there was absolutely nothing I could do about it. *Nothing*." He hits the steering wheel so hard that you'd think this whole thing was the wheel's fault.

It's like I'm seeing Brent for the first time. He doesn't love the Food Network? He wasn't trying to get away from me? What else am I missing?

"And I haven't been here for you tonight, either. You could have been hurt."

"I wasn't going to be hurt, Brent. I was on my way to . . . Well, that doesn't really matter. I was fine." Looking back, maybe I wasn't fine. Maybe I haven't been fine for a little while now. Now that the world is starting to lose that dazzling glow, dread is starting to bloom inside me. Was that mania? Is it still? I think of the Paris idea and realize it doesn't sound so great anymore.

"You peeled out of Ty's street going fifty, and you told

him you were going to Paris. It doesn't sound like you were fine."

"He called you?" I don't know if I feel betrayed or protected.

"Yeah." He grips his cup so hard that it starts to crinkle. "Because my chemistry lab partner does a better job of taking care of my sister than I do." He shakes his head.

"Are you mad? I know you didn't want me to, um, be with him."

"What?"

"You told him not to ask me out. That was a jerk move, by the way, especially after I had no issue with you dating Cecily." A familiar flush of anger threatens to take over our conversation.

"You and Ty are completely different from me and Cecily."

"How so? If anything, I had more reason to be upset. She's my best friend. Ty's just your lab partner. Which situation is weirder?"

Brent squints in confusion, but then his eyes widen. "Nat, this had nothing to do with the situation being 'weird' for me. That wasn't about me at all. It was—" He breaks off.

Oh. Now I get it.

"It's because I'm crazy, wasn't it? Are you ashamed of me?" Shame mixes with anger and confusion. It's a sickening cocktail.

"Of course not, Nat. I'm sorry. I shouldn't have said anything, and I swear it had nothing to do with being ashamed of you. I was worried. What if it didn't work out, and you ended up hurt, and you were so upset that you . . ."

The silence hangs heavy between us.

"If it didn't work out, then so what, Brent? Am I supposed to hide in my room, never dating anyone, never taking any risks, and letting this illness paralyze the rest of my life?"

"I don't know how to protect you. It's all I've been trying to do, and it's been one giant fail." His eyes are still glassy.

"Maybe that's not your job. You've tried to step up and be a dad, but you're not. You're my brother. Just love me. Don't tell me what to do. Let me be goofy. Let me make mistakes. Let me know stuff about your life, like the fact that you like ESPN. How did I not know that? Be, I don't know, my friend. We can be friends."

He looks like he hasn't considered this before. "Friends?"

"Friends."

We both take another bite of ice cream.

Brent speaks first. "So, what did Ty mean when he said you were going to Paris?"

"It was . . . a thing. I don't know. It sounded like a way better idea a couple of hours ago." I have a feeling I'm not going to Paris anymore.

"Oh." He looks at me, and there's a question in his eyes that he's afraid to ask.

I'm glad he doesn't ask it, but I answer it anyway. "I haven't been on my meds for over a week."

He's quiet, slowly digesting my confession. "Why not?" Another bite of ice cream. He's scraping the bottom now.

"I think I can beat this mental stuff on my own. I'd rather do it without medications."

He looks at me like that is a really stupid idea, but his expression is concerned without being condescending. It's different, and I like it.

"The doctor said you need them, Nat. If you had diabetes, would you try to beat it without insulin?"

"Probably."

He chokes on his ice cream because of a snort of laughter. "Yeah, actually, you probably would. But that would also be stupid."

"I know." Now I smile, too, because I can hear how ridiculous I sound. "But think about it, Brent. In school everyone tells us 'Don't do drugs!' and 'Stay off drugs!' and 'Here is your brain on drugs!' But then I find out I'm sick, and it's like, 'You need drugs!' and 'Your brain is awful without drugs!' and 'Be yourself, but only the type of you that's on drugs!' It sucks."

"Yeah, but there's a difference between street drugs and prescription drugs. Also . . . Paris?" His look implies that I should realize the absurdity of what happened tonight.

Crap. I think I might need the drugs. As much as I want to pretend I've been acting normal, deep down I know I haven't. I can call it "inspiration" or "genius" as much as I want, but it's time to admit that it's mania. "But if I go back on the pills, then I'm bipolar."

"You're bipolar with or without them." Brent says this as if it isn't obvious, which I appreciate. "But you can feel healthy when you're on them."

"Yeah . . ." I don't want to admit that he's right, but he is. If there's treatment that can help me with the issues I'm facing, maybe it is a tad ridiculous to go without it. My heart sinks at this truth, but it may be sinking into a place of tentative acceptance.

It feels too hard to keep considering this, so I change the subject. "Sorry that was how you found out about Dad."

He sighs as if he'd momentarily forgotten about it. "I still don't know what I'm going to do about that. The whole situation's jacked up."

"I seriously don't want Mom to come to Art Connect."

"I don't blame you."

"You don't?" This whole Brent-siding-with-me thing is still new.

"No, I don't." He scrapes the bottom of the cup again, but the shake is all gone. He looks up at me. "It feels like everything's about to change."

Brent's eyes are wide, his mouth is set in a firm line, and he's once again gripping his cup a little too hard. He looks vulnerable, almost small. My strong, always-put-together brother seems nervous.

Yes, things are changing. But is that really so awful? Perhaps they could be changing for the better. Maybe Brent and I have a chance to have a more authentic relationship with each other. Or maybe I've messed everything up. Only time will tell, but I feel ready to find out what the future holds.

I hold up my empty cup. "Another round of milkshakes?"

Brent thinks a moment, then shrugs and gives a half smile. "Not a bad place to start." He turns on the car and heads back toward the drive-through.

Chapter 25

Psychiatrists can be frustrating because they make you dig up all sorts of feelings that you spend most of your life avoiding. Sometimes when they're talking, I mentally play Psychiatrist Office Bingo. I can only play against myself, but that's okay. Perhaps I should create an online forum for this. Here are the items that people would need to find on universal psychiatrist bingo:

1. Potted plants. Nothing says "sanity" like polyester leaves.

2. Tranquil posters. Beach or woods scenes are supposed to make you forget you're nuts and instead feel completely at ease. Bonus point if the tranquil poster has an

inspiring quote on it, but minus one point if you feel inspired by it.

3. Intelligent-sounding book titles, like *The Relationship Between Isoenzymes and Depression Tendencies in Children Ages Seven to Eight*. Someone apparently wrote eight hundred pages on that.

4. Kleenex box. There's always a Kleenex box. Bonus point if it's empty, because doctors are very careful to keep these filled for your inevitable breakdown.

5. A clock placed behind you. Doctors need to secretly figure out how many more minutes of your drama they have to endure but still look like they're paying attention. They're sneaky people, these doctors.

"So tell me what happened last week," the doctor says. "Your mom was really worried about you."

Dr. Levine is the fourth psychiatrist I've seen in the past three years. Here's my cycle: I do something my mom deems "concerning"; she makes me see a psychiatrist; he or she puts me on drugs; the drugs don't work (or I go off them); and then, after I do something else "concerning," Mom makes me see someone new for another opinion. Lather, rinse, repeat. I told my mom I didn't want to see Dr. VanderFleet again, which maybe wasn't entirely fair to Dr. VanderFleet, but we compromised on me going to see a new doctor.

This one's not awful so far. I'm busy looking for a pen/magnet/notepad promoting some pharmaceutical product (bingo item #6), so at first I don't realize that he's expecting me to answer.

"I thought my dad was dead, because that's what my mom told me, but it turns out he isn't."

The doctor nods. Even for a psychiatrist, a dead-dad-coming-back-to-life has got to be pretty shocking, but he doesn't show it.

"So how did you feel when you found that out?"

Hmm. Betrayed? Angry? Inadequate, because clearly my mother doesn't want to deal with mentally ill family members? I won't say that because it's too personal.

"Mad at my mom for lying. Brent was pretty freaked out, too. He was all, 'You said he died!' and Mom said, 'I know, but it was what was best for you.' Brent and Mom argued about that for a while, even though Mom was clearly wrong."

"So, you blame your mom. What about your dad? How do you feel about him?"

I've only known I had a dad for a couple of weeks or so, and I'm already supposed to have all these feelings about him? I don't know how I feel yet. Why do psychiatrists ask ridiculously unanswerable questions?

"I'm upset that he left. That choice was wrong, and I don't care what his reasoning was. There are no good reasons. I'm mad, I guess, but it feels like trying to be mad at a stranger.

I'd rather like him. He seems so cool. So much . . . like me. I wish we could put this whole thing behind us and pretend it never happened. But you can't really throw fourteen years of lies away like that."

"So is your frustration more toward your dad or your mom?"

"I don't know. . . . Both? They both lied. They were in this together. It's easier to be mad at my mom. I know her better. I'm even mad at myself, really. I should have found him sooner. I mean, come on. I'm eighteen. Who has a missing dad and doesn't look for him for fourteen years?"

"To be fair, you didn't think he was missing."

"I know. But still. I should have suspected something sooner. Do you know what a game changer it would have been if I found him a few years ago? Maybe all this mental health stuff would have played out differently. I wouldn't have thrown all my art off a bridge, I wouldn't be here talking to you, and you would be off playing a nice round of golf with your fellow doctor people while discussing polos and Cadillacs. I bet you'd be three under par at this very moment."

He chews on his pen cap before responding. "I see you turn to humor to deflect stressful situations."

Tough crowd.

He puts his pen down. "It's not a bad thing; I just want to make sure you are really accessing your true emotions. This is a safe space."

There is no such thing as a safe space. I would hide my emotions from everyone in the world if I could.

"Tell me, why did you stop taking your medications in the days leading up to this incident?"

"Because I'm done being bipolar." It's not stubborn or aggressive; I'm simply stating it. It's like, "I used to like applesauce, but I don't anymore."

My doctor looks confused. "And why do you think that?"

"I don't know. . . . I think I can beat this mental stuff on my own. I'd rather do it without medications." I lick my thumb and try to get a scuff off my shoe.

"You think you can heal your body by yourself?"

"Not always, but when it comes to a mental illness . . . maybe."

We're quiet while he takes some more notes. I notice his degree proudly hanging in the corner of the room. (Hooray! #7!)

"I don't want people to treat me differently because of an illness," I say to fill the awkward silence, "so it's better if I don't have one."

"Right," he says, "but you tried to kill yourself this past summer, you tried to run away to Paris in the middle of the night after disposing of your best artwork, and you still say you don't have a problem. That's interesting."

He waits for me to speak. "I don't want bipolar disorder."

"That's understandable. People who have cancer don't want cancer. Unfortunately, neglecting medical attention does not make the disease go away. It makes it worse."

Obviously, he's right. But it's easy for him to say, over in his posh brown leather chair. He doesn't have to live with this struggle for sanity. He's like a hiker watching someone scramble to hang on to the edge of a cliff and just saying, "Hmm . . . that looks like a tricky situation."

"I could be on meds forever," I say. "If I have bipolar disorder, it doesn't go away."

"It might not go away, but it's manageable. There are lots of ways to manage it, but you have to acknowledge it to manage it."

This guy's good.

"It doesn't have to be a big deal," he adds, and puts his notebook down. He looks at me like we're pals chatting over lattes. "It can be a small part of your life. You take some pills, you go to therapy, you do what you've got to do, and in exchange you can be healthy."

I think back on the past couple of weeks since I stopped taking my pills. It's time to acknowledge the fact that I'm not healthy without them. Maybe I could be someday, or maybe I'm someone who needs them for life, but I'm not good without them now.

It's not healthy to think I'm being attacked by an octopus. It's not healthy to think that running away to Paris is a good idea. The memory of going Ty's house at three in the morning during a storm makes me blush in shame. I haven't seen him since then, and I don't know what I'm going to say next time I do. Also, what if my dad hadn't insisted on driving me home? I was driving so fast. What if I'd gotten hurt? Killed? What if I hurt someone else? The last thing I needed was another car accident. Not to mention that I was putting Petunia in danger, too.

I picture my mom's face when she heard that I found my

dad. I think of what Soo will say when she knows I threw away all my best paintings. What am I going to put in the show now? Everything's a mess, and it's all my fault. I knew I couldn't handle this kind of pressure. Why did I ever think I could enter Art Connect? This is a thousand times worse than the clay pot in ninth grade.

I reach for a Kleenex. (There's a full box here, so I don't get the bonus point.) Would this manic episode have happened if I had stayed on my meds? The answer makes me want to throw up. It's a terrifying feeling to be scared of your own brain, so I think of something else.

I think of my dad and how things might have ended differently if he had accepted help sooner. Was I making the same mistakes he did? Am I willing to take the steps he didn't?

"How do you feel when you're on your medications?" Dr. Levine asks.

My mom refilled the prescriptions, so I've been on them again for a few days now.

I sigh because I don't like my answer, but I might as well be honest. "Clear. I can think better. But I also feel helpless, like I'm a loser who can't function without drugs."

"You can function without drugs. You simply function better with them."

"But what if they stop working? Some people can be on drugs for a long time, and then something switches and they have to start all over trying to figure out what to take. That's scary. I could be fine for, say, two years, then everything can upend and I'll be unstable again."

"That's why you have your support system. You have your mom and your brother, you have your friends, you have me. We'll help you if you need it."

He's right, of course, but it seems like the kind of thing he would say to every patient. "You don't understand. Needing this kind of help is different."

"Why don't you tell me what it's like?"

I don't want to tell him. I don't want to access those parts of my brain that hurt so bad I'll do almost anything to avoid talking about them. I'd rather make a joke and move on to the next boring question.

Then again, maybe if I let these parts of me come into the light, they would stop feeling so dark and terrifying. It's worth a try.

There's a chance this could go poorly. My throat feels a little dry as I prepare to speak, like the words are stuck in there. Other mental health professionals have let me down. On the other hand, I can't get help if I don't reach out. It's time to really invest in my own mental health, and investing in that means opening up to the people trying to help me. I cough to clear my throat, and the words start flowing.

"I feel so . . . small. Having bipolar disorder makes me feel like I'm broken, like there's a piece of me that needs to be fixed, but nothing will ever fix it. And it's like a filter on my life that colors everything I do, but almost no one knows about it. I hide from my friends, I'm hiding from this guy who might like me, I even hide from my own family. I hang out in my closet a lot. It's safer in there. I've never told doctors that before, because I'm afraid they'll think I'm *really* crazy. And I mean, yeah, that's why I'm here, but a piece of me wants to pretend that I'm only here to make my mom happy."

He stops writing. "Why are you here, really?"

Why am I here? I sit in room after room and play Psychiatrist Office Bingo so I can distract myself until the appointment's over. What if I stopped trying to distract myself and really gave this a try? An honest, hard try that might make a difference?

I take a deep breath. "Because I want to be healthy, and I'm ready to do whatever it takes to get there."

He nods. "That's big, Natalie. Even that one statement is major progress for you. I can tell that you mean it. That's a huge step."

I smile a little. Maybe it is.

So, I agree to take my medicine until winter break, and we can reevaluate then. I'm glad that he doesn't use words like *forever*, because forever scares me. Maybe I will need drugs forever, but right now I don't have to think past winter break.

Now I have to think about how I'm going to undo the mess I made last week, and that's almost as daunting as being on medication forever. My chance at a college scholarship is almost nil, Mom is mad at me, my brother and my dad are going to have a lot to deal with, Ty—okay, I don't even want to think about Ty—and Soo is going to kill me.

As a tiny source of comfort, I notice on my way out of the office that there are self-help books on the shelf in the waiting room. Bingo item #8—a new record for me.

Chapter 26

One good thing about going to the psychiatrist appointment today is that it makes me late for art class, which means Ty won't have a chance to talk to me alone. I still have no good way to explain my actions last Friday. Well, there's the truth, but obviously I'm not going with that. Now that I'm back on my medications, I'm mortified about what I did. Ty is in the corner sorting paints when I walk in.

Talking to Soo is going to be rough, too. Today's the day we're supposed to tell her which pieces we're displaying at Art Connect next week. The pieces I planned to enter are now floating somewhere down the river. Maybe a beaver has made a lodge out of the scraps.

My winter scene won't be that bad if I can finish it in time. There's also the painting in my mom's room, but it's not my best work. Even with that one, I'm still one short—one and a half if you consider the fact that the winter piece isn't finished. This is like having a week to make Petunia a show dog.

What can I paint in a week? A blade of grass? The painting blurs in front of me, and I blink a few times. Ty comes over to wipe our table, startling me. He knocks my paintbrush to the floor. Crouching next to me, one hand searching for the paintbrush that's rolled under my chair, he whispers, "You all right, Paris?"

Oh, I get it. The paintbrush was a ploy to talk to me. It's kind of sweet seeing him on bended knee, with his dark curly hair close enough to touch.

"Sorry about that. It was super weird." I reach for the brush he's offering, and my fingers tangle with his.

"Not all of it was weird." His gaze is soft and intense at the same time. "But I was really worried when you left. I still am."

Our hands are touching, and heat rises in my cheeks. I pull my hand back, freeing the brush from his grasp. "It was no big deal. Just one of those things."

"One of what things?" Ty looks exasperated. "You come over to my house at three in the morning, and you—" He cuts himself off. Jill is leaning toward us, clearly listening but pretending to focus on her painting. He lowers his voice even more, and I have to lean closer to hear. "You know what happened."

Now Jill's not even trying to hide it. She's going to fall out of her chair if she leans any farther.

"I don't know, okay?"

"Yes, you do." Ty isn't buying it.

"Natalie," Soo calls from her desk. "You know Art Connect is next week, right? Perhaps you should focus a bit more on your painting?"

My face turns blotchy as everyone looks up from their paintings. All eyes see Ty crouched close to my station. Starr's eyebrows shoot up. Jill looks disappointed that Soo interrupted us. Tim and Karl look up, then quickly go back to painting. I nod at Soo and try to look appropriately chastened. "Sorry," I say to Ty, full volume this time. "I've got to focus." I return to painting.

"Nat," Ty whispers. He looks a bit desperate. "Go somewhere with me after class so we can talk? Please?" He puts his hand on my arm, and I wonder how many times he can touch me before it stops feeling like he's made of electricity.

I nod once and go back to painting. He stands up to clean things. I almost immediately regret this decision because now I'm going to have to talk to him, but it's not like this is my fault. The electricity addled my brain.

When class is over, Ty's waiting for me by his car. "Coffee okay with you?"

"Sure." A breeze whips through the trees and announces that winter will be here soon. My hair flies in front of my face. His is held secure by his baseball cap. Kansas City Royals. "Starbucks?" I suggest. "There's one on Eighth."

"I've got a better idea. Get in the car."

We mostly talk about Art Connect on the way to wherever we're going. Ty's pieces are finished. We don't discuss mine.

Ty pulls his car into the parking lot of a tiny building. The black awning says COASTAL COFFEE. It's a hipster joint—exposed brick walls, neon-colored windowpanes, baristas with purple hair.

"Not quite Starbucks." Ty smiles at me. "Will it work?"

It's so artsy. My mom would hate it. "I love it."

We order drinks—black coffee for him, chai for me—and sit. I wonder how I'm going to bring up The Subject, but Ty saves me the awkward intro.

"I have two things to say," he starts. "One is a question: Why you didn't go to Paris? Wait, no. I mean, what made you decide to go there in the first place? The second thing is"—he pauses to take a deep breath here—"I'd like to apologize for my bad breath that night, because you can't expect a guy to have pleasant breath at three o'clock in the morning."

I laugh. Is he serious right now? That never crossed my mind. I feign disappointment and shake my head. "You could have eaten a Tic Tac or two, or five, before coming out to see me."

"Are you kidding?" He throws his hands up. "I thought something was wrong. I didn't know what was going on. I didn't know you were going to *kiss* me!"

Three guys at the next table turn to stare. One has ear gauges, one is wearing a fedora, and one has some fantastic striped skinny jeans.

Ty reddens, leaning in and lowering his voice. "You gotta give a guy a break."

I lean in and match his quiet tone. Our faces are close together. Personal space is overrated. I wish I had even less of it right now. "Ty, I didn't notice your breath. I'm sure it was great."

"Really? I think you're lying."

"Not lying." I catch a whiff of something minty and sit back up. "Did you eat mints before we came in here?"

Ty gets even redder. "No."

I give him a skeptical look.

"Okay, fine, yes, but only because I'm in damage control mode."

I smile. "How many Tic Tacs?"

He takes another sip of his coffee. "Four. But they weren't Tic Tacs, they were Ice Breakers." He says this with a satisfied smile, like I don't know him as well as I think I do.

"*Four* Ice Breakers? That's a lot of minty freshness."

"I had a lot of damage control to do."

"Consider it managed." I smile again.

He takes another sip of coffee and then puts the cup down definitively. "So. You didn't answer my question."

Oh yeah, that.

Where do I start? Maybe I can brush it off. "I was having a weird night. You're right. I needed sleep. I went home like you said, got some sleep, and whoo-wee, did I feel better the next morning." None of that is a lie, is it? I'm just leaving out a few details.

Ty pauses. He's waiting for me to continue, but I don't. Instead, I take a sip of tea and look at a picture on the wall. It's an abstract piece done in varying shades of blue.

He raises an eyebrow and says, "You are a very bad liar."

"I am not!" Defending my prowess as a liar is a lose-lose situation. After another sip of tea, I admit, "Yeah, okay. I am."

"You're a bad liar, but I bet you're pretty baller at telling the truth. Give that a try."

But the truth will ruin what he thinks of me. I've already lost my reputation at school, and the night at the bridge cost me my reputation as an artist. Can't I keep this one thing? I don't want to lose Ty. Come on, life. Don't I have some good karma saved up somewhere?

After fishing around in my head for a lie that makes sense, I come up empty. A piece of me knew that confessing the truth to Ty was inevitable. Now I almost wish Brent had sold me out. Then Ty could have faded into the background instead of making me say this to his face.

I look down into my chai like I'm talking to it instead of Ty, but then I realize I'm sick of talking to drinks and floors and windows instead of the person in front of me. If I have to ruin this relationship, I will at least be strong while I do it.

I look Ty straight in the eye.

"I have bipolar disorder. I was manic that night, and a lot of things didn't make sense. I'm so sorry. I'm back on my meds now, but that's what happened." I hold eye contact, but my hands shake. Gripping my cup helps keep them steady. Can he hear my heart hitting my rib cage?

I expect to see fear or pity in Ty's eyes, and I'm not sure which I hate more. What I get instead is a look of recognition and a face that seems to say, "Oh, okay, that makes sense."

"Gotcha," Ty says. He doesn't look scared, he doesn't look sad, and I see no pity. It's as if I just said, "I sprained my ankle, and that's why I couldn't play in the game last week." No big deal.

"You're not freaked out?" That's probably not the best thing to say, but I can't help it.

"Why would I be freaked out?" He takes another sip of coffee and wipes a stray drop from his mouth. He tilts his head questioningly, as if he honestly doesn't know why he should be freaked out.

Am I talking to Ella? What is going on? Does he not understand that I confessed to having a *mental illness*?

"I don't know." I brush some hair behind my ear. "That, um . . . I guess it freaks some people out."

"My uncle has bipolar disorder. It's not that big of a deal."

"Really?"

"Yeah, he's awesome. He's had problems or whatever, but when he's around for family events, he's super cool. He's my favorite uncle."

I've recently discovered that mental illness is in a lot of places. It's in schools, friend groups, family trees. It's not the stuff of *CSI*; it's the stuff of friends and family. The more I look, the more I find it.

"I'm glad you're feeling better," Ty says. "It would be a shame for the American artistic community if we lost you to the French."

"Yes. My mom would have much preferred I go to England, anyway. She loves it."

"The British are so proper," says Ty. "I don't think I could hack it there."

"You could be proper if you get rid of the baseball cap and stop wearing ripped jeans." I reach over and take off his hat.

"Whoa. No one messes with my hats. Especially not my lucky one." He grabs the hat from my hand, but he's smiling.

"That's your lucky hat?"

"Yep. It's from the first major league game I ever went to. We were on a road trip, and my dad and I begged my mom to stop in Kansas City for the night." He fingers the brim. "Come to think of it, it's pretty un-American of you to never wear baseball caps. Let's see how you'd look." He puts it on my head and pauses. "You don't look awful in hats. You should wear them more."

We're definitely flirting. I told the guy that I have bipolar disorder, and he's flirting with me.

Ty has some major hat hair going on, so he runs his fingers through it. It sticks up, and I almost reach over to smooth it. Then I decide I like it mussed. I wonder if it looked like that after I kissed him.

"I used to be jealous of my uncle when I was a kid. Mental illness seemed cool."

The absurdity of this makes me laugh. "I assure you that it's not."

"I know, but the way my parents explained it to me was that Uncle Gary's brain worked differently than mine. It seemed cool to have a brain that didn't work the same as everyone else's—maybe that's what made him so fun. When I was old enough, I did some research on it. I found out that it's not something to be jealous of. At the same time, it does allow people to see the world in a different way. Lots of important people have had it. Did you know that Van Gogh was probably bipolar?"

"Of course. *Starry Night* was inspired by the view outside his insane asylum."

"And you don't find it just a tiny bit awesome that you have something in common with Vincent van Gogh?"

"Not until now." I can't believe Ty is finding a bright side of mental illness. Thank you, Uncle Gary. "Sometimes I do see things . . . differently. My favorite paintings are abstracts."

"But you're so good at landscapes."

My eyes roll almost involuntarily. I've had this conversation *so* many times. "I know I am."

Ty chokes on his coffee, and I quickly amend.

"I mean, thank you. I know they look okay, but I like abstracts better. Here."

I pull out my phone and let him flip through pictures of my abstracts. I can tell he's impressed. This warms me even more than my tea.

"These are seriously good," he says. "They have movement and depth and . . . meaning. They make you think."

This sounds out of place coming from the guy with hat hair and ripped jeans, but I'll take it.

He pauses over a photo. "Is this one on a paper plate?"

"Oh, yeah." I forgot those ones were in there. "I have a bunch on paper plates. They're in a stack in my closet."

"Why paper plates?"

"They're how I mess around while I think about whatever I'm supposed to be painting."

"They're good." He finishes looking at the pictures and slides the phone back to me. "Are you going to put any of those in Art Connect?"

I wrinkle my nose. "No, Soo says I have to do my landscapes. She says colleges will be more impressed by those."

Ty pauses. "She's probably right. She knows the art community really well."

"I threw all of my landscapes off a bridge last week."

Ty looks confused, like I made a joke and he didn't get it.

"No, seriously, I did. It was right before I came over to your house."

"No need for landscapes in Paris?"

"Nope. It was going to be a whole new life over there."

"Were you really going to go?"

I sigh. "Yeah, I was. It's one of the things about being manic. Everything seems like a good idea, and everything seems possible. It's wonderful and terrible. And this time the episode was my own fault. I went off my meds. Flushed them down the toilet."

He sits up, surprised. "That doesn't seem . . . wise."

"I wanted to beat bipolar on my own. You don't have any idea what it's like to have an illness that makes people scared to be around you." I poke at my tea bag and wrinkle my nose as I try to stay composed.

"That can't be true. From the moment I met you I wanted to be around you as much as possible. There's no reason for anyone to be scared."

I breeze past the compliment, even though I want to cherish it. "But they're scared of a piece of me that I can't ever get rid of. That makes it feel like they're scared of all of me."

His smile vanishes. "That's . . . awful. You seriously feel that way?"

"If you had any idea what I've been through at school the past few weeks, you'd understand."

"Whoa." He's quiet for a few seconds. "I'm really sorry. I don't know what to say. For what it's worth, I'm glad you told me. And I think you're awesome, every part of you, funky brain and all."

It feels good to hear. "Thanks." I stop poking at my tea bag and give a small smile.

We continue drinking our coffee and chai, and talking about Art Connect. Ty halfheartedly suggests that I could put abstracts in with the landscape that's still at the studio, but we both know that it would make the series seem very strange. The pieces need to make sense together.

I ask Ty to tell me about his pieces.

"You'll have to wait and see. You'll be the only one to appreciate them, though. I couldn't invite any of my friends or family, because I don't want my parents to find out about the art thing." He gets up and goes over to the coffee dispenser to fill up his cup.

When he sits back down, I resume the conversation like he never got up. "The art thing? Seriously?" Art isn't a "thing." It's a lifestyle. Ty knows this.

He takes his hat off my head and adjusts it back on his. "I'm not supposed to be an artist," he says. "Remember?"

"I know, but it's your life."

"True, but it's my parents' tuition money." He smiles, but it looks sad. "Wanna get out of here?"

We walk into the chilled evening air.

"My parents think art is kid stuff," he continues. "Crayons and finger paints and macaroni ornaments. They don't see that kids who love art sometimes grow up to be adults who love art. They kept waiting for me to grow out of it, but I didn't."

We get in the car and drive back to the studio.

It's odd to me that he needs to hide a talent, something that most people would be proud of. Me hiding a mental illness? Now, that makes sense. Then again, it hasn't been going that well. Maybe we both need to stop hiding and square with the truth. As I always say, "It is what it is."

Actually, I never say that. It was on a TV show last week. But I'm going to start saying it. Really. Then people will say, "As Natalie always says, 'It is what it is.'"

When we pull into the studio parking lot, Ty pops another Ice Breaker. Is it a coincidence or is he planning to need that fresh breath soon? The sun is setting behind the art gallery, and the shadows of the trees cast a lacy pattern on the parking lot.

I gather my backpack and put my hand on the door handle. "Thanks for the ride and for the chai."

"Anytime."

Now's the part when I should get out of the car, but I linger for a second. Just in case.

"Sorry you have to hide your talent," I say. "That really sucks."

"It's no big deal," he says (even though it is). "Sorry that you feel like you have to hide, too."

"Yeah, it's not a big deal," I say (even though it is).

There's a question mark hanging between us. It smells like Ice Breaker.

This is the part where I'd usually chicken out and make an excuse for why answering that question is a terrible idea. But Ty's different from other guys, the ones who failed me in the past. I'm different from the person I was a few weeks ago. He knows I'm bipolar, and he doesn't care. Maybe it doesn't have to keep us apart like I thought it did.

I take my hand off the door handle. "When you asked me to go with you to the Crow's Nest concert, I said no because I didn't want you to know about the bipolar stuff."

"Now that I know, does it change anything?"

I get my keys out of my purse. "I'm not sure. I think so."

He eyes light up. "Really?"

"But what if I'm not always stable? I could have another episode. There aren't any guarantees. I can't ask you to take that on. It's not fair to you." I'm scared that I'm going to mess this up, but I'm even more scared about not taking the chance.

"What if I want to take it on? What if you're worth it?"

"You can't know what it will take. I don't even know."

Ty looks frustrated by this. I wonder if he's considering making promises that we both know he can't make right now. I hope he won't try.

He sighs. "How about we play it one day at a time? We can take it slow."

I give a rueful laugh. "I didn't start things out too slow, did I? I'm sorry I kissed you in the pouring rain. It's not how I pictured our first kiss."

"You'd pictured our first kiss? How did it go?"

"I don't know, but not like that."

Ty's shoulders tense, and he messes with the brim of his hat. He looks away, and a small smile plays on his lips. "Did it, by any chance, take place in my car in the art gallery parking lot?"

There's a second of tense silence. "Well, that's definitely how I'm picturing our second kiss." I meet his smile with one of my own.

Ty visibly relaxes. The question mark has been turned into a period.

This is happening.

He shifts in his seat and leans toward me. I lean in, too. I'm locked on his eyes in a sizzle of anticipation, and then my eyelids flutter closed. It feels like someone poured fizzy champagne into my veins.

His lips are so soft.

This kiss is sweet and light, not hungry and frantic like the last one. It feels like a true first kiss. I want this one to count instead of that one.

My eyes open. "That's better than how I pictured it."

"I think so, too."

His smile makes me all melty.

I don't want to break the moment, but I also want to cut it off while it's still perfect. "I should get going." I pick up my backpack and open the door.

Ty takes off his hat and points it at me. "Told you this hat was lucky."

I pretend to be very confused. "But we both wore it. How do you know *you* got the luck?" I smile and shut the door before he can answer.

As I'm walking to my car, Ty rolls down his window. "Hey, Nat."

I turn around.

"Any chance you've pictured our third kiss?"

"Can't say that I have," I tease. "You'll have to hang out with me more and see if anything comes to mind."

I grin and head to my car without looking back.

Chapter 27

I'm in my bedroom three days before the Art Connect deadline. The half-finished painting in front of me, palm trees silhouetted against a tropical sunset, would be impressive—if I were in eighth grade. Maybe the judges will be so blinded by the brilliance of my other two paintings that they'll completely overlook this one.

Wishful thinking never hurt anyone, right?

My phone pings with a new email. It's from the University of Oxford. That's odd.

To Natalie Cordova:

Thank you for your interest in our Summer Scholars art program. We are delighted to offer you admission to our workshop next

July. Your portfolio is impressive. Students with your talent are an asset to the international art community, and we look forward to hosting you next summer. Please fill out the attached financial aid forms and the confirmation of your acceptance. All forms are due 15 November.

Sincerely,
Jane McLaughlin
Director of the Oxford Summer Art Institute

Is this a scam? I didn't apply for anything at Oxford. There's no way I'm talented enough to get into a summer program there.

The sending email address looks legit. A quick Google search of the Oxford Summer Art Institute reveals that Jane McLaughlin is indeed the director. Right as I'm about to email back and ask how she got my information, I stop. What if I *did* apply for this? What if, when I was manic or something, I did this application and don't even remember?

My phone screen stares blankly at me, and I stare back. I've practically memorized the email by the time Petunia makes a snorting noise that breaks my trance.

She's sniffing my paints and stepping on my paper plate.

"Toons, no!" I yell. She looks up, guilty, and there is a blob of yellow paint on her nose. She runs away, leaving tiny orange footprints on my wood floor.

"Arrrgh! Toons!" When I catch her, she squirms in my arms while I run to the bathroom and turn on the bath with my toe. The water runs toward the drain in shades of orange and yellow while I battle to keep Toons from jumping out. She wiggles and slides all around the bottom of the tub. I'm drenched.

When I think the paint is finally off, I pick Toons up and examine her. Finding no paint, I put her down to reach for a towel. Petunia makes a break for it and runs out of the bathroom. At least her footprints are water now.

This is a two-person job. I wish Ella were here.

Wait a minute—Ella.

Ella has pictures of my landscapes on her phone.

Did Ella enter that Oxford program for me? That makes way more sense than me doing it. She could have put together a digital portfolio and sent it in.

Who else could have applied to an art program for me? Ty thinks I'm talented, but would he really go that far? Even if he *would*, he couldn't have gotten access to my paintings. So, who did this?

Also, will Mom let me go?

The last of the orange paint is scrubbed off the floor, so I go downstairs to hunt for the dog. She's on the couch chewing on a throw pillow. There is a giant wet spot under her, and the wall clock tells me I only have about ten minutes until my mom gets home. I scramble for the wet vac, do my best with it, and ultimately grab the blanket off the back of the couch to cover the spot.

The doorbell rings. It's Brynn and Cecily. Brynn's wearing a football jersey, Cecily's in her cheer uniform with maroon and gold ribbons tied around her curled ponytail, and they're both in full makeup.

"Hey, Nat," Cecily starts. "Intervention here. We're headed to the football game, and you're coming with us. It will be like old times. I brought you a jersey." She holds up an away-game jersey from one of the players. "Also a cinnamon spice latte." She pulls back the jersey to reveal a Starbucks cup. "It's fall. It's your last year of high school. You're going to this football game. Plus, the dance is after the game. You don't want to miss it."

Our homecoming dance is pretty informal—it takes place in the gym, and everyone wears whatever they wore to the football game—but it could be fun to go.

The latte smells delicious, and I really need a break from this painting. Maybe going to the game will help clear my head and give me fresh inspiration. Plus, they could have gone without me. It's a relief to feel included again. I look at the clock and then back at my friends. "Give me five minutes."

They cheer, and I rush upstairs to change my clothes and attempt to get the paint out of my hair.

We pile into Brynn's car and head to the game. Brynn and I sit with some other friends in our usual spot in the bleachers, Cecily joins the cheerleaders, and I smile when I see Ella in her normal spot reading textbooks. She looks up, and I wave. She salutes.

Everyone cheers and hugs when our kicker makes a perfect field goal. I wonder if my dad played football in high school. If he was athletic, maybe that will be a good way for him to connect with Brent. They're both going to be at Art Connect, and I'm worried about how that's going to go. Brent says he's fine with it, but I don't think he'd tell me if he wasn't. I'd emailed Dad to tell him that Mom knows I found him and would be fine with him coming to the show. It was half true, so if you round up, then it is all true.

"Check out Jenny and Chloe," says Brynn. "They look fantastic."

Sure enough, Jenny and Chloe walk by wearing new clothes that I can almost guarantee my mom picked out.

"Did you know that the QuizBowl state finals are next week?" I ask. "We should go."

"Why?" asks Brynn.

"It's our school. We should support it."

"I'm busy that day," Brynn says without taking her eyes off the game. I never said what day it was. Why can't Brynn at least pretend to care?

There's a first down, and all talk of QuizBowl is forgotten. I cheer with my friends and boo when there's a bad call by the ref, but it feels a little hollow. There's a moment when the teams are lined up on a third down—key play—where I'm shaking my keys with everyone. Suddenly, I shake a little more slowly, and then stop altogether. The lights illuminate the field and the intensity of the players. The crowd roars amid the jingle of hundreds of keys. A bouncy cheerleader lands a back handspring. And a thought crystallizes in my mind: I don't care who wins this game.

I try to reason with myself. Of course I care who wins this game. The whole school comes out. We all care. I give my keys a halfhearted shake.

I don't care who wins this game.

My friends scream like lives depend on this play. I love them, but things are different now. We're different now. I care about things they don't, and I've had experiences they haven't. Maybe we can stay friends, but things won't be the same.

I get out my phone and text Ty to see if he wants to come over later for pizza while I paint. That sounds more fun than going to the dance, and he could possibly give me some feedback on how to fix the horrific palm tree. Just as my phone pings with Ty's answer, everyone cheers wildly. We got the first down. That's great. Even better, Ty has said yes.

"Everything okay?" asks Brynn. She nods to my phone.

"Yes," I yell over the crowd, "but I've gotta leave at the half to go over art-show stuff with someone from class. It's going to take a while."

"Bummer." Her face scrunches. "Are you sure? It can't wait?"

"Positive." I try to look disappointed. "Have fun at the dance, though."

"All right," she says. "Do you need a ride home?"

"No, I'm good." And I realize that I am.

At halftime, I walk down to the front gate to wait for

Ty. I'll probably never fit Brynn and Cecily's definition of "normal," and that's starting to feel okay. It's not worth going off my meds and trying to shoehorn myself into becoming a person I can't be. I'm not the same girl who drove into a tree. I don't want to die anymore, now that I'm starting to understand how to live. It's the beginning of a long road, but I think I'm finally on the right one.

Four senior girls are drinking hot chocolate by the concession stand, and Alyssa Jackson is speaking.

"Guess what I found out? Chloe's sister is on the spectrum. Isn't that awful?"

The girl next to her takes a sip of her cocoa. "Doesn't that mean she's slow or something?"

"Yeah, I think so." Alyssa leans against the brick wall of the concession stand.

The friend looks confused. "Isn't she super smart, though? She was in calculus when she was in ninth grade."

Alyssa pauses, and I turn to watch from my seemingly invisible post by the gate.

She furrows her brow. "Maybe she's not slow per se, but she's not like everyone else. She is super weird."

I check my phone to see if Ty has texted, and I'm gripping it so hard that my knuckles are white.

"She *is* really weird," chimes in a third girl, "but I thought that was her personality."

"Me too," Alyssa says, "but it turns out there was more to it all along. Can you believe it? This must be so hard on Chloe, you know? Imagine having a sister like that."

Her friends nod solemnly as they take a moment of silence to feel bad for Chloe. My jaw clenches, and I put the hood of my jacket up to muffle the conversation.

"It's so sad," one of them says. "Chloe's sister always sits by herself at games and at lunch. I mean, she doesn't have any friends."

That's it. I put my hood down, throw my phone in my purse, and walk over to the group of girls.

"*Ella*," I say. "Her name is Ella. Also, she does have friends. I'm her friend."

"Oh!" Alyssa looks surprised and embarrassed. "Sorry, I didn't know you could hear us. That's great that you're her friend. It's really kind of you."

"No." Tears sting the back of my eyes. "It's not *kind* of me. She's awesome. She's genuinely one of the best friends I have ever had."

"Good, that's great," says the girl next to Alyssa. She looks uncomfortable. "Sorry, we didn't know."

"Right." Finally, something we can agree upon. "You're right you didn't know. You didn't know that Ella is one of the kindest, least judgmental people in the entire school. You didn't know. You decided to assume bad things because it seemed easier to you than getting to know her at all."

All four girls stare at me in surprise. It takes me a few seconds to realize I'm holding my breath. My face is hot.

Alyssa crosses her arms. "You don't have to be rude about it," she says. "It's not like we said she's a bad person."

"Maybe you didn't say she's a *bad* person," I concede, "but you made her sound like a lesser person. Like she's on a different level from you."

Alyssa's friend is quick to defend her. "It's not bad to say she's on a different level. You have to acknowledge that when someone has, you know, brain issues, it's not like they're on the same level as everyone else."

"Yes, they are absolutely on the same level." My balled fists are going to rip holes straight through the bottom of my jacket pockets if I don't relax.

"Okay." Alyssa holds up her hands in surrender. "Okay, you're right. It's fine. She's on the same level. Whatever. I don't know why you care so much."

After she says that, I realize that this isn't only about Ella.

"This is personal for me. I have bipolar disorder." My breath is visible in the cold air as if I watched the secret leave my lips.

"I knew it," says Alyssa triumphantly. She stands up from leaning on the brick wall and narrows her eyes. "I knew Brynn's story about Natalie Smithson was made up. It didn't make any sense. You *lied*."

"Yeah, I did." A cold wind stings my face. "Because I knew people like you would stand by concession stands and talk about me. But if you can't see past a disorder, then that's on you. My brain is why I'm good at art. It's made me who I am. Love it or hate it, it is what it is."

I knew I liked that phrase.

Alyssa's friends are staring at me like I announced I have fifteen toes. One of them eventually speaks.

"Thanks for being honest," she says. "Your secret is safe with us."

"No, it's not." This will be all over the student section by the end of the football game. "But that's okay. It's not a secret anymore." For some reason, this doesn't bother me half as much as I thought it would. My phone dings. Ty has arrived. "Gotta go," I say to the girls.

I head to the gate, hands in my pockets, and leave them to their hot chocolates.

Chapter 28

We're in the kitchen, and Ty is painting an abstract compilation of benzene rings on the now-empty pizza box when there's a knock at the door. He's painting on the pizza box because I'm out of canvases, and he's painting chemical formations because then he can count this as studying for his upcoming chemistry exam.

He gave me some ideas for my beach silhouette, and I'm trying to implement them. I keep asking him to come over and see if I'm doing it right, mostly because when he stands by me I can smell his cologne. I want Febreze to make that scent. I would buy the spray, the candle, and those weird little car thingies that go in your vents. It smells like safety and adventure and, well, Ty. It smells like Ty.

Oh, also—I keep asking for his advice because his advice is good; he's a talented artist. Somewhere along the line, his artistic skills became secondary. I think it was somewhere between the fourth and seventh kiss. Now I'm not counting. I'm busy making sure my mom stays out of the kitchen.

My mom goes to answer the door, so it must be one of her friends. But wait a minute, it's almost ten o'clock. That's late to have someone over. I look up from my painting and strain to hear who it is.

"Hello, Ella darling," Mom says. "Natalie's in the kitchen."

Ella's here?

Ella rushes around the corner, puts her hand on her chest, and breathes a giant sigh. "Good. You haven't been kidnapped."

I raise my eyebrows, and Ty puts his paintbrush down. Instead of offering an explanation, Ella heads to my cupboard, grabs a glass, and goes to the sink to fill it. Once she's taken a long drink, she says, "Where is your phone?"

"It's upstairs charging. Sorry. Did you text me?"

Ella takes another drink and then puts her glass down. "Yes. I did. You left the game in a car with a strange man, and when I texted to make sure you were okay, you didn't text back. But I convinced Chloe to drop me off here on the way to the dance, so now I'm here, and you're fine, and the strange man is sitting at your kitchen table painting—" She breaks off and stares. "Are those benzene rings?"

"Nice work," says Ty, impressed. He stands and holds out his hand. "I'm Ty—the strange man."

"Ella," she responds. "The concerned friend."

"Nice to meet you." They shake hands.

"Why are you painting on a pizza box?" Ella asks. "Is this a statement against the establishment or something? Because if it is, I don't get it."

I should probably make an adequate introduction. "Ella's my friend from school. Petunia was her grandma's dog." I turn to Ella. "Ty's the studio tech for my art class, and he's painting on a pizza box because I couldn't find any canvases. He's helping me get this piece ready for the show." Ella comes over and looks at the beach scene. She puts her face close to the canvas to appreciate the detail and then stands back to see it all at once.

"Not your best work," she sighs. "But it will still be better than a lot of paintings there."

"Thanks." I think that was a compliment.

"Why don't you use the piece that's over the fireplace?" she asks. "That one's electric!"

"It's an abstract. My mom didn't like it much, so it's in the guest room now. No one likes abstracts, so I have to do landscapes."

"Says who?"

"My art teacher."

Ella thinks about this and then nods to Ty. "Talk to him about that. He's antiestablishment. It's obvious from the piece he's painting. Maybe he can inspire you to do abstracts."

Ty puts his brush down and surveys his pizza box. "This must be deeper than I thought it was," he says. He looks up at me, and his eyes sparkle with laughter.

Ella takes a seat at the table. "I read in *How to Survive High School* that you have to follow your heart. That's mostly junk, because what if your heart tells you to eat an entire pie in one sitting or draw polka dots all over yourself? But in this case, I think it applies. Do the art you want. You're the artist."

"It's not quite that easy."

"Hmm." She looks around my kitchen while I go back to painting. "If you're that talented at abstracts, Natalie, you should do them. Don't let the man keep you down."

That reminds me of a question I've been meaning to ask her. "Did you sign me up for an art workshop at the University of Oxford?"

"Excuse me?" She looks confused.

"I got an email for a summer art thing at Oxford, and you had all of those pictures of my paintings on your phone. Did you put them in a portfolio for me and send them in?"

"That would be super nice of me if I did that." She tilts her head to the side. "Dang. I should have thought of it."

"So it wasn't you?"

"Nope, but if you don't find out who did it, then I'll be happy to take the credit." She grabs a lunch pack of Doritos out of our cupboard and starts munching. "Hey, maybe he did it." She points at Ty.

"Nope, not me," Ty says. "I'm with you that it's great of whoever did it, but I don't have pictures of Nat's paintings. Couldn't have done it if I tried."

There's only one person I know besides Ty who loves art as much as I do, but how could *he* have done it? This doesn't make any sense.

My reverie is broken by Ella standing up. "I'd like to paint," she announces. "It looks fun. Can you please go get me a canvas or another pizza box?" She wipes Dorito cheese on her jeans.

"I didn't know you paint," I say.

"I don't yet. Maybe I'm great at this and don't know it."

Ty laughs out loud, then sees she's not joking and says, "Hey, only one way to find out." He looks up at me as if to say, "Go get her something to paint."

Maybe the basement has something she can paint on. I head down the stairs. It takes me a while, but I eventually find a box that holds Petunia's toys, and I grab the lid off that. It won't matter what Ella puts on it.

When I get back to the kitchen I hear the front door closing. "Did she leave?" I ask Ty.

He shakes his head. "No, I think she stepped outside to make a call."

Just then, Ella rounds the corner into the kitchen. She looks startled to see me standing there and looks around frantically for a moment before speaking.

"Gee, Ty, looks like the humane society is closed, so I wasn't able to contact them regarding the adoption of that lizard we discussed. Perhaps I will call them tomorrow."

Ty gives her a you've-got-to-be-kidding-me look, then says, "That's cool, Ella. No problem." He goes back to working on making an ethyl alcohol 3D.

Ella says the lid to Petunia's toy box is perfect for her painting debut. I tell her all about the dog bath from earlier, and Ty and Ella both find it hilarious. We whisper so my mom won't hear about the paint that got on the floor, and it's fun to feel like the three of us have a secret. It's a light secret—the best kind.

Ella's still hungry, so I pop some popcorn and put it in the middle of the table. We are working in silence, but my brush gets slippery from popcorn grease. We decide to take a break.

"Fun fact," says Ty. "In middle school, I was the best in our class at catching popcorn kernels in my mouth. I would be a pro if there were a league for popcorn catching."

"You're going to have to back that up with some proof." I hold a popcorn kernel like I'm ready to throw it.

Ty hops out of his chair and stands at the ready. I throw the kernel in a perfect arc. Sure enough, he catches it. He looks at me smugly and holds out his arms. "Come on, at least make it a challenge."

"Let me try," says Ella. She picks up a kernel and walks across the room. She throws it in a high arc, but far to the right. Ty manages to get under it just in time and catches it with a satisfying crunch.

We take turns throwing popcorn, and Ty tries to teach us the technique. When we get bored with that, we go back to painting. When we get bored with painting, we go back to throwing popcorn.

By the end of the night, I know three things for certain:

1. Ty is very good at catching popcorn kernels.

2. Ella is not secretly great at painting.

3. This is the best Friday night I've had in a very long time.

Chapter 29

The morning of the Art Connect show dawns brighter than I feel. Ty picks me up after school, and we ride to Greater Falls together. It's weird knowing my mom won't be there. She's been to all my other art shows, but I'm not backing down on my position—especially now that my dad is coming.

The look Soo gave me yesterday when I handed in my third piece made me cry all the way home. Whatever it takes, I'm going to get healthy. If I need pills, fine. Bring 'em on. I'm not tossing any more opportunities off a bridge.

On the ride up, I get good-luck texts from both Brynn and Cecily. Cecily has a cheer competition today, so she can't come. Brynn offered to come cover the show for her YouTube channel, but I said no thanks. After seeing what I'm putting in the show, I didn't want it to have any internet coverage. The three of us have plans to "celebrate" later tonight, though I'm not in the mood to celebrate. Hopefully they'll be able to cheer me up. Our friendship has been on rocky ground lately, but I'm not ready to let it go entirely. After all, they're trying to support me—they're just not great at it yet.

Outside of the Art Connect gallery, Ty stops me.

"You ready for this?" he asks. He looks amazing in his gray dress pants, black blazer, and checkered tie.

"Not really." I try to fluff my hair, as if college admissions people will be so astounded by wonderful hair that it will distract them from my paintings.

"Listen." Ty takes my hand in his and holds it tightly. "You're a phenomenal artist, okay? No matter what happens today, you're strong. You're talented." He lets out a chuckle. "I still can't believe you want to be holding hands with me right now." He kisses my forehead. "I'm the luckiest guy here."

There's a familiar rush of disbelief. He knows about my bipolar disorder and still feels like the lucky one. How long will it take for me to trust that it's real? "Will you still feel that way if everyone hates my paintings?"

Ty's eyes glitter like he knows something I don't. "Trust me, they won't."

What is he talking about? Before I can ask, he heads toward the doors, pulling me behind him.

We walk into the Art Connect hall and consult our maps to find Soo's studio display. Maybe it's the excited buzz in the room, maybe it's the fancy display boards and lighting, but everyone's art looks fantastic. Jill's grasshopper looks completely realistic. Tim's candy looks good enough to eat. Karl's fruit looks so realistic that I want to pick a piece off the canvas, and Starr's fox has the perfect surprised facial expression.

Jill gives me a hug. "Can you believe it's finally here?"

I hope she won't recognize that the smile I give her is strained. "No, it's unreal. Your display looks great!"

"Yours does, too, but why didn't you use any of your class pieces?"

"What?" I'm confused. "I did. The winter piece I finished last week is in there."

"Um, no, it isn't." She points to the right. "Your display is around that corner. The winter scene isn't in it."

How could Soo forget the winter scene? That was my best one. I rush around the corner and stop still. My hand flies to my mouth.

None of my landscapes are there.

The center of my display is the abstract piece I hung over my fireplace the night I decided to go to Paris. With the art lighting, it looks ten times better than it did in my living room. The tendrils fly back from the silhouette in a way that gives astonishing movement to the piece. The colors dance off the canvas. It is, as Ella said, electric.

On either side are thin, tall canvases painted solid black. Ten paper-plate abstracts are attached to each canvas, and the black background makes the colors pop. The plates have been sprayed with an acrylic gloss finish, so they look glassy and reflect the light. The overall effect is breathtaking.

"Do you like it?" asks a familiar voice.

I turn with tears in my eyes. "Ella?"

She's wearing a floral-print dress and Converse high-tops. A headband is lurking in her mess of curls. I suspect this is as dressed up as she ever gets.

"I didn't do it alone. As we deduced, I have no artistic talent." She nods at Ty, who followed me around the corner.

"If you don't like it, Soo has all three landscapes stored in a back room," he says. "We switched the displays this morning. What do you think?"

"I love it!" I look at the pieces again. I feel a rush of pride and a flicker of hope. They don't look bad. Actually, they look fantastic. "How did you get all of my paper plates?"

"You told me about them at the coffee shop last week," Ty says. "When Ella suggested stealing the abstract from the guest room, I figured putting it with the plates would make a logical series."

"And, last Friday, when you went downstairs, I snuck upstairs, grabbed the plates, and stashed them in Ty's car. And I made you think Ty was going to adopt a lizard," Ella says smugly. "I played that so well I should get an Oscar."

I nod, speechless, but there's an obvious flaw in their plan. "What did Soo say?"

Ty laughs. "No offense, but your beach scene is kind of . . . not your best. She thought this series looked much better than your other one."

My face flushes, and I'm not sure if it's from happiness or embarrassment.

"Come see Ty's display," says Ella. "You two would have very artistic children."

"Ella!"

I'm mortified, but Ty gives me a look that says, "It's Ella. I get it."

His display has the eye picture I saw in the studio, the one with the now-finished tear. It also has a painting of some dogs sleeping by an old farmhouse. The last piece makes me smile so wide that my jaw hurts—it's the corn picture. Ty took his drawing from our draw-off and made it into a painting with incredible detail. Anyone would be impressed by it.

I turn to him. "I can't believe you painted the corn."

"My drawing was better than yours, and I needed to rub that in," he says. Then he shakes his head and looks at the floor. "Nah, I just liked thinking about that day. It was a good day." He meets my eyes.

The rest of the room fades. I can see him by the cornfield again, the wind playing with his curls. No one else could make a cornfield exciting.

Ella totally interrupts the moment. "What I don't understand is how this relates to Ty's antiestablishment themes. Is this a statement against the agricultural monopolies in America? The eye with the tear is mourning the loss of our agrarian past?"

Ty sighs and looks at his work. "Um, yes."

Ella nods. "Thought so. I am nailing this art thing today." She walks over to survey the next display.

I'd love to gaze our way back to wherever it was Ty and

I just were, but the gallery is filling. "I'd better get back to my display. Gotta guard the paper plates. I don't want the concession stand to plan a heist."

"Good luck. You deserve all of the attention I know you'll get." For a second, I think he's going to kiss me again. My pulse quickens, but Karl and Tim walk over to talk to him.

The next hour is filled with talking to people about my art pieces and the meanings hidden in the madness of my abstractions. I try to imagine talking about landscapes for this long: "Yes, this is a winter scene. It looks like winter. Please notice the snow." Boring. Now I get to talk about movement and colored emotions and all the things I was thinking when I painted my abstracts. People might not fully understand me, but no one can deny that I'm passionate about these paintings.

As I'm talking to a representative from Indiana University's art school, someone familiar rounds the corner. "Please excuse me," I say. "My dad is here."

I give my dad a huge hug. He looks at my display, and he's clearly impressed. "Holy mackerel, Nat. How did you get this good?" I know parents can be biased, but he sounds sincere.

I tell him about the meanings behind each plate, and he listens attentively, mentioning specifics about my technique. He says he's never seen abstracts this good, on paper plates or otherwise.

"After the show, maybe you could display these in my gallery. If you wanted to." He looks unsure, like maybe I won't want to be a part of his life after today.

I'm shocked but honored. I can't believe he thinks my pieces are at his level. I'm so happy to have found him, but I also understand his uncertainty.

I don't know how to have a dad in my life. I haven't had one for as long as I can remember. I want to imagine that everything is going to be fine and we'll have a great relationship immediately, but that seems optimistic. There's still a piece of me that resents him for leaving. There are still so many unanswered questions. Some of them will never be answered. How would my life be different if he never left? Maybe I never would have driven my car into a tree. If he could have kept that from happening and didn't, how am I supposed to forgive him?

Trying to wade through all of that emotion makes me feel like I'm drowning. I can't get enough air right now. Instead of diving into the deep end, I'll be the kid that sits on the steps and starts by getting my ankles wet. I'll get to the deep end eventually. Right now, I'll keep it light. I'll focus on the fact that he's here, he really seems to care about me, and I finally have a family member who loves art as much as I do.

"I'd be happy to put a display in your gallery. Maybe you could teach me some of your techniques sometime."

"That'd be great. I'll teach you everything I know. Pretty sure you could teach me a thing or two yourself." He shakes his head. "Normal family businesses are 'Highsmith and Sons Plumbing,' but normal's not our style."

I laugh. "I'll take this over plumbing."

"Art is still a messy business."

"But the best kind of messy." There's a spatter of yellow paint near the bottom of his plaid shirt, but I don't mention it. I like it. I remember my whitewashed closet and promise myself I'll mess it up again soon. "Hey, by the way, I don't know how you signed me up for that Oxford summer program, but thanks for that."

"Oxford program?" He looks surprised.

"Someone applied for me, and you went to Oxford. I figured it was you."

"I did go there, and I'd fully support you studying there, but I didn't sign you up for any programs. How could I sign you up without your portfolio?"

Blast. I thought he was going to fill me in on how he secretly did that.

"Um, I don't know." I was *sure* he did it.

"You'd be a great candidate. Good thinking to whoever submitted you. Maybe your art teacher?"

My eyes widen. Soo! Of course. "That's it. I've got to find her and thank her. Thanks so much for coming." I give him another hug.

"Wouldn't miss it. I really appreciate that your mother didn't mind. It was generous of her, considering . . . Well, all things considered."

"Yeah, she's super generous." Did he notice my voice get higher?

His eyes narrow. "She doesn't know I'm here, does she?"

Before I can answer, I'm rescued by an approaching man in a suit. "Hello, are you the artist of these pieces?"

"Yes, I am." I brush my fingers through my hair and try to look professional. "Do you have any questions?" I shoot my dad an apologetic look. The family business calls. He mouths, "I'll be back later," and goes to look at some of the other displays.

Suit Man shakes my hand. "I'm Jacob Webster with the Kendall College of Art and Design. Soo Ahn mentioned that you're a senior. Have you made any decisions regarding college for next year?"

"No." I work to keep my voice steady so I don't jump for excitement and freak this man out. "No, I haven't."

"I'd love to talk to you about our program. Your talent could be a good fit for what we have to offer."

"Sure." I nod. "I'd be interested in what you have to say."

Ahhhhhhhhhhhhhhhh!

A Kendall scout is talking to me! He thinks I could be a good fit for their program! Nothing could ruin this day.

After I talk with Suit Man for about fifteen minutes, he gives me his card. He wants to set up a meeting regarding potential scholarship opportunities. In my excitement, I don't notice that someone is standing to the side, listening to my conversation. As soon as Suit Man walks away, that someone gives me a hug.

"That's wonderful, darling! Kendall is what you've wanted for so long."

"Mom?"

Oh bad. Bad, bad, bad. I take back what I said about nothing ruining this day. Where's my dad? "Mom! You're . . . here."

"Natalie, I know you didn't want me to come, but how can I not support my daughter in the biggest art show of her life? I can't sit around and pretend I don't care, when I'm so proud of you." Her eyes are pleading.

Should I hug her? Should I tell her to leave? I take a deep breath. "Are you really proud of me?" It's an honest question.

She looks confused. "Of course. How can you question that?"

"Because all I've ever wanted was to make you proud, but I've never been able to get there. My art wasn't good enough to be a career option, I was never as good as Brent at anything, and with my brain stuff . . . I don't know. I feel like you see me as a defective kid."

"No." She looks defeated.

Guilt flickers through me, but I need to know the truth. I'm tired of trying so hard and not measuring up.

"You're not defective," my mother says. "If I made you feel that way, I'm sorry. After your accident"—she lowers her voice—"I was heartbroken. I saw what mental illness did to your father, and I hated that you were going to experience that. I felt helpless, but it shouldn't have been about me. I should have done more to make you feel supported." She reaches for me, but changes her mind and drops her arm. "This is your day. I'll leave if you want me to, but either way, I love you, Natalie. I'll try harder to be the mom you need me to be."

Trying harder—it's all any of us can do. I'm trying harder to be okay with my bipolar disorder, trying harder to be a better sister for Brent, a better friend for Ella. How can I freeze my mother out when she's promising to do the same thing?

I take a deep breath, like the air is full of forgiveness and I am finally ready to breathe it in. I pull her into a tight hug. "Please stay. I want you here."

After we hug, she surveys my display. "I didn't know you decided to go with your abstracts."

"Neither did I."

She gives me an odd look.

"Long story."

"Are those paper plates? When did you do those?"

"Yeah, they are. They lived in my closet until recently." It's still surreal to see them out here, under the bright lights.

"Do you think they'll let you do more of this when you're at Oxford next summer?" She says this casually, and it takes a second for her meaning to sink in.

"*You* signed me up? But you hate art!"

"I don't hate art. I may be nervous about you choosing it for your career, but the truth is that you're talented. Soo told me about the opportunity, and I couldn't resist giving it a try. She supplied your portfolio, and I filled out the forms. I told you, I really am proud of you. Maybe it will give me a good reason to go visit my old friends from college. I hear Oxford is lovely in the summer."

I hug her again. "Thank you, thank you, *thank you*!"

As she pulls away, she gives me a huge smile. "We can include your offer from Oxford and your Art Connect display in this year's Christmas card. What do you think?"

"Sure, Mom." I don't really care about the Christmas card right now. Count on my mom to take a promising moment and bring up something like the Christmas card. She has said a lot of hurtful things to me in the past, and one (really, really awesome) gesture like the art application can't erase all of that. Maybe we should all go to family therapy, honestly. It's going to take us a while to move on from this. But, as they say, a snail's pace is still a pace, and maybe we're slowly moving in the right direction.

Another college rep asks about my display, and my mom is beaming. Suddenly, her smile vanishes and she turns as white as a sheet. No need to follow her gaze to have a solid guess at what she sees. Still, when I turn, my stomach drops to my feet.

Not only is my mom looking at my dad, but my dad is walking toward my brother. Brent's still in his baseball uniform, and my dad is wringing his own hands as he approaches him. Brent knew my dad would be here, but I'm not sure how this is going to go down. I thought I'd be the one introducing them.

My dad gently taps Brent on the shoulder, and he turns around. Brent's shoulders tense when he realizes who it is, but he holds out his hand for an awkward shake. I wish I could hear what they're saying. They look so much alike. To everyone in the room this must look like a completely normal father/son conversation. No one would guess it's the first one they've had in fourteen years.

I touch my mom's shoulder and she jumps. "So, when I thought you weren't coming today, I, uh . . ."

I don't need to explain. It's pretty clear what happened.

"I see."

"Are you mad?"

She pauses. "I'm not sure. I think so."

"Oh." We both watch the interaction going on across the room. "Should we go over there?"

"I think not." She smooths her hair, like she's trying to be even more put together than usual. "They'll come over here to see your display. We can handle it then."

I think she wants to give them time to talk, but I'm anxious to hear what's going on.

"Oh great, here they come." My mom closes her eyes, like she's psyching herself up for battle. What is the protocol in this situation? I have no idea what to do.

I wait until they're close and then ask Brent if he won his game.

"Yup. Four-zip."

"Awesome."

We both look awkwardly at our parents.

"How've you been, Henry? Are you doing well?"

Mom's rattled, but I have no doubt she'll stay composed.

"I'm doing great, Maggie. You look beautiful."

My dad's eyes are softer than my mom's.

"Yes, well." She smooths her dress. "I try to look presentable on occasion."

"You never look unpresentable."

Ella walks up holding a bag of Chex Mix. At that moment, I could not be happier to see her.

"Do you need a snack?" Ella asks. "Soo sent me to bring these to people." She sees my mom. "Oh, hi, Mrs. Cordova. I didn't think you were coming."

My mom nods tightly.

Ella sees my dad and gasps when the situation clicks. "No way. Are you Natalie's dead dad? Welcome back, sir." She hands me the Chex Mix and turns to shake his hand. "I'm very glad you're not dead."

"Me too," he says. He looks right at me. "Dying was the worst mistake I ever made."

"I'll make it a point to avoid it at all costs," says Ella. "Thank you for the advice." She turns back to me. "This looks like an emotional moment. I suddenly remembered that I have to go calculate the parabolic functions of drinking fountain water."

"Me too," I say. "I've been wondering about those for a while."

My mom gives me a death glare.

"I should go say hey to Ty," Brent says. "I haven't seen his display yet." He hasn't seen mine yet, either, but both of us want to be far away right now.

When we get to the drinking fountain, Ella says, "Full disclosure—I made up that thing about calculating parabolic functions. I don't know how to do that without a ruler and my graphing calculator."

"It's okay." I take a drink of water. "I don't even know what a parabolic function is."

"Really? They're so easy." She turns on the drinking fountain and shows me different parts of the path the water takes. She's talking about gravity and algebra and a lot of those things that teachers say you'll need in life but only Ella ever uses.

My parents are talking. It looks tense, but neither of them is running from the building. That's positive. Brent catches my eye from over at Ty's display, and we both shrug as if to say, "Not much we can do to make this less weird." We go back to watching my parents.

We're clearly not the picture-perfect family of my mom's dreams, but I think we are at the beginning of something new. Maybe my parents won't ever see eye to eye or be what they once were, but I can still love them both. Brent can love them both. We can be a new kind of family—an abstract kind of one.

"So basically, that's all there is to it," Ella is saying. "Does that make sense?"

"Not really, but you know what? That's okay. You're my friend, so whenever I need parabolic functions calculated, I'll call you."

"Fine by me."

Jill comes up behind us. "There you are. Soo wants pictures of her studio's team. She won an honorable mention!"

"Awesome!" I'm relieved to have an option that doesn't include awkwardness or algebra lessons. The students have assembled in front of Soo's display. Ty ends up next to me, and he holds my hand. I'm going to frame this picture.

As we're smiling for the camera, I see Brent notice our hands. My chest momentarily tightens—what is he going to do?—but he meets my eyes and nods once, showing his acceptance. Maybe even approval. These bright lights make it hard to tell. I squeeze Ty's hand tighter, light with relief and happiness. Maybe the future looks bright not only for Ty and me, but for my relationship with Brent, too.

Soon after the picture is taken, it's time for my dad to leave. He gives me a big hug. "I'm so proud of you," he says, his smile taking over his face. I notice my mom's tight grin as she witnesses this with her arms crossed, and I know things are going to be a little weird for a while. Will they be able to find a way to get along?

As if he read my mind, my dad walks over to my mom next. "See you around, Maggie?" Those four words have paragraphs of guilt and hope folded into them.

For a moment my mom doesn't say anything. Then she uncrosses her arms and sighs. "I suppose you will."

She doesn't exactly smile as she says this, but her eyes are soft. I have hope that we'll find a way to exist in each other's lives. Now that I've found my dad, I don't ever want to lose him again.

After we've said our goodbyes, Ty finds me at my display. "What time is it?"

"Six o'clock. Why?"

He puts his hands in his pockets and looks around in anticipation. "I have something I should probably tell you before seven."

"That sounds mysterious and oddly time-specific."

He stops scanning the room and meets my eyes. "My parents are coming at seven."

I tilt my head and raise my eyebrows. "Are these the same parents that said artists spend all their money on drugs and paintbrushes?"

He nods once. "Yep. Those are the ones. Hopefully being around this many artists doesn't give my dad a heart attack."

I smooth my hair as if I'm going to meet them in the next five seconds. "Why are they coming? How do they know you're here?"

"I was thinking about you last night. Watching you take control of your life inspired me. I told my parents the truth about my 'lab job.' I asked if I could keep working at Soo's as long as I kept my GPA up, and you're not going to believe what happened."

"They grounded you for your entire life?"

Ty laughs. "I'm in college, Nat. My parents don't ground me. Not even for art. What happened is they said *okay*. They heard me out, and they made a deal. As long as I'm above a three-point-eight, I can stay. And then they asked to come to the show, because if I'm displaying at Art Connect, there's a solid chance that I don't suck."

I laugh. "That's not what they said."

Ty grins. "Not exactly, no. But that's the gist."

I inspired Ty? I've never felt so humbled and proud at the same time. I hold both of his hands. "What if a four-year college offers you a scholarship? Could you study art?"

"Whoa, Nat. Baby steps. The fact that I'm not murdered on my living room floor is a big win right now." He smiles.

"But the conversation is open, and that feels like someone took a boulder off my back. Not sure where it will go from here. First I have to hope that they like my paintings."

I let my hands run up his arms and around his neck. "They're going to love them. If they're half as proud of you as I am, they'll have pride coming out of their eyeballs." I point to my own glassy eyes. "See? Look at all of this pride."

Ty laughs and kisses me. Someone walks up to my display, and I peel myself away in an attempt to be professional. We'll celebrate later.

My mom stays and enjoys the rest of the show. She tries to talk intelligently about art with some of the artists, but it reminds me of when she used to talk about recipes with other moms at Brent's Little League games. It never sounded quite right.

She tries, though. That's worth something.

Later, I'm talking to Ty and Ella when an alarm goes off on my phone. I pull it out and turn it off.

"What's that for?" asks Ella.

"My pills. Be right back."

The familiar orange bottle doesn't seem so scary now. At the drinking fountain, I try to remember what on earth Ella was talking about with the para-something functions. Hmm, no clue. My friends might be a little bizarre, but I wouldn't trade them for anything.

I open the pill bottle, take a drink of water, and swallow my pill without hesitation.

ACKNOWLEDGMENTS

———

I have a small army of people to thank for the fact that this book exists. Thanks first to my Pitch Wars team (#TeamVictoryFleet): Katherine Fleet and Kacey Vanderkarr. Katherine, thank you for believing in Natalie's story and choosing me to be your Pitch Wars mentee. You helped transform the story into something worth selling. Kacey, thanks for being not only a great critique partner but also a phenomenal friend. Here's to many more writing retreats where we lament the ups and downs of publishing, drink lots of tea, and eat pretzels and those turquoise Dove chocolates. Thanks to both of you for the awesome days we spent on the beaches of Curaçao talking in-depth about writing.

Thanks to my fantastic agent, Emily Keyes, who has been a champion for Natalie's story. Thanks for introducing me to the world of publishing and being patient with me when it was clear that I had no idea what I was doing.

Thanks to Jonah Heller, my awesome editor at Peachtree, who has an eagle eye for what makes a story better. Thanks for believing in Natalie (and in me) and helping me make this story what it is today. Thanks for fielding my many emails and reminding me that this story is worth telling.

Thanks also to Janet Renard, who went through this book with a fine-tooth comb and untangled many snags. And to Carling Mars and Matthew Broberg-Moffitt, for the feedback that helped make the story better. Thanks to Kaitlin Severini, who proofread the book and caught mistakes that had somehow slipped through the cracks.

Thanks to Maggie Edkins Willis for designing a cover that brings the story to life.

Thanks to Becky McLaughlin, who told me to enter Pitch Wars and got me started on the journey to serious publication.

Thanks to Sheila King, my elementary school librarian turned critique partner, who was the first one to think this story had merit. Thanks for drinking lots of tea and coffee with me as we plotted this thing out. Natalie wouldn't exist without you convincing me her story was worth telling. Thanks for going beyond the call of duty and caring about me waaaaay past elementary school.

While writing this story, I spent a ridiculous number of hours at Fourth Coast, a coffee shop in Kalamazoo. Thanks to the baristas there for countless cups of mango Ceylon tea (wow, I'm realizing I drink a lot of tea). Now that this book has sold, I think I'll buy a scone, too, because I like to dream big like that.

Thanks to the numerous readers who saw this story in various states of completion. Thanks also to those who have followed my various blogs and other writing projects. I know I'll always have fans in Cara Knasel, Dan and Linda Knasel, the Webb family members (especially Jake, who has been a blog follower since the beginning), Elle Poustforoush, Lynn and Larson Sholander, Janell and Dave Colao, Lauren Westerman, Leandra Quinn, Sarah Gerger, Carly Kellerman, Beth Fryling, Krista Moored, and Nana and the Fab Four. Thanks for being great friends/family members, and for always encouraging my writing. I know I wouldn't have gotten to this point without you. I also need to give a shout-out to Missy the pug for inspiring the character of Petunia. Never has there been a pug as fabulously *weird* as Missy.

A special thanks goes to Rex Webb: my husband, best friend, and editor before the editors. Thanks for reading my work, laughing at my jokes even when they aren't funny, and keeping a constant supply of tea and pretzels coming when you know I'm hard at work. Thanks for the long walks where you help me clear up plot holes. You do a good job of acting like you care about my characters as much as I do, even though I think who you really care about is me. I couldn't imagine a better supporter of my work or a better life partner in general.

Finally, thanks to you, reader, for taking the time to read these words. I hope you enjoyed the world I created half as much as I enjoyed writing it.

RESOURCES

If you or someone you know is in crisis, resources are available to help.

United States

National Suicide Prevention Lifeline
https://suicidepreventionlifeline.org
Phone: 1-800-273-TALK (8255)
En español: 1-888-628-9454
Deaf or hard of hearing, TTY: Use your preferred relay service or dial 711 then 1-800-273-8255
Online chat: *https://suicidepreventionlifeline.org/chat*

Canada

Canadian Association for Suicide Prevention
https://www.suicideprevention.ca
Phone: 1-833-456-4566
Kids Help Phone: 1-800-668-6868

International

Find a Helpline
https://www.findahelpline.com

TO LEARN MORE, VISIT:

#BeThe1To
https://www.bethe1to.com/bethe1to-steps-evidence

International Society for Bipolar Disorders
https://www.isbd.org

National Alliance on Mental Illness
https://www.nami.org

National Institute of Mental Health
https://www.nimh.nih.gov

Substance Abuse and Mental Health Services
Administration
https://www.samhsa.gov

Youth.Gov
https://www.youth.gov/youth-topics/youth-mental-health

*These resources are provided for
informational purposes only.*

CHRISTINE WEBB is a middle school teacher from Kalamazoo, Michigan. When she's not teaching or writing, she enjoys hanging out with her zoo (three goofy dogs, an evil cat, twenty nameless pigeons, and a friendly rat) or traveling with her husband. She also loves studying British history and laments the fact that she will never be Queen. Follow her on Twitter @cwebbwrites.